D1590766

The Decision

Robert Cort

Clink
Street

Published by Clink Street Publishing 2022

Copyright © 2022

First edition.

ISBNs:
978-1-915229-37-3 Paperback
978-1-915229-38-0 Ebook

ALSO WRITTEN BY ROBERT CORT

THE IAN CAXTON THRILLER SERIES

Volume 1 - The Opportunity
Volume 2 - The Challenge

To Fiona, Philip and all the team responsible for the fascinating television series, 'Fake or Fortune?'. The programme inspired me to write the Ian Caxton thriller series.

Chapter 1

It was 9.50am when a member of the 'Harbour Heights' reception team telephoned the Penthouse apartment. Ian answered the call. The receptionist asked if Julian could come straight up to the apartment. Ian was confused as he knew it had been agreed that he and his wife would meet Julian in reception at 10am. Nevertheless, Ian assumed Julian must have a good reason for changing the arrangements, so he asked the receptionist to send him up.

Five minutes later Julian pressed the doorbell. Ian opened the door. Julian was not dressed in his usual smart chauffeur attire but in casual clothes. He was unshaven, shaking and had a very white complexion.

Ian was surprised with Julian's appearance. "Julian are you alright? You look in shock. Come in and sit down. What's the matter? Emma! Can you bring a glass of water!?"

Ian helped Julian to the nearest sofa and suggested he sit down.

Emma, Ian's wife, arrived with a glass of water and handed it to Julian. She looked at Ian and asked, "What's the matter?"

Ian shrugged his shoulders and waited for Julian to speak.

Julian took two small sips of the water and then looked

up into both their faces. Tears had appeared in both of his eyes and now they were slowly trickling down his cheek.

"It's Andrei. He's dead!!"

"What!!" exclaimed Ian. "When!? How did he die!?"

Julian put the glass down on the small table in front of him. He lowered his head, covered his face with his hands and said, "I don't know!"

Ian looked across to Emma, who was also shocked and wide eyed. He then sat down next to Julian and put his arm on Julian's shoulder. "I'm so sorry. You don't know what happened?"

"He died on the cruise," explained Julian, still with his head in his hands. "Just two days after Sydney. I don't know how he died… or what happened."

Ian leaned back on the sofa and glanced up at Emma. She looked back with a confused expression on her face.

Ian leaned forward again to Julian's side and asked, "What do we do now? What can I do to help?"

"Sergei telephoned me. He knows what Andrei's wishes were."

"Oh. Maybe I need to speak to him."

"Andrei was more than an employer. He was… I know this will sound ridiculous, but he was like a father to me."

"He was a very special person," said Ian, with genuine feeling. The reality of the situation was now beginning to hit him. He forced back his own tears and looked up to Emma for help.

Emma quickly read the situation. "Come on, Julian, I'll make you breakfast. Ian can telephone Sergei."

Julian picked up his glass of water and followed Emma into the kitchen area. Ian meanwhile stood up and walked into the dining area to collect his mobile phone. He wiped both of his eyes. From his contact list, he selected Sergei's home telephone number. After five rings Sergei answered the call.

"Hello, Sergei. It's Ian Caxton. We are in Monaco. Julian is with us and he's just told us about Andrei."

"Hello, Ian. I telephoned your home number earlier but just got the answerphone."

"Sergei, what can I do to help? Julian says Andrei gave you his instructions."

"I've just been talking to the cruise company and they say that the cruise ship has got to dock at Brisbane. The police have been informed and they need to establish the cause of death."

"Right," said Ian. He was not sure how to proceed, or what to say.

"There will probably be a post mortem," continued Sergei. "The cruise company representative said that Andrei died in his sleep, possibly from a heart attack."

"I see. Do you want me to go to Australia?"

"No, no. That won't be necessary. The police and Andrei's travel insurers, they're already both on the scene. I think we should wait until we hear from them first."

"Okay, but, is there anything I can do in the meantime? We are due back in the UK in three days' time, but I could see if we can get an earlier flight."

"I'm sure there are people that you, or Julian, know who need to be informed. Both in Monaco and France. Maybe you could do that for me, please. We can discuss the matter again when you have returned home."

"I'll do that, Sergei. I'll telephone you when we are back in the UK." Both men said their goodbyes and Ian wandered into the kitchen area where Emma had prepared a cup of tea and some toast for Julian.

"Sergei says there is little we can do at the moment other than inform local friends in Monaco and France."

Julian put down his cup of tea and looked up to Ian. "Andrei only had a few local friends. Lady friends mainly…

like Marie. He was often away on business, so he didn't have a large circle of friends. He really didn't trust many people."

"We have Marie's telephone number, but do you know the others?"

"Yes. I can contact them... and I'll also speak to Marie."

"You must let us help you, Julian."

"It will be better coming from me. I know these people... and they know me." Julian stood up and looked from Emma to Ian. "I must go... and get on. Thank you for the breakfast. I also need to speak to Andrei's legal people." Julian walked towards the door.

"Are you sure you're okay?" asked Emma. She really didn't think that he should be leaving at that moment.

Julian opened the door and looked back. "No, not really... I've just lost my best friend." He exited the apartment and slowly closed the door behind him.

Ian and Emma looked at each other. After a few seconds Emma said, "I hope he'll be alright." She picked up the teacup and plate that Julian had used and placed them next to the sink.

"It's a shock for all of us. I think he'll be okay though." Ian looked down at his mobile phone, it was still in his hand. He wondered why Sergei had not tried to contact him via his mobile number.

Three days later Ian and Emma were back in the UK. Emma's plans for a romantic few days away in Monaco had evaporated after Julian's devastating two words – 'Andrei's dead'. During the rest of the Monaco break, Ian was largely very quiet and preoccupied with his thoughts about Andrei. He also spent some of his time sending and receiving emails.

When they arrived back at their home, Emma telephoned her mother-in-law. She wanted to check to see how Robert was. Everything there was fine and everybody appeared to be happy. At least somebody had a good time, she thought. However, she was looking forward to collecting Robert the following day.

The next morning Ian was up early and just about to leave to go to his office, when he called to Emma, "I'll try and see Sergei after work this evening. You and Robert have your dinner and I will eat something when I get home." He picked up his laptop bag and headed towards the front door.

"Okay," called Emma. She came down the stairs and gave Ian a kiss.

Ian then left their home and walked towards the railway station. There was a light shower in the air, although Ian didn't really notice it. During his 15 minute walk he couldn't get Andrei out of his mind. His thoughts kept swinging from memories of his dealings with his friend to concerns about his own future. He wondered what more surprises he was going to find out over the coming weeks and months? Hopefully, Sergei would soon have some of these answers.

When Ian arrived at his office he telephoned Sergei. They briefly exchanged pleasantries and Sergei agreed to a meeting, later that evening, at 7 o'clock.

It was just after 7pm when Ian pressed the front door bell of the Kuznetsov family home. He stood back and, once again, surveyed the street and noted the opulence of the surrounding Eaton Square properties. The whole area exuded wealth and mystery, he thought, and not for the first time, Ian felt as though he was, what was it… trespassing?

About 30 seconds later the door was opened by Sergei. He gave Ian a big smile and invited him in. The two men shook hands and Sergei pointed to his study, inviting Ian to enter.

The two men sat down and Ian began to speak. "Thank you for seeing me, Sergei. I'm still in shock with Andrei's death. Have you received any more news from Australia?"

"The cruise ship people are still officially saying the post mortem results are likely to state that Andrei died of heart failure. Natural causes. The insurers are arranging for Andrei's body to be transferred to Scotland."

"Scotland!" exclaimed Ian, in surprise. "Why Scotland?"

Sergei pulled a file of papers out of his desk drawer. "A few weeks ago I met with Andrei at the Savoy hotel for lunch. He had just returned from Scotland. He gave me all these legal papers and his instructions in the event of his death. Amongst the instructions, Andrei said that he wanted to be cremated and his ashes to be scattered in the grounds at Baltoun Castle. I have spoken with the Laird and he confirms that he already knew of Andrei's wishes and had also agreed to his request during his last visit to the castle."

"Wow. So, did Andrei think he was going to die soon? What other surprises are there?"

"He was certainly not a well man when we met the last time at the Savoy. He was also in a very serious mood. Not like him at all! He also thought one of his enemies was now looking for him. However, he didn't elaborate any further."

Ian wondered how many more surprises were going to be revealed.

Sergei continued. "The paperwork confirming full and final transfer of the Monaco apartment to you is in the hands of Andrei's legal people. The rest of Andrei's assets are to be distributed as per his will."

"I see. Do you know when the funeral will be?"

"Not yet. The Australian police are being very coy about when they will give permission for the body to be released. The insurers will then make all the necessary arrangements for his body to be transferred to the UK."

"Why would the Australian police do that? Surely they would be keen to release Andrei's body as soon as possible."

"I know. I'm wondering if there is more to Andrei's death

than the cruise ship company wants, or is willing, to say. I'm waiting for a telephone call from the insurers, we may know more then."

After Ian left his meeting with Sergei, he slowly wandered along the streets and back towards Victoria underground station. His mind was spinning. He was certainly feeling somewhat guilty. He wondered if Andrei believed that he had really taken full advantage of 'the opportunity' he had opened up for him whilst he was alive. Now that he was going to fully inherit the Monaco apartment, and the 10 year annuity that Andrei had also set aside to help with the apartment's financial upkeep, he wondered if he really deserved it all.

Ian knew, however, that his main concern was with Emma and Robert. He could not afford to put their livelihoods at stake. Andrei, after all, was a bachelor with very few responsibilities. He could afford to take all the risks he'd taken. Even so, Ian still pondered and worried, that there must be something he could do to clear his conscience and prove that Andrei's belief in him was not completely misguided.

Later that evening, Ian explained all the details of his meeting with Sergei to Emma.

When he'd finished, she said, "It's all a bit strange. Surely if the Australian police are happy that Andrei died of natural causes, then why are they not releasing the body?"

"My only guess is that they think it wasn't due to natural causes! Sergei has only spoken to the cruise company and, for public relations reasons, they probably don't want to say anything else… at least, not until the full details of the post mortem have been issued."

"I see. So what are you going to do now?"

"I'm not sure. I don't know if there is anything I can do. I need to speak to Andrei's legal people about the apartment, but I would prefer to wait until the situation in Australia has resolved itself first. I don't want to appear grasping or uncaring."

Emma suddenly had a startled look on her face. "You don't think Andrei was murdered do you?"

"To be honest, it wouldn't surprise me. Andrei did have a number of enemies."

"I do hope not, Ian. Let's just pray it was natural causes." Emma suddenly felt quite afraid.

"Mmm, I agree. However, we are just speculating. We need to wait for the Australian police to complete their work," replied Ian. However, in his own mind he was still wondering if indeed the death was the result of murder, and if so, would there be any potential repercussions for him and his family?

It was a week later when Ian received the telephone call that he had been dreading.

Chapter 2

Ian was in his office when his telephone rang. Penny, his PA, was currently out of the office delivering some pictures, so Ian answered the call himself.

"Mr Caxton?" asked the authoritative male voice, with a distinctive Australian accent.

"Yes," replied Ian, hesitantly. "Who's calling?"

"My name is Detective Constable Steven Ponting. I'm with the Brisbane police authorities. I was wondering if I could speak to you about your relationship with the late Mr Andrei Petrov?"

Ian rose from his seat behind his desk, and as he began to reply to the policeman he walked across the room to close his connecting door to the outer office. He then resumed sitting at his desk.

Over the next twenty minutes Ian explained that he and Andrei had enjoyed a successful business relationship centred around Andrei's activities of buying and selling art and paintings. He went on to answer a number of the detective's follow up questions and explained exactly his whereabouts around the time of Andrei's death.

Finally Ian asked his own obvious question. "I thought that Andrei died of natural causes. From your questions it sounds as though this might not be the case?"

"No, Mr Caxton, it is not. Our medical investigations proved conclusively that Mr Petrov was murdered. He was poisoned. Have you ever heard of the nerve gas, 'Novichok'?"

Ian immediately felt the blood drain from his face. His breathing became quicker and he also felt his heart rate beginning to rise. "Oh my god! Are you sure!?" was all he could reply.

"Oh yes, Mr Caxton, we are very sure. Mr Petrov involuntarily inhaled the gas during his sleep on the cruise ship. We are certain Mr Petrov was the victim of a deliberate act of murder!"

"I see," replied Ian, still deeply shocked. "Have you any idea who murdered him?"

"At this stage, we are still following our normal enquiries."

"Yes, of course," responded Ian.

"Thank you for your time, Mr Caxton. We probably won't need to speak to you again."

"Thank you," said Ian. "I hope I was of some help." He put the receiver back on its base and just stared out of the window. His mind seemed to be spinning in all directions. After about ten minutes had elapsed he heard a tap on the connecting door.

"Come in," he shouted, and then tried to refocus his mind back to the present.

The connecting door slowly opened. "Hello, Ian." It was Penny. "Is everything okay? Your door is not usually closed."

"Yes...yes, thanks, Penny. Just a private call and I knew you were not in the outer office," replied Ian. He took a deep breath. "Everything okay with you?"

"Yes, fine. I delivered those two watercolours back to Graingers. They were happy with the valuations and will probably go for the auction option. We should find out in a few days."

"Thanks." Ian rose from his seat and walked towards

where Penny was standing in the doorway. "I think I'm going to get some fresh air. It's a bit stuffy in here with the door closed." Ian passed by Penny. Both briefly smiled at each other and then Ian exited the outer office into the corridor.

From where she was standing, Penny looked around Ian's office. Satisfied that nothing seemed to be amiss, she pushed the connecting door back to its usually wide open position and walked back to her own desk.

When Ian returned he felt a little calmer, but was still worried about the Australian policeman's information. After a few minutes he opened up his computer and googled the word 'Novichok'. He was surprised that there were so many entries! However, he selected a website at random and began to read:

'Novichok' is a class of chemicals, developed in Russia. Translated from Russian, it means "newcomer". Nerve agents, like this poison, are designed to attach to the spaces between nerves and muscles in the human body and thus overwhelm essential bodily functions. Enough of this chemical can easily stop a victim's breathing or heart, leading to a very quick and horrible death.'

Ian closed down his computer, leaned back in his chair and wondered how on earth he was going to explain all this to Emma! He also felt a little nauseous.

The opportunity to tell Emma came later that evening after Ian had put Robert to bed and Emma had put their dinners on the table. Between mouthfuls of his food, Ian explained most of the details of the telephone call he had received from the Australian police detective. He'd decided, however, not to mention the word Novichok, but just referred to 'a poison'.

Emma had listened to Ian's detailed explanation without

interruption, but once he had finished she asked, "Do the police have any idea who was responsible, and why he was poisoned?"

Ian ate the last forkful of food and then laid his cutlery on his plate. "If they do, they didn't tell me. I think it was probably someone finally catching up with him from his past. Repaying a grievance, maybe. I know Andrei was always concerned about the Russian mafia! If that was the case, then it is very unlikely the police will be able to capture him... or her!"

"Yes, poison is often a woman's weapon," replied Emma.

"There were over 3000 passengers on the ship, not to mention all the crew. I'm sure the police will continue to investigate, but it's almost impossible to identify the culprit... unless, of course, someone comes forward with some useful information. My guess is that the murderer is a professional, so it's most unlikely he, or she, will ever be discovered."

Thirty minutes later, both Ian and Emma headed upstairs to get ready for bed.

As Emma sat at her dressing table, she was worried and wondered if, as a result of Andrei's murder, there might be any potential repercussions against Ian, her or, even, Robert! Why in God's name, she cursed to herself, had Ian ever got involved with Andrei in the first place!

It was two weeks later that Sergei emailed Ian to say the Australian authorities had finally agreed that Andrei's body was no longer required and would be released. The police investigation to find the murderer had achieved very little and nobody had been arrested. Witnesses had come forward to say that Andrei had been seen in the company of two different women whilst he was on the ship. One of the women was identified and questioned, but she was quickly dismissed as a possible suspect and the second woman had seemingly just 'disappeared'!

Ian replied to Sergei's email and thanked him for the information. He also asked if a date had yet been finalised for the funeral.

A day later Sergei replied stating that Andrei had left definite instructions. He had said that he didn't want a formal funeral, but was happy for his 'friends' to attend the scattering of his ashes. The scattering of the ashes would take place on the 24th November at Baltoun Castle.

A day later Ian received another email, this time from Richard Forsyth, the Laird of Baltoun. The email read:

Hello Ian,

I hope you are well and you are enjoying the 'pleasure' of fatherhood!

It's with much sadness that I am writing to you. As you are probably aware, Andrei's ashes are to be scattered at Baltoun Castle on the 24th November. You, and your wife, would be very welcome to come and stay with us if it is your intention to attend this sad event. Andrei spoke about you often.

On his last visit, he told me how special he felt Baltoun Castle was to him and he sought my permission, that, when he died, his ashes would be scattered here in the grounds. I had no hesitation in agreeing to his request. After all, his investments in the estate have been a godsend and it is the minimum I can do for him. He will always be in our hearts. Moira, has particularly found the whole business very distressing. She and Andrei both enjoyed their little chats in Russian. Such a nice man.

Please let me know if you will be attending and how long you would like to stay with us.

Best Wishes,
Richard.

Ian looked at his calendar for the period around the 24th November. The 24th was a Monday so he decided he could travel up to Scotland on the Friday evening flight to Edinburgh and return back on the following Tuesday. However, he would still need to discuss this with Emma first before he formally replied to the Laird. He was reasonably sure that Emma would not want to attend. She still had mixed views over his relationship with Andrei and there would also be Robert to consider. As Ian's parents spent most of November and December in the Algarve, the possibility of placing him in their care for a few days was not an option this time.

That evening, after dinner, Ian told Emma about the two emails he'd received from Sergei and Richard. He also suggested that he would like to attend the 'scattering of the ashes' on the 24th. Ian was pleased when Emma suggested he should take advantage of the Laird's offer and stay for a long weekend. That way Ian could also see exactly what Andrei's investments had produced. Emma also said that she hoped Ian would understand that it was not practical for her to go too, as there was Robert to consider.

So it was agreed. Ian was going to convey his answer to Richard's email and book his two flights. He also wondered whether he should contact Sergei to find out what his plans were.

Chapter 3

The opening of the new 'Taylor Fine Art Gallery' had been a success. Bob Taylor had earlier travelled from Monaco and, with Ian's help, they had signed off all the internal alterations and decorations. They had agreed which pictures were going to be displayed and had only tweaked Oscar's suggestions for the final layout slightly. The Isaac Tobar pictures were taking centre stage. Both Ian and Emma had supported Bob on the opening evening and Oscar had emailed his best wishes from Antigua.

Bob had announced to both Ian and Oscar that he planned to manage the Gallery personally for the first two months. During that period he would advertise for, and appoint, a manager, who would be solely responsible for running the business after he had returned to Monaco. Ian had whispered to Bob that he might have just the right person in mind, but he would need to sound out that person first.

The pre-opening marketing of the gallery had gone well and after the first 48 hours of the gallery's trading, six paintings were either 'reserved' or had been sold outright. Two of the Tobars had achieved a nice financial profit. Another two paintings had received offers via the new internet website. 'A successful beginning', was how Bob Taylor described the Gallery's trading position to his wife when he telephoned her later that evening.

Three days after the opening of the gallery, Ian asked Penny what the current state of play was with Vic and his graduate training course. She told him that he would be finishing his course at the end of that month but he was still undecided about what he wanted to do next. He said that if he stayed with Sotheby's, he would prefer to return and work in Ian's department. However, he was also considering a fresh, new challenge, outside of Sotheby's.

"Maybe I ought to have another chat with him," was Ian's response.

Penny set up a meeting for Ian with Viktor at 'The Grapes' for 6pm the following evening. The two men duly met and, after Ian had questioned Viktor about his thoughts for the future, he decided it was obvious from Viktor's answers that he would probably benefit more, and could well excel, with a completely new challenge.

After buying two fresh pints of beer, Ian explained to Viktor about the new Taylor Fine Art Gallery and the opportunities it offered someone of his ability, ambition and enthusiasm. He suggested that Vic would be his own boss and would be solely responsible for driving the business forward in the UK. He continued to explain that the owner, Bob Taylor, was based in Monaco and most of his business was on the mainland of Europe. Therefore he would receive little interference.

This new career opportunity appealed to Viktor. He certainly could see how he might be able to drive the business forward. It would also give him the freedom to be able to develop his career without the perceived restrictions of being employed by Sotheby's. After a few minutes' thought, Viktor told Ian that he had made his decision. He would definitely apply for the Gallery manager's vacancy. Besides, he thought, he had nothing to lose!

A week after advertising the manager's vacancy at the gallery, Bob had received a number of applications. He selected four initially, but then reduced this number down to just two candidates to interview. He decided to keep the other two 'in reserve', just in case. When Bob had received Viktor's application and CV, he noticed that Viktor was currently working for Sotheby's. His profile seemed good and so he decided to interview him. He also made a mental note to speak to Ian if the interview went well.

Bob emailed both his preferred choices and stated that they were in consideration for the manager's job. He then gave both candidates separate dates and times for their interviews.

As the 24th November gradually drew closer Ian decided to email Sergei to see what plans he and Boris had for attending the 'scattering of the ashes'. However, he was quite astonished to receive the following reply:

Hello Ian,

I have made all the necessary arrangements with the undertakers in Edinburgh.

Andrei's cremation was carried out in Brisbane and the insurers arranged for the transfer of the ashes to the undertakers in Edinburgh. The undertakers will transport the ashes to Baltoun Castle on the 23rd November, as per Andrei's wishes.

Everyone knows Andrei was not a religious person so there was no need to involve anyone else. Both Boris and I will not be attending the formalities in Scotland as we have already paid our last respects, in our own personal way.

Whilst these arrangements do not necessarily follow the usual practice carried out in the UK, you have to remember that this is what Andrei had insisted on.

I hope you understand,
Sergei.

Well would you believe that! thought Ian. If they do not want to be involved, well so be it. I still want to say my own farewell… to my friend… and in MY own way!

On Friday the 21st November at 3pm, Ian was in a taxi heading towards London Heathrow airport for his flight to Edinburgh. At the same time Viktor Kuznetsov had just sat down in front of Bob Taylor at the Taylor Fine Art Gallery for his interview. An interview, which if successful, could dramatically alter the career path for this ambitious young man for many years to come!

Inside a small church in Monaco, Julian, Marie and a small number of Andrei's former friends and acquaintances from Monaco, and the surrounding areas, were all gathered together to pay their own personal last respects to Andrei. The local priest gave a short prayer and then, one by one, each member of the congregation made a small speech about Andrei and how their lives had been touched and made much more enjoyable, because of his friendship. After they'd all exited from the church, there was not a dry eye amongst them.

Julian was especially sad and depressed. He had lost his father figure and best friend. No more emails or phone calls in the middle of the night. No more valuable paintings to collect, or deliver, in the Rolls Royce. Life had suddenly become quieter and certainly much duller. A decision, very soon, would have to be made.

When Julian returned back to his apartment he looked at the various provisional bookings he'd already made for Andrei. A number of them were paid for but would not now be used. These bookings were to places that Julian thought he would only ever go to… in his dreams! If he cancelled them then the refunded money would only go back into Andrei's estate. Alternatively, he pondered on a possible different option. Finally, he made his decision. He would replace Andrei and finish Andrei's trip himself! Yes, HE would complete the rest of Andrei's five year travel plan!

When Ian arrived at Edinburgh airport, he spotted the familiar figure of Duncan, the Laird's driver, waiting for him in the 'Arrivals' area.

"Welcome back to Scotland, sir," were Duncan's first words. He took charge of Ian's bags and they headed for the exit.

"Thank you, Duncan. It's just a pity that I'm back in such sad circumstances."

"Aye, Mr Petrov, he'll be sadly missed at Baltoun Castle, sir. His support, and friendship, was very special to the Laird."

Duncan led Ian to where the Range Rover was parked and they both climbed aboard. The journey to the Castle was similar to how Ian remembered. It was pitch black and chilly outside. A heavy frost was forecast and Ian had a similar apprehension to the one he had on his first visit with Andrei. The big difference this time was that Andrei was not sitting at his side whispering that he did not understand a word Duncan had said! Ian smiled and looked out of the window. He occasionally spotted lights emitting from cottages or an isolated farmhouse, but otherwise, there were only brief glimpses of the countryside. That was when the moon temporarily re-appeared from behind light clouds to illuminate fields and trees as they passed by.

Duncan looked back through his rear view mirror. He too was feeling a strange, sad sensation. He too was missing the presence of Andrei and his little broken English jokes and smiles.

When the Range Rover drove into the inner courtyard of the castle, another familiar figure, that of Jenkins, the butler, appeared and he walked over towards the car. He opened the rear passenger door. "Welcome back to Baltoun

Castle, Mr Caxton," he announced. "The family have all been looking forward to your visit."

After Ian had exited the car he thanked Duncan and smiled at Jenkins. "It's lovely to be back again, Jenkins. I only wish it had been under happier circumstances."

"The loss of Mr Petrov... yes, it is all so very sad."

The two men walked towards the large oak double gates to the castle. Duncan followed carrying Ian's bags. Jenkins pushed open the smaller door in one of the gates and they all entered the main entrance hallway. Duncan peeled away and took Ian's bags up the stairs to one of the guest bedrooms, whilst Jenkins led Ian towards the library.

Ian looked around him. There was the familiar chill and the stone walls. All still decorated with swords and old battle fighting equipment. Again he smiled when he remembered Andrei's initial comment that he couldn't believe that people still lived in such cold old buildings.

When the two men arrived at the library Jenkins knocked and pushed the door wide open. He then announced, "Mr Caxton."

Ian walked past Jenkins and into the room. He immediately noticed that the temperature was several degrees warmer in this room due to the roaring log fire. He spotted Richard and Moira as they both walked towards him.

"Hello, Ian, welcome. Sad business." The Laird shook Ian's hand and stepped back.

Moira approached Ian and they both kissed gently on the cheek. "We've all lost a good friend," she said, trying to hold back a tear.

"Hello, both of you. Yes, Andrei was certainly a 'one off' and a true friend," replied Ian. He always felt that he struggled in these sorts of circumstances to say the correct words.

"So how was your journey? We'll be having supper shortly," said Richard, walking over to a small table near the log fire. On the table was a decanter of whisky and four glasses.

"It was fine, thank you. It was also nice that Duncan was waiting for me again."

Richard poured four glasses of whisky and handed one to Moira and then one to Ian. "Warm the cockles on a chilly night."

"Thank you," said Ian, but he was surprised to see Richard holding the remaining two glasses in either hand.

Richard put one of the glasses down on the table next to a large vase – a previous present from Andrei, Ian was told. Richard stepped back and raised his own glass in the air like a salute. "To a special absent friend."

"A very special friend," said Moira. She tried desperately to hold back a tear.

Ian quickly followed suit, raised his glass and said, "Na Zdorovie, my friend."

All three sipped their whisky, but then the men watched as a tearful Moira put her glass down on the table and ran towards the library door.

Chapter 4

When Ian awoke the next morning he immediately noticed that the two leaded windows were covered with frost. He had slept well but had dreamt about meeting up with Andrei to value some paintings in Hong Kong. It was all so very surreal.

He leaned over to pick up his mobile phone from the bedside table. He'd remembered that on his last visit the broadband and wifi connection was very poor and spasmodic. This time there was a good signal! Part of Andrei's investment? he wondered. He looked at his emails and noticed one from Bob Taylor. The message read:

I interviewed Viktor Kuznetsov yesterday for the manager's job. I was very impressed. He says he's currently working at Sotheby's and I wondered if you knew him?

Ian smiled and started to write the following reply:

Yes I know Viktor. He worked in my department for a short period, as part of the Company's graduate programme scheme. He is the person I was hinting at when I said I thought I had someone in mind for the role. I am pleased he interviewed well. He would be a good choice.
Ian.

Ian typed another two business emails and then a short one to Emma saying he had arrived safe and well. He also hoped she and Robert were fine. He finished off by mentioning that his bedroom windows were covered with frost and he was decidedly reluctant to get out of his nice, warm bed!

Ian did finally get out of bed. After visiting the bathroom he got dressed into several layers of warm clothing. He then went downstairs and entered the dining room, where breakfast was being served. Richard was sitting at the table, reading the morning newspaper, which he put down when he saw Ian walk into the room.

"Good morning. Did you sleep well?" asked Richard, as he folded the newspaper and laid it down on his side of the table.

"Yes, fine, thank you. I noticed we had quite a frost last night."

"We've had quite a few lately. Par for the course up here this time of the year I'm afraid. This is not Surrey," replied Richard, with a smile. "Help yourself to breakfast."

"Thank you," said Ian, and he walked over to the side table where there were a number of silver dome plate covers keeping the food warm. Ian lifted several covers, eventually selecting two kippers and some toast. He also poured himself a cup of tea. "Is Moira joining us?"

"No. She was up early and Duncan took her into Edinburgh. She will be back for dinner."

Ian took his food and tea to the table and sat down opposite Richard. "So, what are the plans for today?"

"I thought you might be interested to see Andrei's investments. His generosity has made a massive difference to the fortunes of the estate."

"That sounds very interesting. Yes, I would like that very much. I suppose a lot has changed since I was last here."

"Indeed. When you left I was convinced Andrei was just

going to buy some of our paintings. He obviously had other ideas."

"Yes, it was a total surprise to me too. I had no idea of his plans, but he did love the setting of the estate and told me that there was a lot of potential here."

"Well, as a result of Andrei's generosity, the estate is now more secure and on a much better financial footing. I am sure you will see a big difference."

"I'm sure I will," said Ian. He then concentrated on his kippers.

It was just before 10.30am when the two men met in the courtyard. Richard was going to drive Ian around the estate in Duncan's absence.

When Ian saw the Range Rover parked in the courtyard, he was surprised as he thought Duncan would have used it to take Moira to Edinburgh.

"Come on," said Richard, waving his hand at Ian. "Jump in. Moira and Duncan have gone off to Edinburgh in the Jag, so we've got this. It's ideal for travelling around the estate, especially by the stream banks. It's still quite wet in places down there. Not quite as practical as the Landrover, but certainly more comfortable."

Ian smiled and climbed aboard. They headed out of the courtyard and onto the old drawbridge. Richard then steered the vehicle to the right and onto a track, crossing a large grass field. They headed towards a large wood. To his left, in the far distance, Ian could see a sizable herd of red deer grazing. Mmm, he thought, I don't remember seeing this number of deer on my last visit.

"We'll turn off shortly and I'll then take you onto one of the new estate lanes," said Richard, holding tightly onto the steering wheel as they bumped and crossed the field.

Ian nodded and pointed out of the window. "There seems to be more deer than I remember."

"We have more than doubled the herd's size. The extra venison has increased our turnover and the lodge guests report that they enjoy seeing the deer roaming so freely."

Again Ian nodded.

"This lane coming up is one of the two new lanes we've had built. They both give access from the far end of the estate to the lodges, campsite and the luxury yurts. That's where the new entrance is."

"Wow," said Ian.

Just before the wood Richard steered the Range Rover off the track and onto the tarmac lane. In the distance Ian spotted the first of the lodges.

As they drove closer Richard explained, "The original 12 lodges have all been modernised and a further six new ones have now been built. Occupancy through the first summer has been roughly 70%, and even now, we've still got five of them occupied. Not bad for our first year and bookings are already up again for next year!"

Richard pulled the car over to the frontage of one of the unoccupied lodges and both men got out.

Richard unlocked and opened the front door, but, before either entered they removed their wellingtons and then entered the hallway. Richard led the tour.

Ian was very impressed with the lodge's interior design and furnishings. It had a modern kitchen and a separate useful utility room. A wood burning stove was located in the lounge and new wooden flooring had been laid throughout the ground floor area.

"Each lodge is fractionally different but, basically, they follow the same set up. Upstairs each bedroom has its own ensuite. Andrei was very pleased. On one of his visits he decided to stay in the lodge next door for two nights."

"I can see why he would be pleased, they are very luxurious for a holiday lodge," replied Ian. He was genuinely impressed.

After exiting the lodge the two men put their wellingtons back on and Richard led Ian around to the back. Here he pointed to the new footpath which led down to the stream where there were access points on the bank for trout fishing.

"This was Andrei's favourite spot. He loved wandering down here, listening to the flow of the water and looking out for salmon and trout. He was not really an angler, but he did try it once. He liked to stop to chat with any of the anglers who were present. The very first time I brought him down here he saw his first ever kingfisher. Thereafter he always reported back when he'd seen any others."

Ian smiled and wished he had been here when Andrei had revisited.

"Do you see that temporary white post near the bank?" Richard pointed to a white painted wooden stake a few metres away from one of the allocated angling stations. "I put that in there the other day. It is where Andrei wants his ashes scattered!"

"It's a lovely, quiet and relaxing spot," replied Ian. He was feeling a little emotional. He knew Andrei would have approved.

"I have his written instructions back in the office," said Richard, mentioning this fact just in case Ian decided to query the request.

For the rest of the morning, and into the early afternoon, Ian was guided to the locations of all the other lodges and was driven along both the new lanes. He thought both lanes had been laid out well and didn't detract too much from the wood-land scene. Both lanes also gave easy access to and from the main road. Ian noticed that all vehicles entering the site now had to pass the new check-in cabin. Next to it was a small general store. Just after the check-in cabin there was a four acre field. Richard stopped here and told Ian that in the summer months this was the site for the luxury yurts and extra camping.

"It's a lovely spot," said Ian. He could see that the field was also partly hidden by a variety of mature trees.

"Yes," responded Richard. "The field has good drainage. It's a little higher than the surrounding land. When all the 10 yurts are erected they have a fully equipped kitchen and their own vehicle parking area close to the check-in cabin and shop."

Richard then pointed across the field to a large single storey building. "That building is the permanent toilet and bathroom block. After customer feed-back, we are investigating the possibility of adding ensuite facilities to the yurts. There were ensuite bathrooms on the original plans, but we decided that it would be a little difficult to include because we take the yurts down and put them into storage in the winter. We might consider keeping them up through next winter. It really all depends on the demand."

"It's all very impressive. I'm sure Andrei would have been excited with the results."

"Andrei visited us several times. On his last visit, he said he was very pleased with how his money had been spent. The new website and improvements to both broadband and wifi connections have been very successful too."

"Yes, I noticed that this morning when I sent some emails. It's certainly much better."

"Our guests have praised us for the quality of the connection."

"So are there any future plans?"

"Not major plans, no. But we'll still have the ongoing maintenance costs. Andrei had promised a five year commitment. Said he was going to set up an annuity, but now, well I'm not sure what the position is with that."

"Maybe he has made arrangements in his will. Have you heard from Sergei? He's Andrei's executor."

"Not about the will, no."

"Do you want me to speak to him?"

"Maybe when you get back to London. It would be a great help. It's all a bit embarrassing for me to speak to him directly."

"I'm sure something has been arranged," replied Ian. At least he hoped so. He would hate for Richard and his family to have been put back into the problem position they found themselves in just 12 months ago.

Chapter 5

Andrei's ashes were delivered by the undertakers on Sunday. Ian, meanwhile, had taken the opportunity to borrow Duncan and the Range Rover, to visit Edinburgh. Duncan had suggested he knew where Ian could purchase what he was looking for on a Sunday. Successfully accomplishing this task, they arrived back at the castle in good time for dinner.

Dinner that evening was a sombre affair. Neither Ian, Richard nor Moira were in a mood for talk or much discussion, although Richard did mention that based on the replies he'd received, it was probable that only the three of them would be the attendees witnessing the scattering of the ashes. This comment didn't surprise Ian. He already knew Andrei's Russian colleagues in London had already stated that they wouldn't be attending. He also thought that it was very doubtful that anyone from Monaco would be joining them either.

Just before they'd all decided to retire to their beds, one thing was agreed. Andrei's ashes would be scattered at 12 noon. Richard said that Duncan would be driving them over to the spot reserved for Andrei's final resting place next to the stream.

When Ian arrived in his bedroom he telephoned Emma.

He asked how she and Robert were and summarised his day. He also explained the plans for tomorrow. Emma said she thought Andrei would appreciate Ian's idea of how he was proposing to celebrate Andrei's life and she also wished him good luck.

Once Ian finally got into his bed he lay on his back and stared up at the ceiling. His mind drifted back to some of the events and adventures that had occurred during the relatively brief time he had known and worked with Andrei. He knew he was going to miss his great friend. He switched off his bedside light and rolled over to his sleeping position. His last thought, before drifting off to sleep, was that now he had to definitely commit to the big decision.

Next morning, when he arrived downstairs, Ian found the dining room empty. It appeared that he was the first one down for breakfast. He poured himself a glass of orange juice and a cup of tea and placed them on the table. When he sat down he opened up his mobile phone and read emails and the news headlines. It was about 15 minutes later that Richard finally joined him.

"Duncan will be taking us in the Range Rover at 11.45," announced Richard, as he walked over to the sideboard and poured himself a cup of coffee. "I hope you had a good night's sleep."

"Yes, fine, thanks," replied Ian. He drained the last drops of his tea and walked over to the sideboard to help himself to a bowl of porridge.

Richard helped himself to two kippers and sat at the table directly opposite to where Ian had been sitting.

"Richard, I have a request when we scatter the ashes," said Ian, as he returned and sat down again at the table. "I know it will sound odd, but when Duncan took me into Edinburgh yesterday, I bought two bottles of champagne. During difficult times, or, if he'd heard some personal bad news, Andrei's answer was to open a bottle of champagne. I am not totally sure why, but he always did it. I would like us to toast and celebrate Andrei's life in the same way, please. I hope he would have appreciated this gesture."

"How very interesting. I will arrange for Duncan to bring some glasses."

"Thank you," said Ian. He hoped he was doing the right thing.

At 11.40 Ian and Richard were standing in the castle courtyard when Duncan appeared in the Range Rover. As the car stopped, Moira joined the men from the inside of the castle. Ian gave his two bottles of champagne to Duncan who placed and secured them in a wicker hamper basket. Next, Richard gave Duncan the urn containing Andrei's ashes, which he secured in the car's boot, next to the wicker basket. The three passengers climbed into the vehicle and Duncan returned to the driver's seat.

At 11.55, the group alighted from the car and walked the short journey to where the white painted stake still stood close to the stream. Duncan gave the urn to Richard and removed the champagne bottles from a wicker basket. He passed them to Ian and placed the basket, still containing the glasses, to the side of Ian's feet. He then turned and walked back towards the car.

Richard walked over and pulled the white post out of the ground. He then returned to stand next to the group.

Ian was the first to speak. "Andrei was not a religious man, so can I suggest we just take a moment with our own personal thoughts."

Both Richard and Moira nodded.

Two minutes later Richard pulled the lid off the urn and walked forward towards the stream. He then poured the ashes around the area where the white stake had been standing earlier.

Ian uncorked one of the bottles of champagne and Moira removed four glasses from the basket. After all four glasses had been filled Ian stood one of the filled glasses in the area where the ashes had been scattered and rejoined the group.

Ian was the first to raise his glass and toast, "Na Zdorovie, my friend. Dosvedanya."

Richard followed with, "Goodbye, Andrei and many, many thanks for all your kind help."

Finally Moira lifted her glass and said, "Dosvedanya, dear Andrei." A tear appeared in her right eye.

All three drank some of their champagne. Ian then walked over to where the fourth glass was standing on the ground. He picked it up and slowly poured the contents into the ashes.

"I hope you enjoy your final glass of champagne... my friend. Bless you."

Ian, Richard and Moira all finished their own glasses of champagne in silence and then walked slowly back to the car.

Out of everyone's sight, a kingfisher landed on its favourite low branch. The branch was gently swaying in the breeze. It was just a metre above the stream and very close to where Andrei's ashes had been scattered. It briefly looked down towards where the ashes and champagne had been poured, but then focused its attention on the flowing water... and searched anxiously for its next meal.

After lunch, Richard took Ian for a long walk around the estate. They stopped at the area that Andrei thought could have possibly been converted into a golf course. Richard explained that he and Andrei had a number of discussions on the matter, but finally they'd both agreed, the money would be much better spent in other areas of the estate.

"Not being a golfer myself," replied Ian, "even I can see that without serious improvements to the land's drainage, keeping the course dry enough for regular play would be a major problem."

"Andrei was disappointed, but eventually he could see the logic of the decision. Come on, let's wander down by one of the streams. After that we should head back, dinner should be ready soon. Andrei enjoyed our venison, so that's what we'll be eating tonight."

The two men walked along one of the new lanes and then Richard pointed to a track through the wood for them to follow. Twenty minutes later they arrived at the second of the two estate streams. Except for the gentle breeze through the trees and the occasional bird call, it was all very quiet and peaceful. Even Ian felt that any conversation ought to be spoken in a whisper. They continued their walk following this new track, which ran parallel with the edge of the stream. Richard pointed to more angling points which had just recently been established. He explained that trout were in abundance and a few salmon had started to arrive in the late spring.

Slowly the two men meandered back towards the castle. Jenkins was waiting for them in the library with two 'hot toddies'. A lovely warming sensation after such a bracing afternoon, Ian thought.

"So, Ian," enquired Richard. "Do you approve of all the changes?"

"It's not for me to give my approval, or otherwise, Richard. All I can say is that it looks excellent and I'm sure Andrei would have been very pleased and proud with the estate now, especially compared to when I was here last. It certainly feels a lot more vibrant and inviting for your guests. You and Moira must be very pleased."

"Oh, yes. As I've said before, Andrei's investment has put the estate on a much sounder footing, both short term financially and also for our long term business prospects. We dared not believe that his investments would have resulted in such a large increase in new visitors. I was seriously fearful that I would be the last Laird and the estate would be broken up and sold. Now it's on a far better, and more sustainable, basis going forward. Andrei's lasting legacy will mean that my children will definitely have a future here."

Ian was awake early on Tuesday morning. He was anxious to get back to Emma and Robert and also to catch up on his work at Sotheby's. He'd enjoyed his short break and the hospitality shown by his hosts, but now it was time to get back to a normal life. He was pleased he had attended Andrei's last wishes, but he also hoped that time would eventually prove that Andrei's judgement of him was correct. He packed his clothes, tidied his room and quietly crept down the stairs, leaving his two small luggage bags in the hallway. He then wandered into the dining room for his breakfast.

"Good morning, Mr Caxton," said Jenkins, who was just making the final check that all the breakfast options were ready. "You are the first one to arrive, sir."

"I'm leaving today so I thought it best to get an early breakfast," replied Ian, as he walked across the room.

"Well there is plenty to choose from. Please help yourself. Duncan is aware of your impending departure and he will be ready to take you to the airport when you are ready, sir."

"Thank you, Jenkins, you have all been so very kind."

Jenkins smiled, nodded and left the room. Ian helped himself to a glass of orange juice and a cup of tea. He sat quietly at the table and sipped his juice. As he did so he looked around the room. He was particularly interested in the portrait paintings of the ancestors who had once lived at Baltoun Castle. He smiled at the thought that just one Russian had managed to save all this heritage from being sold.

"Good morning, Ian." It was Moira who had silently entered the room. "Have you finished breakfast already?"

"No, no," said Ian, shifting his attention from the paintings to Moira. "I was just looking at the paintings of Richard's ancestors. There must be, what, over 500 years of history here."

Moira walked over to the sideboard and helped herself to two boiled eggs and two rashers of bacon. "1320 was when the original castle was built, but it was renovated and extended in the 16th century… after a serious fire. We have pictures of many of Richard's ancestors, but not all, some were lost in the fire. Please come and help yourself to some food."

As Moira sat down Ian walked over to the sideboard and helped himself to bacon, sausage, toast and another cup of tea. He then rejoined Moira at the table.

"You and Richard have been very kind in letting me stay with you."

"It's been our pleasure. We know how close you and Andrei were and Andrei has been the family's saviour. I honestly don't know what we would have done without Andrei's kindness."

Ian nodded and started to eat his food. "Where is Richard?"

"He'll be with us shortly. There is a problem with two of the deer, so he has gone with the gamekeeper to try and sort it out."

"Oh," said Ian.

"What time are you leaving us?"

"I understand Duncan is taking me to the airport. I ought to be leaving here at 10.30."

"Please don't forget us, Ian. We would like you to stay in touch."

"I promise I will do that, Moira. I think it would be a

great idea for all my family to visit and stay in one of the lodges. They look wonderful."

"Please remember, Ian, you will always be welcome at Baltoun Castle," said Moira, with a genuine heartfelt smile.

Chapter 6

The postman arrived early at the Kuznetsov home, in Eaton Square, to deliver their post. Viktor eagerly opened the letter he'd received from the Taylor Fine Art Gallery. As he read the contents, slowly a broad smile appeared on his face. 'Yes!' he said to himself. Bob Taylor had offered him the manager's role at the new London gallery... and with 50% of the UK agency! Wow, he thought, that's fabulous! He immediately ran back to his bedroom and picked up his mobile phone. He quickly dialled Penny's mobile number. When she answered he was so excited that it was difficult for Penny to fully comprehend what he was saying.

"Slow down, Vic," said Penny. "Are you saying you have been offered the job at the gallery?"

"Yes! Isn't it great?"

"Vic, I'm so pleased for you and the opportunity it gives you. Although there will be a number of people at Sotheby's who'll be sorry to see you leave."

"I know. But we can still be friends, can't we?"

"Of course. Ian is back in the office early this afternoon, do you want me to tell him?"

"Err, maybe not yet, Penny, please. I still have to reply and give my acceptance and discuss the final terms. Also, I will have to tell my current boss that I will be resigning.

Can we just keep it between ourselves for the time being? When it's all finalised I would like to take you and Ian out for dinner to celebrate. Without you two I would never have been in contention for a job like this."

"Okay, Vic. Let me know when you want it to be public knowledge. Must go now or I'll miss my train. Great news and... well done."

"Thanks, Penny." Viktor switched off the connection and placed the phone on his bed. However, his thoughts now switched from excitement to apprehension. Mmm, he pondered, I've still got to tell my father! That's going to be the tricky one!

Viktor had not mentioned to his father that he had applied for the manager's role at the gallery. He knew his father wanted him to progress steadily with a secure and stable career at Sotheby's. Viktor, however, had decided to bide his time and only tell his parents once he'd finally decided the direction his career was now going to take.

During that same day at work, Viktor struggled to concentrate. His mind kept switching from his new career move and to what he was going to say to his parents and to his current boss. Nevertheless, at lunchtime, he emailed Bob Taylor to confirm that he would accept the manager's position. Within a few minutes he received a reply.

Bob said he was very pleased and suggested they both meet to finalise the terms of the appointment. He suggested a meeting at the gallery at 6pm the following evening. Viktor emailed back to confirm that he would be there.

Later that evening, during dinner, Viktor pondered on whether now was the best time to finally come clean and tell his parents. However, as he watched his father eating his food, he, once again, decided now was still not quite the right time. He continued to eat his own meal quietly, but his mind was certainly elsewhere.

"Viktor." It was his father who had broken the silence, which suddenly dragged Viktor's mind back to the present. "I have some interesting news for you."

Viktor accidentally dropped his knife, apologised, and looked at his father with a surprised gaze.

"Some time ago I had a meeting with my good friend, Andrei. At the end of the meeting he asked if I would be the executor for his will. As you know, Andrei was a wealthy man and had complicated business affairs. Following his recent sad death, I have been trying to fully carry out all his wishes. He left specific legacies to a number of very special friends and colleagues, but he has also left you some money too."

"Oh! Me? Well that's very kind of him, but I hardly knew him," said Viktor, genuinely surprised.

"Andrei didn't have any children of his own so he took a keen interest in your progress as you were growing up. He would always ask about you when we talked."

"I see. Although I didn't know him that well, he always seemed to enjoy an interesting and exciting life."

"Well he's left you a legacy of ten million pounds."

"What! Oh, wow! I don't believe it!"

"Well you had better believe it, because it's true. There is, however, a stipulation attached to the legacy."

Viktor sat back in his chair. After the initial excitement, he wondered what his father was going to say now.

"You will get two million pounds on your 30th birthday, three million on your 33rd and a final five million on your 35th."

"That's still fabulously generous of him. Wow!"

"I'm pleased you see it that way, my boy. It is extremely generous."

Later that same evening in Antigua, Oscar had just returned home from seeing a client who had agreed to purchase a

Pissarro painting. The picture, an oil on canvas painting, showing a section of the Boulevard Montmartre in autumn, was painted in 1895. Oscar had been working on this deal for three weeks and had just finalised the sale for US$5.35 million. He never ceased to be amazed that such a relatively small picture, just 49 x 58cms, could be worth so much money, just because it had an authenticated signature of Camille Pissarro in the bottom left hand corner. Still, after sharing his commission with Wesley Fredericks, at the Shell Gallery, it was worth just over US$250,000 to him. He was certainly not going to complain about the money despite the fact that he was not a great fan of Pissarro's work. He saw the sale as just another very good day's work.

Oscar put a bottle of champagne in the fridge and quickly changed into his beach shorts. Ten minutes later he was swimming in the Caribbean Sea, by moonlight. Most evenings he usually found time for a swim. The beach was just a few metres from his villa and he thoroughly enjoyed the constant warm sea temperatures. After he'd finished, he went back to his villa, poured himself a glass of champagne and congratulated himself again. He then walked through to his office area and switched on the computer. Despite having been based in Antigua for just over six months, he still had to constantly remind himself that 11pm in Antigua was about lunchtime, tomorrow, in Hong Kong!

Oscar read through his emails and savoured the taste of the lovely chilled champagne. Only one item of correspondence caught his interest. It was from May Ling in Hong Kong. Although her normal base was Beijing, she was gradually spending more and more time in Hong Kong. She explained to Oscar that she had recently acquired a new client in Kowloon. She told him that the client had told her that he was originally from Trinidad but that his wife was homesick and he wanted to know if May could acquire any paintings that would remind his wife of Trinidad, or alternatively the Caribbean generally. May now asked if Oscar had any ideas or suggestions… and, if he had, could he email her photographs of the paintings.

Okay, thought Oscar, so how many pictures does she want? What's the price limit the client is willing to pay? He leaned back in his chair and pondered on the sort of paintings the client would maybe want. He knew there were some of the Tobars still for sale in London, but they might be too expensive. I'll pop into the Shell gallery tomorrow and see what I can find, he thought …and also have a chat with Wesley… and pick his brain!

Chapter 7

Emma's luncheon get-together with her former business partner, Bernard Murray, was a nice relaxed meeting. A far cry from their previous partners' business luncheons which were rarely relaxing. It had been many months since Emma had been in contact with anyone from the former partnership, so when Bernard telephoned, out of the blue, she was pleased, but also very curious.

Emma had quickly agreed to Bernard's suggestion of the lunch date and, immediately after the completion of the call, she set about finding a 'sitter' for Robert for that day. That proved not to be a problem as Ian's parents were always keen to see their only grandson. Robert was duly passed on to them for a three day holiday break.

The luncheon meeting went on until well into the afternoon. Bernard updated Emma on what he was now doing in retirement and Emma explained how radically her life had changed after becoming a mother.

"So," said Bernard, after swallowing the last piece of his cheesecake dessert. "You don't miss the world of accountancy?"

"To be honest, Bernard, yes I do. I miss the technical challenges and of course, the social interaction with colleagues and clients, but I certainly don't miss all the politics, hassles and complications attached to being a partner."

Bernard laughed at Emma's comments. He was expecting this sort of a response. He knew Emma very well.

"Exactly my feeling too," said Bernard. "Since retirement, I've been offered two partnerships, and a chairman's role, but in each case I said, 'no thank you'. I'm too old to start again and have earned my free time... my freedom! Audrey and I now intend to spend a large part of the winter abroad and we also help out with the grandchildren during the summer months. Mind, that is becoming less of a chore now. The youngest is taller than me!"

It was now time for Emma to laugh at Bernard's comment. She then asked, "Do you still keep in touch with John Tyler?"

"No. As you know, John had it in his head that you and I had 'stitched him up' – I think they were the words he used – with the sale of the partnership. We both know that was not the case. He still thought that William Jones & Co. would offer him a partnership, but it never materialised. The last I heard was that he and his wife had moved nearer to Edinburgh. He's joined a small accountancy firm there. Apparently his wife comes from that part of the world and her parents live close by."

"I hope he's happy now. Financially he should be okay."

"Do you think you will re-establish your career anytime soon?"

"I'm not sure, Bernard. All my time now is divided between being a mother and a wife."

"Ah, but are they satisfying all your ambitions and aspirations? You're a good accountant and you always had a sound and successful relationship with your clients."

"Bernard, I know you from old. What are you not telling me... yet!?"

"Okay, I'll come to the point. I know the chairman of one of your former large clients, Clinton and Beck, and he was asking after you. I told him your circumstances and he wondered if you would be interested in being their accountant and auditor again? Apparently, David Gould, who you know, he's now their Finance Director by the way, has been 'bending his ear'."

"Oh, I see," said Emma, sitting back in her chair. "I got on well with David, he's a nice man. But surely our agreement with William Jones & Co said that we were not allowed to approach our clients after the sale, for what, two years, wasn't it?"

"Well the two years is nearly up, but since the time when you dealt with them, they've sacked William Jones and are now very unhappy with the current firm they have a contract with."

"I see." Emma pondered the thought of being involved with accountancy again.

"Besides which, you would be doing this on your own. No politics, hassles and complications attached to being a partner, to quote your words."

"Yes... I can see that," said Emma, smiling. As the seconds ticked away the proposition became more and more interesting... and intriguing. "I'll need to discuss the matter with Ian first."

"Of course you will. Can you give me a ring in say, what, a week's time?"

Emma smiled at Bernard. "Yes, okay, Bernard. I'll telephone you within the week."

"Excellent, Emma, excellent."

When Ian arrived home from work later that evening, it was a strange experience for him when there was no Robert to run across the hallway to greet him. He then remembered that Emma had arranged for him to stay with his grandparents for two nights. He put his bags in the hall and walked into the kitchen.

"Hi," said Ian, to Emma, who was preparing his meal. "Isn't it quiet without the whirlwind!?"

Emma walked over and greeted Ian with a kiss. "Yes it is. I will collect him the day after tomorrow and then normal service will resume."

"Well we had better take advantage of all this peace and quiet. By the way, how did your luncheon meeting with Bernard go?"

"It was very interesting. Pour us a couple of glasses of wine and I'll tell you the full details whilst you eat. I'm still really full from lunchtime."

As Ian poured two glasses of chablis, Emma dished up Ian's pasta meal. They then both sat down at the kitchen island. Whilst Ian slowly ate his food, Emma sipped her wine and outlined the discussions she'd had with Bernard earlier that day. Finally she mentioned Bernard's conversation with the chairman of Clinton and Beck… and the proposition.

"Wow! I bet that was a surprise?" asked Ian.

"I know Bernard from old. I knew when he telephoned me that there would be more to the luncheon invitation than just a chat about old times. But yes, I was not expecting this one either."

"So, what do you think?" asked Ian. He'd wondered for a little while if Emma was missing the world of accountancy.

"I think I would like to have a go at this opportunity, Ian. It would be part-time and I could fit a lot of the work around Robert. Mind they're not offering me the job, Bernard is just sounding me out, to see whether I would be available and interested."

"It sounds a bit more certain than that. They've dealt with you before and don't like the firm they're currently using. How much work do you think there would be?"

"On average, perhaps about 10 hours a week. However,

there will be periods when it will be very busy. I might employ some part-time help for these busy periods. Quarter reporting and the like. They're now a listed company, so there would be a lot of extra work to meet with the usual regulations."

"Okay. So what happens next?"

"I promised Bernard that I would contact him within the week. He'll then report back to the chairman."

"So what are you going to tell him?"

Emma sipped her wine and gently put the glass back on its coaster. She looked at Ian and said, "If it's okay with you, I would like to tell Bernard to set me up for the interview."

"Excellent," said Ian, after he had swallowed the last mouthful of his food. "I think it's a great idea."

"You don't think I would be taking on too much work do you?"

Ian picked up his glass of wine and pushed it forward towards Emma's glass. "Cheers. Welcome back to the business world."

Emma, however, decided to sleep on her final decision.

It was during the car journey two days' later, when she was going to collect Robert, that Emma finally made up her mind. She indicated a left turn and steered the car off the main road and into a side street where she found a convenient parking space. She lifted her mobile phone out of her handbag and dialled Bernard's home telephone number. Bernard answered the call and after Emma explained her decision, and why, Bernard confirmed that he would pass on her message to the chairman of Clinton and Beck.

Chapter 8

It was just after 5.40pm when Viktor left the Sotheby's building and started to walk the short journey to the Taylor Fine Art Gallery. During the day, his mind had been a real mixture of excitement and confusion. He was now, in theory, a paper millionaire and had been offered a fabulous new career opportunity. How lucky was all this!

As Viktor slowly walked along New Bond Street, he tried to focus his mind on the meeting with Bob Taylor in a few minutes, but still wondered whether his new inheritance had changed his thoughts and ambitions towards the manager's role. He looked at his watch, 5.45. I've got 15 minutes to finally make up my mind, he thought.

Stopping outside one of the jeweller's shops, he stared through the window, but his eyes were not really focusing on anything for sale. He was just 50 metres away from the gallery, but now wished he'd had the opportunity to discuss his quandary with his former boss, because he knew Ian would have had a less confused and better detached view of the situation. He continued to ponder on his options until gradually the picture became much clearer. Yes, he thought, I now know, definitely, what I'm going to say! He turned away from the jeweller's shop and briskly headed towards the gallery. There was definitely a new sense of purpose in his stride.

When Viktor arrived at the gallery, there was a 'closed' sign hanging in the door window. Bob had told Viktor that although the gallery was closed to the public at 5.30, the entrance door would not be locked. He pushed the door open and, as he entered, the bell above his head rang. After closing the door behind him he clicked the lock into place and walked through the display area towards the office at the back of the building. Bob came out of this room, greeted Viktor and they both walked back into the office.

"Welcome to what will become your new office," said Bob with a smile. "Sit down here and try it on for size." Bob pointed to the comfortable looking chair behind the desk.

"Thank you," said Viktor. He sat down in the chair and made himself comfortable.

Although the room was used as an office, it was also doubling up as a storage and packing area. There were a number of paintings leaning against the far wall and another two still remaining half packed on the work table.

Bob lifted over another chair and put it at the side of where Viktor was now sitting. "Okay," he said, and at the same time moved some papers in front of him. "Do you think you'll still be happy with the manager's role?"

"Yes, I am. Certain," replied Viktor, with convincing confidence.

"Right then. Let's get down to business."

For the next 30 minutes the two men discussed the finer details of Viktor's new role and his contract. The longer the meeting continued, the more Viktor was convinced this was the right career decision. He could see lots of opportunities ahead, although he decided to keep some of his best ideas hidden, 'under-wraps', from Bob, at least for the time being.

The meeting finished when they both agreed on Viktor's starting date. One month after Viktor had handed in his notice at Sotheby's.

That same evening, Emma was cooking the family's dinner when she was interrupted by the telephone ringing. She immediately assumed it would be Ian to say he was going to be late arriving home. To her surprise, however, it was not Ian, but Bernard!

"Emma. You have a meeting with the chairman and David Gould next Tuesday morning at 10 o'clock. I hope that's okay with you?" said Bernard, this time straight to the point.

"Yes," replied Emma. "I'll be there… and, Bernard, thank you."

"My pleasure. Let me know how it goes."

"I will, Bernard. Goodbye." Emma put the phone back on its base and entered the appointment on the family's calendar hanging on the kitchen wall, just at her side. She stood back, smiled and wondered what she had let herself in for!

Emma's thoughts were broken when she heard Ian entering through the front door. Robert put down the toys he was playing with, at the far end of the kitchen area, and ran through the door and into the hallway, shouting, "Daddy".

A few seconds later Ian arrived in the kitchen. He was carrying Robert. He went over to where Emma was standing and gave her a kiss. "Are you okay? You look deep in thought."

"Mmm. Yes, fine," said Emma. "I've just put the telephone down after chatting to Bernard. I've got a meeting next Tuesday with the chairman and David Gould at Clinton and Beck."

"Well that's great… isn't it?" Ian was unsure now what Emma's likely response was going to be.

"Let's all have dinner, put Robert to bed and then we can have a quiet and proper chat," said Emma, who then returned to the two simmering saucepans on the hob.

"Okay… right then, young man come and show me what you have been building over there," said Ian. He turned around and carried Robert over to where there lay a large pile of coloured plastic bricks.

At 11.30pm, Sergei finally put the telephone handset back on its base in his home office. The incoming call had been from an agitated Boris. Following Andrei's murder, both Sergei and Boris had become more concerned about their own futures. They knew that Andrei had 'acquired' an increasing number of enemies, both from his time in Russia and, subsequently, with his 'business dealings' around the world. However, they had assumed that the only organisations capable of carrying out such a skilled and quiet execution, would have been one of either the Russian government, the Russian Mafia or professional agents working under instruction on either of their behalf. They were now fearing that the same organisation might also be thinking that due to their association with Andrei, they could now be targets themselves.

However, following Boris's new information, Sergei's assumptions began to change. Boris had received news from a colleague in Venezuela who had told him that the motivation for Andrei's death was different to what they had all believed. This colleague had told Boris that it was strongly rumoured in South America that Andrei had been murdered because he had cheated one of the heads of a leading narcotics cartel in Colombia… out of US$22 million!

Sergei was partly relieved with this information, but he also wondered what the hell Andrei had been trying to achieve by doing business with a drugs baron in the first place! Especially one who was known as the 'Godfather' of South America! After all, it was not Andrei's normal practice to be involved with such dangerous people. Mmm, thought Sergei, maybe there are just some things one should not want to find out about Andrei's dealings!

Sergei got up from his seat, switched off the desk lamp and headed up the stairs to his and Ludmilla's bedroom. Halfway up the stairs he suddenly stopped and looked at his watch, 11.40. No, he thought, I'll deal with it in the morning… and he carried on climbing up the stairs.

Chapter 9

Emma arrived five minutes early for her appointment with the chairman and finance director of Clinton and Beck. Whilst the receptionist telephoned David Gould's PA, announcing Emma's arrival, Emma sat a little nervously, on a light grey leather seat looking out through a large window and into a small garden area. She tried to remember the last time she'd sat on this particular seat, whilst she'd been waiting to see David. She decided it must be about four years ago. Mmm, she thought, a long time to be away from accountancy!

Emma looked down to her knees and automatically pulled at the hem of her skirt. It was also a long time since she had worn one of her 'work suits' for a business meeting. The previous evening she had tried on a selection of her more formal 'work' clothes and was especially pleased to discover that most of them still fitted. Following the birth of Robert, she had been determined to get her figure back as soon as possible and had diligently followed the regimented exercise programme Zoe Taylor, in Monaco, had recommended. She was now pleased that all the hard work had paid dividends.

"Mrs Caxton?"

"Yes, hello," replied Emma, a little surprised as she'd not heard a young lady arrive at her side.

"Hello, I'm Lucy, Sir Gordon Hawkins' PA. Sir Gordon and David Gould are now ready to see you. Will you follow me please?"

Emma stood up and brushed her skirt down again. She then followed Lucy as requested. Emma guessed the young lady would be about 23. She wondered, was that the age nowadays for a PA?

They travelled up in the elevator together in silence. The elevator eventually stopped at the top floor and the doors opened. Lucy stepped out and Emma followed her again. They walked along a well lit corridor decorated with a number of oil paintings on both walls. I'm sure Ian would be interested in a number of these, she thought.

At the end of the corridor Lucy stopped, knocked and opened the large oak door. The sign on the wall next to it said 'Board Room'. She walked through and held the door ajar for Emma to follow. At the same time she announced, "Mrs Caxton", to the two men sitting around the table.

Emma thanked Lucy and walked past her. She was immediately greeted by a person she already knew very well. About six feet tall, medium build with black hair, Emma decided David hadn't aged one minute since she had last met him.

"Hello Emma, so good to see you again," said David Gould, who had now walked over to greet her. Emma smiled back and they both shook hands.

As Emma walked at David's side around the table, she said to him, "It's nice to meet you again too… and I gather you are now the Finance Director. Congratulations."

They were now standing next to the chairman. David smiled again at Emma in acknowledgement of her congratulations. He then said, "Emma, please meet our chairman, Sir Gordon Hawkins."

Sir Gordon had stood up from his seat and held out his

hand. "Welcome back to Clinton and Beck, Mrs Caxton. David has talked about you often."

Emma shook Sir Gordon's hand and smiled. "It's a pleasure to meet you, sir." Emma did feel slightly embarrassed. It was a few years since she had been to such an important business meeting.

"Right. Let's all take a seat and we can get started," said Sir Gordon, and they all sat down.

For the next hour and a half the three of them discussed the finances of Clinton and Beck. Once Emma had got over her initial nerves she quickly got back into her stride and her old business routine.

At the end of the meeting it was agreed that Emma would take over responsibility for the Company's accounting and auditing needs. Initially for 12 months and with effect from the commencement of the new financial year. At the end of 12 months, both sides would then review their position.

Emma mentally calculated that the new financial year would commence in about six weeks time. A lot to get my teeth into in such a short period of time, she thought.

"Thank you for coming in to see us, Emma. It was a pleasure meeting you at long last. I'll leave you with David," said Sir Gordon. He rose up from the table and once again, held out his hand.

Both David and Emma also stood up and Emma shook the chairman's hand. "It was a pleasure meeting you, Sir Gordon. I hope to see you again soon."

Once Sir Gordon left the room, Emma and David resumed their seats.

"Well done, Emma. A good performance. You've certainly got me out of a tricky position," said David, with a sigh. "Our current accountants have struggled to understand our business and it will be a relief to have you back on board."

"I'm pleased to be dealing with you again, David. You will be my only client going forward."

"Oh! Really!? We are not going to be that demanding are we?"

"No, no. I need to get my feet under the table again, so to speak. And with a young son, I was only looking for a part-time role."

"Yes, I heard you'd had a baby. Congratulations! So, how is motherhood?"

"Like most things, there are good and... well, let's say, more difficult times. But overall I am thoroughly enjoying having had Robert. However, I do realise that I still need to challenge my brain again too."

"Well I'm sure we will be able to help you achieve that!" said David, laughing at his own comment.

Emma smiled back. "It's quite exciting to be back working again, and at least this time, I will not have the politics, hassles and extra complications attached to being a partner."

"Yes, it can be tedious sometimes when you are working in a team. Too many egos and self interests!"

"Mmm. Well, I'm aware that I'm taking up your time. Let me take those files we were discussing earlier and I'll be on my way."

Just over an hour later Emma arrived home. From her car she unloaded three large paper files and several CD disks, all relating to Clinton and Beck's accounting records. She took them through to the home office and placed them on her desk. She suddenly decided she felt hungry, so left the files and went into the kitchen to make herself some lunch.

Whilst eating her tuna and cucumber sandwich, Emma mulled over in her mind the discussions from the earlier meeting. Overall, she was pleased with the way the meeting had gone and also that the work didn't appear to be quite as daunting as she'd earlier feared. The challenge now was to reignite her accountancy brain!

Emma left the kitchen and walked back to the home office. There she sat down and looked at the pile of files and CDs. She began to think about the strategy she was going to adopt for this new business venture. She was convinced that, despite the demands of Robert, it could, and should, all work out well. Robert would be starting nursery school very soon and the arrangement she had come to with her friend, and fellow mum, Brenda. ought to help too. Yes, she thought, it should all really work out just fine.

Right, she thought. First things first. Emma picked up the telephone and rang Bernard. For the next ten minutes she gave him a summary of her meeting with Clinton and Beck

Bernard told Emma that he was very pleased and wished her the very best of luck! Also he asked her to stay in touch.

Chapter 10

Ian was reading a draft catalogue for a forthcoming Sotheby's auction, when Penny appeared at the door to his office. "Ian, I have a Russian gentleman on the telephone wanting to speak to you. He has the same surname as Vic. I was wondering if he is related?"

"Is his first name Sergei?" asked Ian, abandoning the catalogue.

"Yes, do you know him?"

"Yes. He's Vic's father. You'd better put him through."

"Ten seconds later Ian's phone rang and he answered it. "Hello, Sergei, how are you?"

"I'm very well, Ian. Thank you. I've been finalising Andrei's affairs and have come across a letter that's addressed to you. It's sealed and just has your name on the envelope. I don't know what it says."

Curious, thought Ian. "Maybe it's something to do with the Monaco apartment?"

"I don't think so. As you know, that's all finalised. No, I feel it could be something more sinister," replied Sergei. His voice had genuine concern.

"Sinister!" exclaimed Ian. He sat up immediately. "What do you mean?"

"As you know, Ian, my English is not too good. Maybe

sinister is not the word I mean. I just feel it might be trouble."

"I see." Was trouble better than sinister? Ian wondered.

"Can we meet and I will give you this letter. Also there's some more information you should know. They may be connected. I don't want to say too much over the telephone."

"Yes of course," replied Ian. He was now partly intrigued and partly worried. "When and where do you suggest?"

"I have to go to a meeting near Trafalgar Square this afternoon. There is an inn close by in Duke Street called 'The Green Man'. Do you know it?"

"No, but I know where Duke Street is. What time will your meeting finish?"

"It's a social meeting with a few Russian colleagues, so I can leave when I need to. Shall we say 6 o'clock?"

Ian quickly checked his diary as he remembered he was supposed to be meeting with a work colleague to discuss the auction catalogue at 5.15. "Can we make it nearer 6.30? I should be free by then."

"Of course. I'll see you later."

Ian heard a click and the line went dead. He slowly replaced the handset on its base and wondered why Sergei thought the letter might be spelling trouble… or worse, sinister!

Penny broke Ian's thinking when she re-appeared at his door. "So was he Vic's father?"

"Yes, he is," replied Ian. "I've met him a couple of times with Vic. I think he wants to chat about Vic's career," replied Ian. He was concerned not to give Penny any details of his real dealings with Sergei.

Penny nodded to Ian and walked back to her desk. Strange, she thought, why would Mr Kuznetsov want to discuss Vic's career now that he has only a few days left before leaving Sotheby's?

Ian leaned across his desk and reached for the draft catalogue once again. He tried to concentrate on the forthcoming auction, but after 10 minutes he gave up and decided to try and clear his mind. As he passed Penny's desk he told her he was going to get a cup of coffee. Did she want him to bring her one back?

"No, I'm fine at the moment. Thank you for asking," replied Penny. Ian smiled and walked out of the room and into the corridor. Penny leaned back in her chair deep in thought. There is definitely something not quite right here.

Sergei arrived at 'The Green Man' at 6.20. He walked into the lounge bar and ordered a double vodka. He took his drink and sat down at a vacant table where he could see the entrance door. He only had to wait five minutes for Ian to appear. Ian immediately spotted Sergei and walked over to join him. The two men shook hands. "Let me buy you a drink, Ian," said Sergei. "What would you like?"

"Oh, thank you, Sergei. I will have a small glass of chablis please."

Ian sat down and looked around the bar area. He'd never been to this pub before and looked at the decor, deciding that despite some of the modern renovations and due to the pub's location, it must be several hundred years' old. It was reasonably busy with some early drinkers, but not busy enough to be noisy.

"Here we are." Sergei handed Ian his glass of wine and then sat down.

"Thank you, Sergei, Cheers."

"Cheers," responded Sergei, and they both gently clinked glasses. Sergei drank a small mouthful of his vodka and then put the glass back on the table. He then looked around the bar area and, after seemingly being satisfied that nothing appeared to be out of the ordinary, he removed a white sealed envelope from the inside of his coat pocket and handed it across to Ian.

Ian took hold of the envelope and looked at the front. There was just the handwritten name, 'Ian Caxton'.

"That is Andrei's writing," said Sergei. "It was amongst some of his Swiss bank papers."

"Oh," said Ian, none the wiser. He just stared at the envelope and wondered what was inside.

"You do not have to open it here, but before you do, I had better tell you that I think I know who killed Andrei and why."

Ian put the unopened envelope on the table in front of him, sipped his wine and waited for Sergei to explain more.

Sergei told Ian about the conversation Boris had with a colleague in Venezuela. He explained that this colleague had a connection with a high ranking member of the Colombian government and he'd informed him that Andrei was murdered because he had cheated the head of one of the leading narcotics cartels, out of US$22 million!

"Oh, wow!" replied Ian, picking up the envelope again. "And you think this letter has something to do with Andrei's murder?"

"I sometimes have unusual feelings, Ian, and when I first found and handled this letter I felt a very strange sensation."

"Do you think I should open it?"

"It's up to you. Once it's open you will not be able to forget the contents."

Ian stared at the envelope, turned it over and looked at the back. "Andrei obviously wanted me to have this information."

"Yes, that would seem to be the case."

Ian took another sip of his wine. He then made the decision and ripped across the top and pulled out three typed A4 sheets of paper. He scanned all three sheets. There was no covering message. He said to Sergei, "It is just a list of names and addresses of people… around the world. Look, there are also some numbers at the end of each address." Ian handed the papers to Sergei, who was not overly keen to read the contents. Nevertheless he did briefly glance at each sheet before handing them back to Ian.

"I think you will find that it's probably a list of all Andrei's business connections, around the world. My guess is that if you look at the Colombian name it will be Gonzales, Georges Gonzales. He's the person that Andrei apparently cheated!"

Ian read down the list until he came to Colombia. There it was, Georges Gonzales!

When Ian had finished his meeting with Sergei, he slowly walked back to Victoria Underground station to connect with the first leg of his journey home. He pondered this latest news and wondered what, if anything, he would do with all this information. Why had Andrei given him these details? Why was there not a covering note?

Once he was sitting in the train going home to Esher, Ian removed Andrei's list of business connections from his inside pocket. He had only scanned the listing briefly in the pub with Sergei, so he now began to read each entry in more detail. He noted the countries listed, the contact name and the addresses. He concluded that the numbers listed in the end column must equate to the turnover, or was it profit, with that particular connection. He mentally added up all the numbers and gave a quiet whistle at the final total. He smiled at the thought of Andrei's likely comment of, "And it's all tax free, my friend!"

Ian looked again at each country's entry and noted there were two names listed in Monaco. Just a minute, he thought, I know that one! Surely that's Bob Taylor's father-in-law?

The entry read :

Monaco3: Antoine Allard, Les Roses Rouges. Euros 25.2 million.

The train began to slow down as it approached Esher station. Ian decided there was a lot of information here to digest. He definitely needed a lot more time to consider the full implications. Was this part of the opportunity Andrei had always promised?

Chapter 11

Oscar made himself an early morning cup of coffee and walked into the small office area. One of the first jobs Oscar had completed when he moved into the villa was to change a small, single bedroom into a working office. It was situated on the north facing side of his villa, so it didn't get too hot during the day.

It had been over a week since he had emailed 20 photographs of the paintings depicting scenes from the Caribbean to May Ling. He had asked Wesley's advice beforehand and Wesley had shown him about thirty paintings that he thought might be suitable options for a Trinidadian lady who was homesick in Hong Kong. Most of the paintings were of colourful flowers, but there were also four seascapes with palm trees as well. Oscar decided on 20 and took a photograph of each picture.

He put the coffee cup on his desk and opened up his laptop computer. He scanned through the new emails in the inbox, but was quickly disappointed, there was still no email from May Ling. He sat back in his chair and was now feeling definitely frustrated. This could be another big deal, he thought. I wonder if I should email a reminder to May? He looked at his watch and roughly calculated the time in Hong Kong. Eventually he decided that he would leave it for one more day. He looked through his other emails, but decided nothing was urgent… or even very important. After finishing drinking his coffee he went into his bedroom and changed into beach shorts. Five minutes later he was swimming in the Caribbean Sea. Even though it was still early in the morning, the water was calm and warm, just as Oscar liked it.

When Oscar returned to his villa he was in a better mood. He had swum for nearly half a mile and was feeling refreshed and more relaxed. Once again he checked his emails, but this time with hope rather than expectation. However, and to his surprise, there was the email he'd been waiting for! He opened it and quickly read through the contents. May Ling apologised for not coming back to him sooner, but she had been waiting on her client's decision. The decision was that he wanted six of the original list of paintings. Well that's better than none, he thought, but he did feel a little disappointed. Maybe it was unrealistic to think the client would buy all 20 from the photographs he'd sent. But just six… oh well… better than nothing, he supposed.

Oscar checked the six named paintings against his price chart and totted up the total. He then calculated his commission. After allowing for packaging and postage, he thought he would be making just over US$50,000 in profit. Okay, not a fortune, but it would pay the bills for a while… and it would, of course, all help to cement his relationship with Wesley at the Shell gallery. That arrangement was beginning to work very nicely.

Emma had spent the last few days scrutinising Clinton and Beck's last three years' accounting records. Because of the volume of paperwork, she'd decided to move all the files from the home office to the dining room. Here she was using the dining table as her temporary office desk. Now spread across the table were several open paper files, six CD discs and her laptop computer.

For the last few hours she had been slowly coming to the conclusion that the figures didn't fully tie up with the high level of information she'd been given by Clinton and Beck's accounts department. Also she had checked her own files from four years ago when she was last handling the Clinton and Beck's accounting records. Again the recent figures didn't seem to follow the same trend that had been established in those earlier years. Was she just rusty or was she actually missing something important? Or was there something, possibly more sinister or devious, going on?

Emma laid down her reading spectacles, stood up, yawned, stretched and decided to make herself a cup of coffee. She checked her watch. Mmm, I'll have to collect Robert in half an hour. I think I'd better call it quits for the time being and return to these files again tomorrow.

She walked into the kitchen, filled the kettle and switched it on to boil. Whilst it was heating up she made a decision. She picked up her telephone contact book and flicked through the pages until she came to the letter 'F'. There she found the number she was looking for and put the book face down on the worktop whilst she made the coffee. Two minutes later she was ringing Susan Flewin.

"Susan Flewin," came the reply from the other end of the line.

"Hello, Susan. Emma here."

"Oh, hi, Emma. What a lovely surprise. How are you… and Robert? He must be, what, two now?"

I'm fine thank you… and Robert, he was three, six weeks ago."

"Oh, wow. How time flies."

"Susan," Emma was eager to get to the point before she

had to rush off to collect Robert. "Would you be interested in a part-time job?"

"That depends, Emma. You know I received a nice redundancy package following the takeover of the old partnership by William Jones & Co. Well, since then, I've been quite happy just looking after the family."

"I would like you to work for me. Very part-time, some busy periods but mostly very little."

"Are you working again then, Emma?"

Emma spent the next five minutes explaining the background details leading up to her agreement to take on the accounting and auditing work for Clinton and Beck. Susan listened patiently. When Emma had finished, Susan asked a few questions and then finally said yes, she would help Emma.

Emma's final words before she put the phone down back on its base were, "It should be just like old times!"

Later that evening, after dinner, and after Robert had been put to bed, Emma and Ian finally sat down on the sofa together in the lounge. It was Emma who broke the silence. "Ian, remember the anonymous telephone call I received just before the partnership takeover?"

"Mmm," replied Ian, trying to remember. "Didn't you think it was from one of your former PAs?"

"Yes, Susan Flewin. I spoke to her on the telephone earlier today."

"Oh, okay. Did she have another mysterious message?" joked Ian.

"No, not this time," smiled Emma. "I actually telephoned her. I've offered her a part-time job helping me with the Clinton and Beck account."

"Oh, I see," said Ian, but truthfully he was none the wiser, "...and?"

"She agreed, which is really useful because she had some

dealings with the account with me, in the very early days."

Ian leaned forward, picked up his glass of wine and waited for Emma to come to the point she obviously wanted to make.

Emma continued, "Over the last two days I've been going through Clinton and Beck's papers and records and now I'm a bit worried, because they don't seem to fully tie up. I'm hoping that Susan, with a fresh pair of eyes, will spot my error."

"Do you think you have made a mistake?"

"I don't think so, but of course I'm still a bit rusty. It would be great for Susan to double check my thoughts and calculations before I go back to David so soon. The current auditors are contracted to deal with the accounts until the end of the financial year, but honestly, Ian, I don't think they have all the information!"

"But surely, I mean, these auditors are professional, won't they come to the same conclusion as you?"

"The world of auditing has changed quite a bit since my partnership days. Competition is a lot fiercer between the big companies and some have cut corners to save costs. So there's been quite a reduction in professional standards and, sometimes, poorer investigations!"

This was all news to Ian. He had heard of a few big companies collapsing, sometimes involving fraud, but he had no idea that maybe poor auditing contributed to the collapse as well.

"Audit profit margins have been slowly reducing," continued Emma. "This has resulted in corners being cut even more. After several years of high profile company collapses and rising shareholder anger over auditors' failures to spot fraud some severe fines have been imposed by the regulator. Unfortunately, this has only marginally improved the situation. A lot of audit companies are now having to be extra careful, but there are still some continuing to cut the same corners."

Ian looked slightly puzzled. "So why don't the government bodies come in to protect shareholders and of course, the company's employees? Big accountants shouldn't be allowed to just shrug their shoulders and walk away from difficult jobs and their responsibilities."

"I agree. The Financial Reporting Council is being put under ever increasing pressure to act. They are responding with heavier fines, but the business world as a whole needs to accept higher market fees. Also accountants should then be hit by even larger fines for continuing with poor quality auditing."

"So why do you want to get involved in all this again?"

"I miss the challenge, Ian. I've missed the world of accountancy and the people. Clinton and Beck were one of my favourite clients and I really want to make sure their accounts are in first class order. I've made sure that I'll be paid well and, in return, I will not be cutting any corners. I owe it to their directors, shareholders and of course, all their employees."

"Mmm," responded Ian, "so no pressure then!"

However, neither Ian, nor Emma, were laughing at Ian's joke.

Chapter 12

In the weeks leading up to when Viktor would be starting his new job at Taylor Fine Art Gallery, he had repeatedly been putting off the inevitable discussion with his parents to inform them of his impending change of career. It was during today's Sunday lunch with his parents that he finally plucked up the courage. Just one day prior to him starting at the gallery.

His father had not shouted or interrupted whilst Viktor had explained everything. To Viktor's relief all his father had to say was that he hoped Viktor was making the right decision and wished him well. Viktor was astonished and just a little disappointed. His father had previously emphasised on many occasions how important it was to achieve. To achieve the best results at school, at university and to achieve a successful career. Viktor was not sure why his father was not being so pushy. Had he finally decided that Viktor was now old enough to make his own decisions in life, or was it more the fact that Sergei knew that if Viktor did fail, he still had Andrei's inheritance to fall back on? Either way, Viktor was determined to display to his father, and to anybody else who might cast a doubt on his decision, that he had definitely made the correct call.

During his first week working at the gallery, Viktor had spent most of the time listening to Bob as he explained how he wanted the gallery to operate. He'd also taught Viktor some of the tricks of the trade and advised some special points to look out for when negotiating to buy and sell paintings. Some of these tips Viktor already knew as he had used them previously at Sotheby's, but a number were new to him and he thought they would come in very useful. Bob had also told Viktor that he would be returning to Monaco at the end of the next week, so if he had any queries this was the week to ask. However, Bob did emphasise that he would still be only a telephone call, or an email message, away.

On Tuesday morning, whilst Bob was out delivering a painting, a gentleman walked into the gallery. He wandered across to view the four remaining unsold Tobar pictures. After a few seconds, Viktor joined him and explained the background history of the artist and the picture's provenance.

"An interesting story," said the man, with a slight North American accent. He then went on to ask Viktor some questions.

Viktor noticed that this middle aged man was both well dressed and seemed to be quite knowledgeable about the techniques Tobar had employed. As a result he was feeling a little nervous and hesitant to push towards a sale, just yet. Let the man think about what he'd been told, but don't let him out of the gallery!

The man thanked Viktor and said he would look at some of the other pictures. He then walked away and went further into the gallery's display area.

Two minutes later, Bob Taylor returned to the gallery and noticed the visitor. He looked across at Viktor and Viktor flicked his head gently towards the four Tobar pictures. Bob nodded and sat down on a nearby sofa. He picked up the gallery catalogue and pretended to be reading it.

Viktor immediately knew that this was his cue to demonstrate to Bob his newly acquired selling skills. No more prevarications. Another two minutes passed and the man returned back to the four Tobars. Viktor joined him.

"These are pretty good," said the man, not taking his eyes off the pictures.

"Yes, we had fourteen, but ten have already been sold. These are the last four in the collection. We've got a couple of inquiries still outstanding."

"Interesting. Tell me, are these the best prices you can offer?" said the man, his eyes moving from the paintings to the price tags.

Viktor quickly glanced over the man's shoulder to where Bob was sitting. He knew Bob could hear the conversation, but he'd made no move to look up from the catalogue.

"We could come to a special arrangement for the sale of all four paintings," replied Viktor. He was conscious that he was beginning to perspire a little.

"Mmm, I see… and what would that be?"

"We could offer a 5% discount and free delivery," replied Viktor.

"I was thinking more like 15%."

"No, I'm sorry, we already turned down 12% last week. I could move a little more to 7%."

The man continued to look at each painting closely. "My final offer is 10% for all four."

"How would you like to pay that, sir?"

"I could do cash, by bank transfer, but I would still want free delivery."

"Where would you want the pictures to be delivered?"

"Epsom in Surrey."

"That should be fine, sir. Should we go over to my desk to complete the paperwork?"

Viktor guided the gentleman to his desk where they both sat down.

Bob folded up the catalogue and placed it back on the small table at the side of the sofa. He stood up, deliberately made a noise, and wandered across to look at the Tobars.

"Sorry, buddy, but those have just been sold," said the man, looking across to Bob from Viktor's desk.

"I think you've made a good investment," replied Bob, walking away and looking at some other pictures.

"It looks as though you were just in time, Mr...?" asked Viktor.

"Crosby, Aaron Crosby. When will the pictures be delivered?"

"Would Friday suit you, Mr Crosby?"

"Friday afternoon would be great."

When the paperwork and transaction were finally completed, Viktor shook Mr Crosby's hand.

"It has been a pleasure doing business with you, sir," responded Viktor. He was now beginning to relax.

After Mr Crosby had departed, Bob walked over to join Viktor. "Well done, Vic. That was an excellent sale. I can see I've definitely made the right managerial choice."

Viktor smiled back and wiped the sweat from his brow. He was feeling both relieved and excited.

Later that same day Viktor met up with Penny at 'The Grapes'. It was a meeting they had set up just before Viktor had left Sotheby's. Penny was eager to find out how Viktor was progressing in his new career.

"So, Vic, how's it all going?" asked Penny, once they had sat down with their drinks.

"It's going well, thanks, Penny. It's been useful to have Bob alongside me, but I've also managed to make a few sales on my own," replied Viktor. He sipped the first pint of beer he'd had for a few days. "Bob goes back to Monaco at the end of this week, so I'll be on my own from then on."

"Are you going to be okay? It's quite a responsibility."

"Of course. Bob told me that if there was anything to discuss he was always available by telephone or email. Hopefully, I won't have to contact him very often. So, how are Sotheby's existing without me?" asked Viktor, smiling at his own comment.

"Oh, we're just about surviving," joked Penny. "Life goes on." They both laughed.

"How's Ian?"

"The usual I guess. Mind he has been a little more pre-occupied recently. I think it was following a meeting with your father. I didn't know he knew your father."

"Mmm." Viktor had to think quickly. He didn't know his father had spoken to Ian recently. He also didn't want to tell Penny the whole truth but he certainly didn't want to tell her any lies either. "I introduced my father to Ian a few years ago. We met in a pub by accident. They discovered that they both knew the same colleague in the art business. Small world!"

Penny was not totally convinced, but decided to let it go. "So what are your mega plans in the art world then, Vic? Once you've been let loose on your own next week."

"My main aim is to grow the agency. The gallery is really just the start. I want to seriously get involved in buying and selling paintings, both for clients and myself. There's a lot of money to be made out there. I did some calculations this afternoon. The Isaac Tobar paintings have all been sold now and I think Ian made a profit of about five million pounds! That's the sort of money that I intend to make."

"Wow, you are thinking big. I hope you have enough investment money," said Penny, smiling at Viktor's ambitions.

"I don't think I've told you about my inheritance, have I?"

Chapter 13

It was just after 9 o'clock in the evening and Ian was sitting at his desk in the home office. Emma was out at a meeting with some friends and Robert was tucked up and sleeping in his bed. Ian decided to take this rare quiet opportunity to read Andrei's list of clients once again. He wanted to be able to think more clearly about what all this information meant to him and how he was going to use it now, or in the future. He was convinced that whatever decision he finally made, it was going to be the biggest business decision he had made in his life!

He retrieved the envelope containing the listing out of the safe and then sat down behind his desk. After removing the three sheets of paper, he started with sheet one and slowly worked down the page making notes and comments at the end of each entry. Against 'Colombia. Georges Gonzales', he simply wrote, *'Don't touch with a barge pole!'* Against 'Monaco3, Antoine Allard, Les Roses Rouges', he wrote, *'To be discussed in more detail with Bob Taylor – asap'*.

Gradually he read and commented on each entry. Slowly a picture began to materialise in his head. Andrei had listed connections throughout the world, but Ian realised that he had to be a bit more limited, more selective – maybe just to pick certain locations at this stage.

Eventually he also concluded that some clients looked more potential than others.

After he'd entered his final comment on the last sheet, he returned all the papers to the safe. He now needed to think carefully about what his next steps would be. He also thought about telling Emma his initial thinking, but then decided maybe it was just a bit early to involve her.

After locking the safe, he was just going to return to his desk when he heard Robert calling for his mother. Ian climbed the stairs and entered Robert's bedroom. There he found Robert sitting up in his bed.

"Well, my little man, what's the problem with you?" asked Ian, as he sat down next to Robert on his bed.

"I want mummy," demanded Robert, still half asleep and rubbing his eyes.

"Mummy is out at the moment. She's meeting some friends. What do you need her for?"

"I'm thirsty."

"Do you want some water?"

Robert nodded his head.

"Okay, I'll go and get your beaker." Ian left the room and went back downstairs to the kitchen. He removed a plastic beaker from the cupboard and half filled it with cold water. He then returned to Robert's bedroom. Robert was still sitting up. He took the beaker from his father with both hands and sipped half the contents. Happy once again, he passed the beaker back to his father and settled back down.

Ian put the beaker at the side of his bed. "Are we okay, now?"

Robert's eyes were closed, but he smiled and nodded his head.

"Well I've left the beaker on the side here if you need any more."

Robert did not stir again and Ian quietly kissed him on

his head and whispered, "goodnight". He then walked out of Robert's bedroom. His intention was to go straight back to the home office, but he decided he needed a drink himself, not water though. It was a cold glass of chablis that was needed from the fridge.

He carried his drink back towards the office, but briefly stopped at the bottom of the stairs and listened. Satisfied that all was quiet again upstairs, he walked back to the office and sat down on the small armchair in the corner of the room. He sipped his wine and then picked up the article he had torn out of the Sunday newspaper magazine some days ago. After placing the glass of wine on the side of his desk he started to read:

In Greek mythology, Sisyphus was a king who annoyed the gods with his trickery. As a consequence, he was condemned for eternity to roll a huge rock up a long, steep hill in the underworld, only to watch it roll back down again. The story of Sisyphus is often told in conjunction with that of Tantalus, who was condemned to stand beneath fruit-laden boughs, up to his chin in water. Whenever he bent his head to drink, the water receded, and whenever he reached for the fruit, the branches moved beyond his grasp. Thus to tantalise is to tease or torment by offering something desirable but keeping it out of reach. Both these stories are often referred to in more modern times when comparing career ambitions at work with the reality of glass ceilings, lack of recognition and curtailment of promotions. The feeling that work has gradually become just an unending, thankless, and ultimately unsuccessful, effort. This situation mainly occurs in 'middle age' and mainly to men!

Middle age is when career ambitions often get stuck. After leaving university the world is your oyster. The only way is up. Efforts are recognised, promotions happen and your income increases. Wonderful. Life is so good. No, life is excellent! Get married, live in a lovely house, nice car, good friends, exotic holidays, little stress. Yes, life is seriously wonderful.

But suddenly, oh dear, middle age happens! Children arrive and are growing up. Two incomes become one. A bigger house is needed, which comes with a larger mortgage. Promotions stop, there is no recognition of the extra effort anymore. This is seen by the boss as just part and parcel of the job. Stress levels start to increase. Now, life is no longer so wonderful! It's all changed!

So what are the options? There are several, but none of them are great. There might be another step up on the ladder, but that comes with more stress, more demands and responsibilities and possibly little increase in salary. Stepping downwards is a no no and sideways, well that is frowned upon and is a strong sign that you've reached your peak – and with still another 20 years before retirement.

You look around your workplace. Colleagues 15 years older than you can see the retirement light at the end of the tunnel. Children have flown the nest and their mortgage is almost paid off. People 15 years younger? They are what you were 15 years ago! Hungry, ambitious, cheaper, work longer hours and will lick the boss's boots!

You have two options. One, you can try and compete, keep slogging away, but inwardly knowing you have reached the peak of your career… or, you can just accept your midlife crisis! Ah, I hear you shout, what about moving to another job? Okay, let's investigate that option. Why are you stuck where you are, why are you discontent with your lot? Why are you unhappy? Is it the long hours, the long commute, the work too dull and/or unchallenging/unrewarding? Moving to a similar job elsewhere won't change these issues. Situational change is no 'real' change at all.

The answer is between your ears, i.e psychological!

You have to work out what makes you happy and to stop

believing that slogging away for 40 years will be rewarded. To go with 'happy' there should be a 'purpose'. Think of Sisyphus and his fighting a losing battle! Is that you?

Do you honestly know your strengths and weaknesses? Are your weaknesses holding you back from the next rung on the career ladder? Ask friends and colleagues to tell you their opinion of your strengths and particularly, your weaknesses. Plan ways to strengthen them.

Don't throw in the towel, change the towel! Think positively and plan your transition to your new future. It might just be a minor shift. Working from home more often or taking a short sabbatical.

Whilst we all still need to pay the bills, money, on its own, will not 'buy' us happiness. It may make us feel more secure financially, but not necessarily happy. Some suggest a more altruistic approach often brings happiness, but that is down to the individual. Until you know exactly what you want from the rest of your life you will still be stuck in the worlds of Sisyphus and Tantalus. Not a very happy prospect is it? So what are YOU going to do about it!?

Ian put the article back on his desk, picked up his glass of wine and tried to picture himself in just a few years time – middle aged! Still working for Sotheby's. Still working in London, the daily commute. Would his work still give him the buzz he experienced in New York and Hong Kong? Would he be happy, still challenged and excited? Even if he was offered the top job – and that's not certain – is that what he was really striving for? Suddenly Moscow and the Kremlin challenge came to mind. Dangerous? certainly. Silly? probably. But wow, was it an exciting time… and he had been successful and financially well rewarded as well! Working with Andrei was always exciting! Yes, that was when he was really happy … then!

Then!? Not now?

Ian leaned back in his armchair and closed his eyes. He saw Emma, Robert and… Andrei! He walked over to speak to him… "Hello, my friend…"

"So you're in here!" It was Emma who had returned from the meeting with her friends. "Did I wake you up? Has Robert been okay?"

Ian was brought back to his present world and opened his eyes. "Hello, Emma, did you have a good evening?"

"Mmm. It was very nice. Julie was there. It must have been 10 years since I last saw her. We had quite a long chat."

"Good. Robert woke up and wanted a drink of water, but otherwise it's been a quiet evening." A very quiet evening indeed, thought Ian. I wonder how many quiet evenings Andrei used to have?

Chapter 14

It was just after 11am and Emma was finishing making a pot of coffee. She had already put the milk, sugar, mugs and biscuits on the tray and carried them all through to the dining room. The table was still covered with Clinton and Beck's papers, files and CD discs. The doorbell rang and Emma placed the tray on the table and then walked through to the hallway to open the front door.

"Hello, Susan, so good of you to come. You found the house okay?"

Susan Flewin walked through the doorway. She was ten years older than Emma, but still very trim and young in her outlook on life. "Yes, thanks. Your instructions were fine."

"Come into the dining room, my temporary office. I've got all the files ready... and I've just made some fresh coffee."

Susan followed Emma into the dining room. She looked around the room and was impressed with the simple, but very fashionable, decor and furnishings.

"Let's start with a cup of coffee first. Sorry, I can't remember if you take sugar?" said Emma, picking up the coffee pot.

"Black, with no sugar, is fine for me. By the way, where's Robert?"

Emma poured the coffee and offered Susan the biscuits.

"He's staying with Ian's parents for a couple of days. They spoil him, so he loves that!"

Susan smiled. "Yes, grandparents are like that." Having just become a grandmother for the first time, she was looking forward to doing something similar with her new granddaughter.

"As I mentioned on the telephone, I have agreed to look after the Clinton and Beck accounts again. Do you remember them?"

"Yes, of course. That's some time ago. Didn't we deal with David Gould? If I remember correctly it was a well run company," said Susan, helping herself to a chocolate biscuit.

"David Gould is now the finance director."

"He's done well."

"Mmm, but I have a problem. There is something odd about their accounts and I want you to check them for me, to see if you come to the same conclusion."

Over the next two hours Emma showed Susan all the files and the last five years' Report and Accounts. Susan asked questions and made some notes.

Finally Susan put down her pen and re-read her notes. "I can't see where the tax payment for their Irish subsidiary has been reported for the last two completed years," said Susan, still looking at her notes.

"Exactly my conclusion! They have been excluded for those two years!"

"Wow," said Susan, removing her reading spectacles. "That is serious. It means that the audited and published Report and Accounts for those years are not accurate. They show a bigger profit than the company has actually made."

"Mmm, I know. I wonder if David is aware of the situation?" pondered Emma.

"If he's the finance director, he jolly well should know!"

"He was only appointed six months ago… after Hugo Stapleton retired."

"Well done you. So what are you going to tell David?"

"I'm not sure," said Emma, pouring the last remaining drops of the coffee into her mug.

Later that evening, on the train back to Esher, Ian was still pondering on the connection between Bob Taylor's Monaco gallery and Andrei. He had remembered back to the dinner in the Taylors' apartment in Monaco when Bob said he and his father-in-law had done some business with a Russian… located in 'Harbour Heights'. But, at that time, he had no idea that their dealings amounted to 25.2 million Euros! Ian pondered on whether he should speak to Bob and find out what exactly was going on. But then again, he wondered, was it really any of his business? He wouldn't blame Bob if he told Ian that it was, indeed, none of his business! But then again, Bob did suggest he and Ian might be able to do some business together in the future.

Ian checked his watch. About another 10 minutes to his station. His mind wandered back to Andrei's client listing. Do I really want to get involved? It's back to Andrei again… it always is! Even from his grave he's still trying to pull my strings! Emma would be furious if she knew. Maybe I'd better just keep this information to myself until… until when? Ian pondered on that thought. Until, until… I've made my final decision, I guess. But then he thought again about the stories of Sisyphus and Tantalus. Procrastination!

When Ian arrived home he found Emma in the dining room, sitting at the table. The table was still covered with papers, files and CD discs. Screwed up papers had been thrown onto the floor and the laptop blinked with the CD tray still laying open.

"Well who's had a busy day then?" said Ian, as he walked over and kissed Emma on the head.

"Oh, hi, Ian. I didn't hear you come in," said Emma,

removing her reading glasses and placing them on a green folder. She stood up and gave Ian a brief kiss. "Susan and I have been working on these files for most of the day. She only went home about an hour ago. I've got a serious problem!"

"Already!? You haven't officially taken over the account yet!" exclaimed Ian, somewhat confused.

Emma explained her and Susan's findings about the Irish subsidy's tax payments and another error to do with the company's Capital Additions two years ago.

"How is that a serious problem for you?" asked Ian. "Surely that's a problem for the current auditors?"

"Yes, but it's me who has to explain the errors to David Gould!"

"So, I repeat, why is that a problem?"

"Because I don't know if these errors are deliberate or just poor auditing. David may be involved in the cover up! There may be fraud involved!"

"Ahh. I now see your dilemma. You are not sure who you should announce the errors to. That's a little bit more tricky."

"I'm sorry, Ian. I've been so wrapped in this." Emma pointed to the paper strewn table. "That I haven't prepared any dinner."

"No problem. It's just the two of us so let's go down to the 'Lamb and Flag'. Isn't it their 'fish special', tonight?"

Emma tied up the table a little and left all the files in the room. She closed down the computer and took the used coffee pot and mugs into the kitchen. Suddenly she felt hungry. She and Susan had only had a biscuit with her coffee and a cheese sandwich for lunch. Now her stomach was complaining.

"I think we should walk to the pub, Ian. I could do with some fresh air, exercise… and a large glass of wine!"

Ian changed into his casual clothes and ten minutes later they were walking towards the pub.

"Do you fancy a trip to Monaco?" asked Ian, as they crossed their avenue and headed towards the main road.

"It would be nice, but can we just wait until I've sorted out these tax issues with Clinton and Beck, first please?" replied Emma. She was still unsure as to how she was going to deal with that situation.

"Okay, but I think we should go back there as soon as possible," said Ian. He had finally decided that he would speak to Bob Taylor, face to face, about the gallery's involvement with Andrei. He wanted to see how Bob reacted!

Chapter 15

When Ian and Emma arrived at the 'Lamb and Flag', Emma found an empty table whilst Ian went over to the bar to order their drinks. A few minutes later he brought the two drinks over to the table. Emma sipped her large glass of chablis and gave a deep sigh. Ian smiled and drank some of his pint of beer.

The dinner menus were already on the table and both considered the various fish options. Emma decided on the fish pie and Ian went for the beer battered fish and chips. A waitress came over and took their order.

After the waitress walked away, Ian was the first to speak, "I've been thinking about what you were saying earlier about David Gould and the tax issues. You know the man very well, so my suggestion would be to speak to him 'face to face' and state your findings. I'm sure you'll be able to judge from his facial reaction whether he's involved or if it's all a total surprise."

"That's the sort of conclusion I've been gradually coming to. I really don't think David is directly involved, but, obviously, I don't know that for sure," replied Emma. She was still a little uncertain.

Whilst they ate their food, they discussed the pros and cons of other options, but finally Emma agreed, she would telephone David's PA tomorrow morning and make an appointment and have a 'face to face' meeting.

An appointment was duly made for later that same day at 3 o'clock. At 10am Emma dropped Robert off at Brenda's and returned home. She'd decided she wanted to complete one final check of her figures before challenging David. At 2 o'clock all the checking was finished. Nothing had changed, so she now packed her car with the three relevant Clinton and Beck files for the meeting. A meeting she was certainly not looking forward to… but at the same time, she knew it had to be done!

The journey to the client's office was quicker than Emma had anticipated and she was parked in the office car park at 2.45pm. Sitting in the car, and to help kill some time, she checked her emails. Susan had sent her a 'good luck' text message and asked Emma to let her know the outcome of the meeting.

Five minutes later, Emma locked her car door and headed towards reception. It was a cold and blustery day and the dry autumn leaves were being blown around the car park. She wondered if she would receive a similar chilly reception from David.

"Hello. I'm Emma Caxton. I have an appointment with David Gould," she announced, to the receptionist.

"Mr Gould is expecting you, Mrs Caxton. He's in this office today…" The receptionist pointed to a room to Emma's right hand side "…I'll just let him know you're here."

About 10 seconds later David came out of the room and over to greet Emma. "Hello, Emma." He shook her hand. "Come this way. I'm afraid I've been relegated to this office for two days. My main office is being redecorated. Couldn't stand the horrible purple colour my predecessor seemed to prefer. Please, sit down. Would you like a cup of tea? I've had one specially brewed."

"That would be nice, David. Thank you."

"I'll be mother. Help yourself to milk and sugar. I gather you want to speak to me about some queries on the accounts?"

Emma put a small drop of milk in her cup and sat back looking at David. She had thought long and hard as to how she would open the conversation and concluded that it would be best just to adopt her normal professional approach.

"I've been going back over Clinton and Beck's Report and Accounts for the last five years and I've discovered some errors."

For the next 20 minutes, Emma explained the results of her and Susan's investigations. She showed David the files and pointed to the errors. Both during her explanation and after she'd finished, she had searched David's face for any possible guilty or knowing reaction. There was none. David rubbed his chin and concentrated his mind on Emma's findings.

Finally, David leaned back in his chair and said, "I'm not totally surprised, Emma. For the last three years we've had two different auditors and well, I know I shouldn't really be saying this, but Hugo was not up to his usual standard either. His wife was suffering from a horrible cancer and, to be frank, his mind was not fully on the job. That's why he was eased out into early retirement and I took over. I have looked thoroughly into our current year's figures, but as the previous years had all been signed off, I had assumed they were all okay."

"Are there any similar problems for the current financial year?" said Emma, sipping the remains of her now cold tea.

"Not as far as I'm aware. They looked okay. Oh hell!" David suddenly shouted. "Oops, sorry Emma, but the chairman is going to have a fit!"

"This is all very serious, David. As you know, the Financial Reporting Council will need to be informed. There could be a very hefty fine! Then there are the shareholders."

"That's all we need at the moment. Look, Emma…" David leaned forward towards her and dropped his voice to a whisper, "…you must promise me to keep this confidential, but we have been approached by a possible buyer. This information about the accounts… well, as I say, the chairman is going to have a fit!"

It was about 30 minutes later when Emma left Clinton and Beck's head office building. David had promised Emma he would telephone her after he had spoken with the chairman. He said that there would undoubtedly be an emergency board meeting and a statement to the shareholders would have to be issued.

When Emma sat back in her car, she took a deep breath, pleased that the meeting was finally over. She had never experienced such a similar case, in her career, before. Nevertheless, she was fairly sure that David was not directly responsible, or involved, as far as the inaccurately published accounts were concerned. However, she certainly didn't envy his task in trying to explain the situation to the chairman.

After a couple of minutes reflecting on the meeting, Emma picked up her mobile phone and telephoned Susan. She gave Susan a brief summary of the discussion, but deliberately excluded David's comment about a possible buyer. Emma promised to contact Susan again, once she had heard further from David.

Emma then texted Ian a brief message.

Hi. Meeting finished. I managed to survive unscathed! Discuss more later. Love Emma, x.

Emma checked her watch. Mmm, she thought, time to get back to mother duties and collect Robert.

Later that evening Ian had put Robert to bed. He'd read him a story about the continuing adventures of Jackdaw and his friends. He was never sure if it would be Robert or himself who was the most likely to fall asleep first! This time, fortunately, it was Robert.

Ian walked into the lounge where he found Emma sitting on the sofa sipping her glass of wine. His glass had been placed on his side of the coffee table.

"Right," said Ian, joining Emma on the sofa. "You can now give me the blow by blow account of your meeting with Mr Gould."

Emma gave Ian a similar summary that she had told Susan, and again, she deliberately excluded referring to the company's possible sale.

"So what happens now, for you I mean?"

"I'm not sure. It might be the shortest contract ever!"

"I don't think so," said Ian, smiling at Emma's comment. "You seem to be the only person doing their job properly!"

"I'll just have to wait for David's call. I've still got most of their files."

"So maybe now we can have a break in Monaco? It's been quite a while since we were last there."

"I think we should take Robert, this time. It will be his first flight."

"Good idea. How about I book tickets for about ten days' time?"

"I think I could do with the break. We might even get some late summer sunshine in Monaco. Yes, do book the tickets, please."

Ian sat back on the sofa and sipped his wine. "What about me contacting Bob and Zoe to see if they are free for a meal? We could try and find somewhere where the kids could run around and mix together."

"Okay, it would be nice to meet up with Zoe again. I

can show off my new figure! The last time she saw me I was about seven months' pregnant and looked like a bloated whale!"

Ian smiled and patted Emma on her stomach. Good, he thought. Maybe I could then have a chat with Bob and try to sneak in a word about Andrei and see what reaction transpires!

"Oh! I've just had a thought," announced Emma. "Robert will need a passport!"

"Heck, you're right. Mind I think he can initially be added on to one of our passports."

"I'll check it out tomorrow."

It was two days later when Emma received David's telephone call.

"Hello, Emma. I was right, the chairman went ballistic! Once he had calmed down he did manage to ask me to pass on his thanks to you for unearthing the errors. Unfortunately, Hugo's name is now mud!"

"Oh dear," said Emma. She doubted Hugo would have been as negligent had his wife not been suffering from her medical problems. "So what's going to happen now? Is there anything you want me to do?"

"No, Emma. Not at the moment. Thank you. The chairman has been speaking to the two auditors and tearing strips off them both. He's putting all the blame on them. As you can guess, they are not coming out of this very well either."

"I see."

"We've got an emergency board meeting tomorrow and after that we'll have to tell the financial authorities and, of course, our shareholders as well. Mind, they will probably find out much sooner, the press can smell there's a problem already."

"Well thank you for keeping me informed, David, and please, let me know if you need my help," said Emma, with genuine feeling and concern.

"Thanks again, Emma. I'll be in touch."

The line went dead and Emma considered David's comments. She then telephoned Susan and informed her of the latest developments.

"Is there anything we can do in the meantime?" asked Susan.

"It appears not, but I'm still going to have a deeper delve into their accounts. There might be some more issues that I wouldn't want to be responsible for when I take over the account properly."

"So are you glad to be back in the workplace?"

"I wanted a challenge, but I didn't, in my wildest dreams, expect to be opening up such a large can of worms! Goodbye, Susan. Speak to you again soon."

"Goodbye, Emma… and good luck!"

Chapter 16

Ian sat in his usual early morning commuter train heading towards London. He'd earlier purchased a copy of *The Times* from the station kiosk as he knew there was going to be a review published today about the forthcoming Bonhams auction. It was always important to know what the opposition was up to. He slowly flicked through the pages, but suddenly stopped when he came to the financial section. It was the headlines that caught his attention and he immediately started to read the full article:

Clinton and Beck *look set to become the latest company to fall into private hands after a conglomerate founded by Hong Kong's richest man swooped in with a £1.6bn approach.*

RB Hutchins, part of the Li Fong empire, that owns several other British brands, sprung a surprise on Tuesday afternoon with an 350p-a-share deal offer. This offer, if accepted by the shareholders, values the 110-year-old company at a premium of more than 30pc on yesterday's closing price. The deal, recommended by Clinton and Beck's board, comes just weeks after private equity firm PP Capital struck a £3bn deal for Software Enterprises. This is now the third foreign transaction in a flurry of multibillion-pound deals this autumn…

Oh, wow! thought Ian, I wonder if Emma is aware. He quickly removed his mobile phone from his jacket pocket, and texted her. *Emma. Check the financial news, C & B are being taken over! Ian x.*

Emma was in the kitchen. She was just finishing washing the breakfast plates, mugs and cutlery when she heard her mobile phone ping. After she'd dried her hands, she picked up the mobile and accessed her text messages.

"What!" she exclaimed out loud, which caught Robert's immediate attention at the far end of the room. She quickly switched her mobile setting to the internet and then to the financial news section on the BBC website. There half way down the list of business articles was one headed *'Clinton and Beck, Hong Kong takeover!'*

Emma read the brief article and yes, it said the board were recommending the sale! Well, well, well, she thought, so it will be the shortest contract I've ever had after all! No wonder David has been so quiet. Emma logged off and put her phone into sleep mode. Robert had now appeared at her side. He was obviously concerned about Emma's outburst.

Emma picked him up. "I'm sorry if I made you jump, it was because Mummy received some surprising news."

Robert gave Emma a cuddle and then wanted to get back to building his Lego building. Emma put him down and he ran back to his play area.

Emma stood and watched him run away, but her mind was focused on Clinton and Beck. What's going on? she wondered. Suddenly the landline telephone rang. Emma assumed it would be Ian with some more information.

"Hello, Emma, David Gould."

"David!"

"You sound surprised."

"Well yes, I've just read the news!"

"Ahh, yes. Well that's why I'm ringing."

"To tell me that my services are no longer required?"

"No! Well… yes, sort of. Let me explain. I told you that we had been approached about a possible sale. Well this was also discussed at the emergency board meeting along with the accounting issues. It was agreed by the board that the chairman would speak to the potential buyer and put our cards on the table about the accounting errors. If they still wanted to go ahead with the purchase then the board was in full agreement and their offer should be accepted. After all, they were offering a premium of 30% on our current share price. Such a windfall was obviously going to be snapped up by a large majority of our shareholders. The chairman has subsequently telephoned the buyer's contact and explained everything about the accounts issues. The upshot is that the Hong Kong people said that they still wanted to go ahead on the original offer. So, as they say, 'it was all a no brainer', for us!"

"I see. So am I involved now or not?"

"Yes. What we would like you to do is to complete an in depth final check on the draft Report and Accounts for this last financial year before we publish them. As you know we had already told the current auditors that we would not be continuing with their services into the new financial year, but my worry is they may do another poor job. We would like you to check over their work… please. We cannot afford any errors this time! Also, and until the takeover is completed, we would like you to continue as our auditor. We will also double your fees as compensation."

"Mmm… and if I say no?" said Emma, teasing.

"Emma, we really do need you."

"Double my fees you say?"

"Double your fees… and a £10,000… apology!"

"Okay, David, you have a deal!" said Emma, with a big smile on her face.

"Thank you, Emma. Thanks a lot. I'll inform the chairman."

As soon as Emma had finished the telephone call, she rang Susan and explained what had happened.

"What a surprise," replied Susan.

"Actually David did hint earlier that there was a possible offer on the table, but he also told me that he was telling me in the strictest of confidence. Nevertheless, seeing the details on the BBC website was still a bit of a shock."

"So where do we go from here?"

"Well that's the other point I wanted to ask you. What are you doing next week?"

"Which days?"

"All of them!"

"Really! Oh, gosh."

"Mmm, afraid so. The current draft Report and Accounts are being delivered to David tomorrow. David wants to drop them off to me tomorrow evening on his way home from work. That means I have the weekend to start initial checking. But the main work will be next week. David would like my comments as soon as possible. He's increased my fees so I will double what I'm paying you."

"That's very generous of you, Emma. I will need to change some of my arrangements, but I can be with you on Monday morning for about 9.30, if that's okay?"

"Thanks, Susan. You're a star!"

Susan laughed at the other end of the line. "See you on Monday then, Emma. Bye."

"Goodbye… and, thanks again."

Emma put the telephone back on its base and turned towards Robert. "Come on, Robert, let's get you ready for nursery school. After that we'll go and have a walk through the park." I could do with some extra thinking time, she decided.

Robert dropped the Lego bricks. He was trying to build a castle, but now he ran across and joined Emma. They both went upstairs to get ready to go out for their walk.

The following evening David arrived not only with all the accounts files, but also with a huge bouquet of flowers.

"Wow, David, that's very kind of you. They are beautiful. But you're already paying me well, remember?" said Emma, trying to take the flowers from him. "Come in," she said and headed towards the kitchen.

David closed the door and followed Emma into the kitchen. "We all feel quite guilty messing you about like this. It's the least we can do to say sorry."

"Well it's still very nice of you. So, what's the deadline for my report?" said Emma, laying the bouquet gently on the breakfast bar.

"Could you achieve a week today? Next Friday?"

"Do you want me to email you?"

"Okay. But if you find any major problems, again, please ring me first and I will come over straight away."

"Let's hope everyone has learned their lesson," replied Emma, seriously. "I'll get started in the morning."

"I hope you're right. Fingers crossed, eh? The chairman is desperate that nothing else should now go wrong… not at this late stage."

Chapter 17

Viktor was enjoying his first few weeks on his own at the gallery. There had been a few visitors and some small sales, but he was also seeing an increasing number of visits to the gallery's website. Some of these were returning for a second, or even a third, viewing. He particularly studied which people were viewing and wondered whether he should respond to some of these visits with his own email. However, he remembered Bob advising him not to be in too much of a rush otherwise people might feel he was being too pushy. So, at this stage, Viktor just made his notes, produced a large spreadsheet and continued to analyse all of the results.

He also spent a lot of his quiet time looking at different gallery's websites, catalogues and forthcoming auctions. He particularly wanted to gauge what was popular, the prices different paintings were being advertised for and what price they were finally being sold for. He again produced a separate large spreadsheet and annotated it with his findings.

It was late on a quiet Thursday afternoon, just before he was going to close the gallery for the day, when he had an unexpected visitor.

"Hello, Vic. How's it all going?" asked Viktor's former boss, Ian, smiling as he walked up to Viktor's desk.

"Hello, Ian. Well this is a surprise. It's all going okay, thanks. A big learning curve, but I'm certainly enjoying the new adventure!"

"The gallery is looking great. Good lighting and just the right balance of quality and numbers of paintings. Well done."

"Well done you, Ian. I know you had a big input into setting this all up. You will notice the Tobars have all been sold."

"I knew they would. The two that I bought from Yorkshire, have at least doubled in value. Maybe I should get you to sell them for me now?"

"I know at least three people who'd be very keen to buy them."

"I'll remember that." Ian wandered around and looked at the closest paintings to him. "Have you heard from Bob recently?"

"Not for about a week. Nothing really to chat about at the moment. The website activity is busy, but Bob can see that from Monaco."

Ian stopped walking and looked closely at a small water-colour painting by Helen Allingham. It showed a Victorian country scene. Two young girls were playing in front of a lovely thatched cottage. Typical chocolate box, Ian thought. He looked at the name on the frame *Ickford Farm*.

"This is a lovely painting, Vic. It's for sale at £5,750. Interesting," said Ian, trying to gauge Viktor's response.

"Do you want to buy it? I'm selling it on behalf of a client. For you, Ian, I would accept £5,000."

"Tempting, especially as I think it would fetch between £8,000–10,000 at auction."

Viktor got up from behind his desk and walked over to join Ian. He looked very closely at the picture. "Are you sure?"

"Helen is a lovely artist. She worked as an illustrator from an early age. She did some illustrations for a few of the Thomas Hardy novels. *Far from the Madding Crowd* was one. She turned to these watercolours later in life, after she married. I think this scene is either located in Sussex or Surrey. Lovely talent. Some say her work is much too sentimental, a too conservative vision of the countryside, which never really existed. That's probably true, but still a lovely talent nevertheless. Okay, I'll give you £5,000 for it."

"Err, after what you have just said, I'm not so sure."

Ian laughed. "Increase the sale price to £9,000. If you've not sold it by the end of the month, let me know. My £5,000 is still on the table."

"I have a lot to learn," admitted Viktor.

"Come on, Vic. Cheer up. I've been a fan of Helen's for a number of years, that's how I know that much about her and her work."

"Maybe I ought to think more about the artists I really like."

"None of us knows everything about every artist. You initially need to get a good depth of understanding of a few artists – especially those you like and are hoping to sell. Your knowledge and enthusiasm will then come through with the buyers. Your ears pricked up when I told you about Helen's background didn't it?"

"You're right. Until now it was just another picture, but your enthusiasm had a positive effect on me. Thanks."

Ian smiled. "Fancy a beer at 'The Grapes'?"

"Only if you let me buy you a pint… or two."

Both men laughed and Viktor grabbed his coat, switched off all the lights, set the burglar alarm and locked the main door. Ten minutes later they walked into the familiar surroundings of 'The Grapes' main bar. After Viktor had purchased two pints of bitter the two men sat in the far corner, close to the large window which gave them a view into the street.

Viktor opened the conversation. "I had a drink with Penny the other week. She says Sotheby's is managing to survive without me."

"It has done so far, and for a few hundred years, so I guess it can still survive without any of us."

"I like Penny. I had a wonderful time in your department with you and her. It was great fun. It was my happiest period at Sotheby's."

"You've told me that before. Yes, it was an interesting period. Not really very typical though, unfortunately. Most of the time it's... well, just much more, sort of routine."

"That's what Penny said."

"Did you know she has broken up with her boyfriend?" asked Ian, deliberately throwing a pebble in the water.

"She didn't tell me that. I'm really sorry. She must be very sad. She really fancied him."

"I'm not sure of the background, or the reasons, but his work took him away quite a bit. Maybe give her a call?"

"I'll do that. Thanks, Ian."

Ian wanted to get to the main point of why he was meeting with Viktor. "Has Bob mentioned any of the regular clients he and his father-in-law use? Maybe in Britain?"

Viktor thought this was an unusual question for Ian to ask. "No, I don't think so. Certainly not in Britain, because that's why he wanted to set up a separate agency here. Why do you ask?"

Ian picked up his glass of beer and took a sip. "Can you keep this just between the two of us?"

Viktor nodded with a curious look on his face. He leaned forward waiting for Ian to speak.

"Remember Andrei?" Viktor nodded. "I think he was doing some business with Bob's gallery in Monaco."

Viktor's eyes suddenly were wide open, but then he wondered why this was of any interest to Ian. "Andrei did business with a lot of people, all over the world, didn't he?"

"I know. He left me a list of some of his clients. Bob's father-in-law's name is on the list."

"Excuse me for asking, Ian, but why would Andrei do that? Leave you the list, I mean?"

"That's a good question. I'm not exactly sure and I'm also unsure what to do with this information."

"Andrei seemed to like teasing and leaving surprises. My dad says he was always strange that way. Sort of taunting, deliberate acts to see what resulted. Did you know he left me £10 million?"

"No I didn't. Wow! That will set you up very nicely. Good for you."

"Yes, but with Andrei it's never just that straight forward. I only met him a few times, but according to my dad, he enjoyed hearing news about me whilst I was growing up. Maybe it has something to do with him not having any children of his own. Anyway, I don't get any of the money until I'm 30 and then only a proportion. The rest is paid in instalments over the following five years."

"I can understand Andrei's thinking there. He didn't want you to blow the whole amount at one go."

"Ian, I'm sure you know me by now, I'm far too astute and sensible to do that!"

Ian laughed and sipped his beer. He then said, "You would be a nice catch for Penny!"

"No, you are wrong there, Ian. She would be an amazing catch for me!"

Chapter 18

Oscar lay on his lounger, on the patio located at the rear of his villa. He could just see the horizon of the Caribbean Sea over the low hedge of hibiscus bushes. He was listening to the distant tumble of the waves as they gently crashed onto the sandy beach. It was a quiet time, business wise, and he was considering his next move. The problem was 'mañana'! It had slowly crept into his daily way of life and he was finding it much more difficult to re-establish the old levels of motivation. He was certainly adapting to the Caribbean way of life... sort of infectious, he thought. Afterall, 'if you can't beat them, join them... man'!

He also realised it was nearly the end of his first year of residence in Antigua and wondered what he was going to do, if anything, to celebrate.

The tropical sun was still shining in the late afternoon. It seemed to be always shining and warm, thought Oscar. Okay, so there was the occasional heavy downpour that lasted about an hour in some late afternoons, but this only forced him to find shelter, usually in one of the local bars. Then there was always the remote threat of a hurricane, but these only reminded him of the typhoons that occurred, from time to time, in Hong Kong. You just had to be prepared. All in all, this was much more acceptable... a great place to live!

He leaned over to the small table on his right hand side and reached out for his glass of rum and coke. The ice had melted, but Oscar didn't like his drinks to be too cold. He sipped his drink and then, for some reason, began to think about Ian and England. He wondered how his old buddy was doing. He suddenly realised they had not spoken to each other for some time. Then there was the new Taylor gallery, how was that doing? Maybe I should give him a ring? Yes, he would definitely do that… well, maybe tomorrow!

"Hey, man, how's things?" It was the voice of his neighbour, Garfield, peering over the fence. "Looks like you've had another busy day, man!"

"Hi, Garfield. Fancy a beer?" Oscar knew Garfield only drank beers.

"I'll be round in two ticks, man." Garfield's face disappeared from over the fence.

Oscar put down his own drink and sauntered into the kitchen and removed a can of beer from his fridge. When he returned, Garfield was sitting on the second lounger. "Here you are." Oscar passed Garfield the can.

"Nice and cold, man, cheers," replied Garfield, snapping off the tab and taking a long drink.

"So, how's things with you, Garfield? You're home early," said Oscar, picking up his own drink again. "I take it that Ella's not at home."

"You're right there, man. Ella's at her mother's till this evening," replied Garfield, placing his can on the table. "Business is not bad. As my afternoon appointment finished early today I decided not to go back to the office."

Garfield was a partner with a small firm of solicitors based in the financial area of St. Johns. He mainly dealt with commercial business contracts and related issues. "There's a problem about moorings in the harbour for the fishing boats," continued Garfield, "I'm trying to sort it all out. Just a squabble really. I'm more of a mediator. Cheaper for the guys than going to court."

"Yes, I suppose it would be," observed Oscar.

"You not working today then?" asked Garfield, taking another long drink of his beer.

"No. Taking a relaxing day off. I've been pretty lucky with some deals recently and have found another painting by Isaac Tobar that a client wants to sell. The trouble is the client wants too much money at the moment. He's heard about the prices the others have been selling for in London. There, the prices have risen quite a bit over the last few months. I do have two potential buyers who would be interested, but only for the right price, of course," said Oscar. That reminded him to speak to Ian and May Ling as they might also be interested in the picture.

"Are you going to the cricket match tomorrow?"

"Me!? I once saw a game in Hong Kong, many years ago. I didn't have a clue what was going on. Not been to a game since."

"Big match tomorrow. Antigua are playing Barbados. Should be a good game. There's a group of us, about twelve, going. Why don't you come along? It will be a great day. Lots to drink!"

Oscar pondered on Garfield's offer. He had nothing planned and it would be a good opportunity to meet with some more Antiguans. Possibly some new clients!

"Mmm. Okay, I'll come. What time will you be leaving home?"

"That's great, man. Come around for about 10 o'clock. We'll pick up the beers on the way!"

The day after the cricket match, Oscar was recovering from his hangover. He had never before been with a group of men who drank so much beer! He'd enjoyed the 20/20 cricket match, which the home side had apparently won, and this had naturally meant more celebrating… more beers and then rum and cokes… and it all went on well into the evening!

At the start of the match Oscar had chatted to some of the group and picked up some very useful information. Two of them in particular, once they heard that Oscar was involved with buying and selling paintings, said they wanted to stay in touch. By the afternoon Oscar had given up on trying to obtain more possible business clients and just enjoyed their company, the noise and the beers! He still didn't understand the game, but hey, he thought, it was still a great day!

Oscar didn't remember arriving home and slept through until 11 o'clock that morning. It was now lunchtime but he knew he couldn't face anything to eat. Instead he drank several glasses of cold water and decided to go for a swim in the sea. Hoping this would sober him up and clear his heavy head!

Whilst Oscar was walking the short distance from the beach back towards his villa, he saw Garfield waving to him from over his back garden fence. Oscar walked over to join him.

"Great time at the cricket yesterday, man. You certainly enjoyed it," said Garfield, who seemed not to be suffering the same after effects of the alcohol excess.

"Yes, it surprised me how much I enjoyed it. Mind I can't remember too much after the match finished."

Garfield laughed. "We went on to a bar near the ground for a while, but I got you back to your villa about 9.30."

"I don't remember any of that. I didn't wake up until about 11 this morning!"

"I don't know if you remember speaking to Frank Hall? He's a surgeon at the main hospital."

Oscar tried to engage his memory cells, but was struggling. He shook his head, and then regretted it. "I'm not sure."

"Big guy, wore a white suit and a straw hat. Anyway he was on the phone to me this morning. He wants to have a chat with you about some paintings." Garfield put his hand in his back pocket and pulled out a small scrap of paper. "Here, these are his contact details. Best to call him later tonight because tomorrow, being Monday, he'll be in theatre most of the day, operating."

Oscar took the paper and briefly looked at the details. "Thanks. I'll ring him later tonight. I must get something to eat, I've not eaten today."

"Okay, man. See you soon. Good luck with Frank. He's a nice bloke, but I wouldn't want to get on the wrong side of him in an argument."

Oscar waved and walked towards his villa. He was not exactly sure what Garfield had meant, but anyway, forewarned is forearmed, as he remembered his buddy, Ian, often used to say!

When Oscar finally arrived back in his villa, he was definitely feeling a lot better. The swim and the walk, breathing in the sea air, all these, he decided, helped to take away his throbbing head. All I need to do now, he thought, is to settle my rumbling stomach.

Later that evening Oscar telephoned Frank. It was a young female voice that answered the call and Oscar asked if Frank was available. In the background he heard the same voice shout, "Dad, it's for you." The line went quiet and then a deep male voice said, "Hello?"

"Hello, Frank," replied Oscar. "This is Oscar Ding. I understand from Garfield that you wanted to speak to me."

"Garfield? Oscar? Oh yes, Oscar, yes, man. We met at the cricket. I gather you are into paintings. What do you know about Boscoe Holder?"

Oscar quickly tried to engage the brain. "Trinidad born contemporary artist. Specialised in painting Caribbean people and their culture. Expert choreographer and musician. Introduced limbo dancing and steel drum playing to Britain in… the 1960s, or thereabouts. Died, I think, around 2007."

"Hey, Oscar, man, that's pretty cool! I'm impressed," replied Frank, somewhat surprised that an Oriental should know so much about a Caribbean artist.

"Did I pass the test?" replied Oscar. He knew that studying the local artist talent would prove useful after the Isaac Tobar experience.

"Yes you do! I have a small collection of Boscoe's paintings. They are quality works of art… and, I hope, a great long term investment. I would like some more. Can you help?"

For the next ten minutes the two men discussed specific details and agreed on Oscar's commission. When he finally put the phone down Oscar said out loud to himself, "Oscar, lazy days are over… man! Back to work. Maybe even a trip to Trinidad is called for."

Chapter 19

Emma and Susan had spent four solid days working on the numbers for Clinton and Beck's past financial year's accounts. It was now Friday morning and Emma had promised David Gould an email... or telephone call, depending on her findings that day. 'An email if all was okay or a telephone call if there were serious problems.' They were David's instructions... his last words.

By lunchtime Emma and Susan had checked, and double checked, all the figures. Emma was pleased that this time all the numbers seemed to be accurate and add up. She hated to unearth other company's mistakes and sloppy professionalism. It portrayed a bad picture of her profession.

Susan was feeling exhausted. "I thought you said this was going to be just part-time work?"

"I said there would be some busy periods and some less so," replied Emma. She knew Susan was mainly joking. But yes, this was a very busy week.

"So when does the part-time working bit begin?" Susan could not help but smile, teasing Emma.

"Tomorrow. I promise. At least for a while. David wants me, i.e. us, to oversee the accounts until the takeover has been completed."

"I see. So what are you going to do then?"

"To tell you the truth, I'm not quite sure. I've already had two other former clients asking whether I was back in the market. How about you? What do you think?"

"It's been interesting, Emma, but really, I am getting too old for this full time pressurised work. Maybe you should be thinking about someone a bit younger?" replied Susan. She was wondering why Emma had decided to return to the accountancy world. It all seemed much more complicated now. More so than she could remember.

Emma weighed up Susan's comment. "Mmm, there's something in what you say. I don't think I would take on another client without your support, so maybe it would be best for me to retire too. Ian's been so supportive, but I'm sure he'd be pleased with that decision."

Even Emma was beginning to think that maybe it was all a mistake.

The room was quiet for a short period whilst both pondered on what had just been said.

Finally Emma broke the silence, "So, I think we are agreed, these accounts are a fair and accurate representation of the last financial year?"

"As far as we can tell, based on the information given, yes," replied Susan. She took off her reading glasses, put them gently on the table and rubbed her eyes. This was Susan's way of indicating that her work was done for the day! Probably the last job of her accountancy career.

"Right. Last job," said Emma, as she pressed some buttons on her laptop's keypad. "Email David telling him that all is well… this time!

"We should have bought some shares in Clinton and Beck," said Susan, rubbing her eyes, again.

"Nice thought, but as accountants we might have been accused of insider trading."

"Oh well, just a thought," replied Susan, pouring the last of the coffee into her mug.

When Ian arrived home that evening Emma had made her decision. She told Ian that after the run off dealing with the Clinton and Beck accounts, she did not want to take on any new clients. Her career in accountancy was now finished.

Ian was a little surprised, but quietly pleased. It had been a stressful few weeks for Emma… and Robert had been pushed about just a little too much to accommodate all the Clinton and Beck's demands.

"If that's what you want, then that's fine with me," responded Ian. "Good time now to go off to Monaco, I think."

"Yes, I think so too. I've sorted Robert's passport. Are you going to book the tickets?"

"I've already reserved three seats on the flight leaving next Thursday. Hope that's okay."

Emma smiled at Ian. "Yes, Ian, that is very okay."

Viktor was walking towards the gallery. His mind was pre-occupied with a request from Bob Taylor, who had told him that a long standing client of his was moving back to the UK. Apparently his employment contract in France was coming to an end. He and his wife were now moving back to be closer to their daughter and grandchildren. Bob had spoken with the client and told him of Viktor and the new London gallery. The client had indicated that he would appreciate a call from Viktor to discuss the possibility of doing some business. The client, however, was not moving back to the UK until next month but Viktor was already wondering how best to approach this opportunity.

"Hello, good looking!"

Viktor was startled and immediately looked to where the voice had come from. "Oh, hi, Penny. You made me jump!"

They both stopped walking.

Penny laughed. "You were obviously having one of your deeper thinking moments!"

"Mmm, a possible new client, introduced by Bob," replied Viktor. "Mind if I walk with you to your office?"

"No, that would be nice. I'm sure you know the way," joked Penny.

"Only done it about a thousand times! I can almost see my footprints in the pavement… all the way to Sotheby's front door!"

They started walking side by side, a little slower than the usual commuter walk. As a result other people had to dodge them in their rush to get to work.

"I was going to give you a call," said Viktor. He was feeling a little anxious, but wanted to take advantage of the moment. "I was thinking about you the other day and wondered maybe, if you would like to go out for a meal?"

Penny suddenly stopped walking and looked at Viktor a little surprised. She then gave him a tiny smile. "What? Like on a date?"

"Er, well, yes. I thought it might be nice." Viktor could feel his face beginning to blush.

Penny's tiny smile had now expanded into a big grin. "That would be lovely, Vic. When were you thinking of?"

"Er, well, I hadn't gotten that far!" replied Viktor. He really did feel embarrassed.

Penny laughed. "What about this evening? I've not got any plans."

"Oh, wow! Yes. That would be great. I'll find us a nice restaurant."

"I'll want to get changed first. Email me details of the restaurant and the time."

They both started walking on again. Viktor couldn't hide the smile on his face and Penny, whilst a little nervous, was excited and very happy. When they arrived at the entrance to Sotheby's, Viktor confirmed he would email the restaurant details for tonight. Penny leaned over and gently kissed Viktor on the cheek and disappeared into the office. Viktor stood and watched her disappear into the building, gently stroking the side of his face.

"Wotcher, Vic. How's it going?" It was Jordan Robson who tapped Viktor on the shoulder and then disappeared into Sotheby's building. Jordan had joined Sotheby's just two weeks after Viktor had started.

Viktor, under his breath said, "It's going absolutely brilliant, Jordan! Thanks for asking." He turned around and almost skipped all the way to the gallery.

When Penny entered her office Ian was behind her desk putting some papers into the filing cabinet. "Good morning, Penny," he announced as she entered the room.

"Good morning, Ian," she said, with a cheery voice and a large smile on her face.

"Well someone sounds pleased with the world," replied Ian, looking at his PA.

"Mmm. I've got a date!"

Ian walked to Penny's side with a congratulatory smile. "So do I know the lucky man?"

"Oh yes. It's Vic!"

"What, our Vic?" asked Ian, deliberately trying to show his surprise.

"Yes. He just asked me on the way to work."

"That's great news, Penny. Yes, really great news."

Penny blushed a little and sat down at her desk with her back to her boss.

Ian looked down at his PA and smiled. Under his breath he said to himself, 'Well done Vic. Well done!'

Chapter 20

Oscar investigated the life and work of Boscoe Holder. He'd looked on the internet and had read a biography that Wesley had let him borrow. There he'd discovered that as well as an accomplished artist and dance choreographer, he was generally well respected during the time that he'd lived in London. Amongst his circle of friends were fellow celebrities, such as the writer and actor, Noel Coward, who was one of his closest friends.

Boscoe had appeared in films and on UK television. His dance company toured all over Europe and in 1953 they'd performed at the coronation of Queen Elizabeth II. As well as performing with his dance company, during this same period, Boscoe had continued to paint and a number of his pictures had been exhibited at several UK galleries, where they'd been generally well received.

In 1970, however, Boscoe and his family returned to Trinidad. He had been based in London for 20 years and now he'd decided it was time to go home. There he found that he'd now got the opportunity to re-establish his painting career. From 1979 he exhibited at many shows each year, both throughout the Caribbean and further afield. In December 2004, the Trinidad and Tobago government recognised his importance by issuing an official Christmas series of postage stamps featuring six of his paintings. Today his paintings are included in many private collections throughout the world.

Boscoe died at the age of 85 at his home in Newtown, Port of Spain, Trinidad.

This guy really had an interesting and varied career, Oscar said to himself. He put his pen down on his desk and closed his notebook. Really good quality paintings too. I can see why Frank is keen to expand his collection.

When Oscar researched the market price of Holder's work, however, he was a little disappointed. A lot of the pictures had sold for less than US$1,000. Only a few had been purchased for between US$2,000–US$10,000. Frank had given him a budget of US$50,000, so Oscar wondered what to do. He accessed some of the main Caribbean based gallery websites and tried to find the very best pictures currently available. Again, he was disappointed that there were so few Boscoe Holder pictures for sale. Was that because they were deemed a collectors item, or was it simply the opposite, that they were no longer popular?

Despite having already checked with the Shell gallery website and found nothing for sale, Oscar decided to call it a night and go to bed. He felt rather sad about Mr Holder and wanted to raise his profile again. Yes, he decided, I'll call at the Shell gallery tomorrow. He hoped Wesley would have some additional advice and, just maybe, some extra useful local information about Boscoe Holder's talented work.

The following evening, after chatting with Wesley earlier that day, Oscar was now sitting at his desk in his home office. He was reviewing all the information he'd gathered together. He re-opened his notebook and jotted down the titles of six good possibilities. He wanted to know what Frank thought of these six suggested paintings before he spent more time researching the wider market.

Forty minutes later Oscar had emailed Frank with his written comments on each of the six selected pictures. He'd also attached photographs of the same. Fingers crossed!

In Monaco, a somewhat depressed Julian had picked up Ian's email request for a taxi service from Nice airport to Harbour Heights. He opened up his diary to see if he would be available. Life for Julian, had become very difficult since Andrei's death. Even after all this time, he was still grieving. He knew he had to move on and still had the rest of Andrei's travel ticket options to use. Andrei had taken him from his troubled background in Scandinavia and given him his opportunity to make something of his life in Monaco. This, Julian had appreciated and was always available for Andrei, no matter what.

Andrei had always been very specific about his require-ments, but because he was abroad for most of his time, this gave Julian a lot of free time to establish a new and better life for himself in the Mediterranean sunshine. Andrei was also very generous too. As a result, whatever and whenever Andrei needed Julian, Julian was always available – any time during the 24 hours of a day. For both men, it was a 'win-win' situation. But, now there was no Andrei, no surprise telephone calls in the middle of the night and no urgent email instructions. Julian was really struggling to cope without his 'father figure' still guiding his hand.

Julian looked at his diary and flicked the pages to the date Ian had mentioned. The page was empty and, after much thought, he sent an email reply to Ian confirming he would be available. He then looked again at all the travel bookings he'd previously set up for Andrei. Most had either been paid for in full or large deposits had already been made. Andrei had set up a special bank account where he'd deposited money for Julian to use to pay for Andrei's arrangements. Julian now looked at the bank account's balance and smiled. There were lots of zeros after the nine. He then read again all the planned travel details, the exotic tropical and adventurous plans that Andrei had been looking forward to. Julian knew he needed to be more positive and get on with this fabulous opportunity. To stop prevaricating any longer and to get a grip on the rest of his life… but life for Julian, was still not yet… quite that simple.

Also in Monaco, Bob Taylor was experiencing problems with his father-in-law, Antoine. He was becoming more and more difficult to communicate with. He rarely answered the telephone and ignored Bob's emails. Bob had told Zoe of his problems. She had tried to mediate, but without success. It was now affecting business, as Bob often needed Antoine's agreement, or signature, to complete deals and contracts. He was seriously wondering whether he should suggest to Zoe that they step away from the Monaco gallery and the French business altogether. But of course, the apartment above the gallery was also their home and he knew Zoe loved living there. He wondered whether to take a trip to France himself and have a face to face meeting with Antoine. However, he was also afraid that such a meeting could lead to irreparable damage to their relationship. But what else could he do!?

Bob, once again, discussed the matter, and his frustrations, with Zoe. Zoe, in turn, had telephoned her mother, Isobelle, but even her mother was finding it a struggle to deal with Antoine's unfamiliar mood swings.

It was finally decided that something legally needed to be done so that Bob and Zoe could carry on handling the business properly and without the negative input, or even downright obstructions, currently demonstrated by Antoine.

Zoe and her mother went to see the family lawyer and

they relayed to him the problems they were experiencing. The lawyer recommended that Antoine should have a full medical assessment first, as any court would need this sort of information before being able to make a sensible judgement.

Both Zoe and her mother doubted that Antoine would agree to have this assessment, but when Zoe's brother Claude's name was mentioned, they were more optimistic. Claude, being a male, and the eldest, was Antoine's favourite child. Isobelle said she would ring Claude, explain the problem and seek his agreement to speak with his father. Isobelle promised she would tell Zoe of the outcome.

When Zoe returned back home to Monaco, she told Bob all the details of the meeting with their lawyer. She also mentioned the possible involvement of Claude. Bob was happy that something was finally being done, although he was concerned with the family giving Claude the control and responsibility to discuss business matters with Antoine. He understood their reasons for this approach, but reminded Zoe that Claude had no involvement in the business and had nothing to lose if he failed to convince their father.

Zoe was becoming more and more frustrated and upset. She was tired and annoyed that, in this modern age, her father still tended to look on a woman's role as only being useful as a wife and mother. When she was a child growing up, Claude was the one who got all the advantages, the better schools and all the encouragement. Whilst she loved her father, she hated his old fashioned attitudes towards women. Right from a young age she had noticed that he treated her mother in the same way. An Aunt had once told her that Isobelle had been half way through her university studies, training to be a doctor, when she had met Antoine. However, once they were married, Antoine had put a stop to her developing a medical career!

This was the main area that Bob struggled to come to

terms with after he'd married into Zoe's family. His only conclusion was that they were French! They had a different language, different standards and a different society approach to the one he'd become accustomed to in England. He knew he would not be able to change his father-in-law's attitude, but he did try his utmost to make sure he himself treated Zoe as his equal and to fully encourage her with all her personal aspirations and ambitions.

Bob reluctantly finally decided that he would just have to wait until Claude had spoken to Antoine. It was not ideal but he would just have to put up with it. He was now, in retrospect, very pleased that his father-in-law had no involvement with the London gallery. Maybe now, he thought, this is the time to consider moving back to England. Or, alternatively, setting up a separate arrangement in Monaco and France… and with just Zoe and him in charge. He could just let Antoine's business run down and slowly transfer the better clients to the Taylors' new business. That was always an option, but for that to happen, he would need Zoe's support. However, he doubted that, at just this very moment, she would be in favour of this dramatic change. But maybe soon, he wondered, she just might want to, or even have to, reconsider her position!

Until then he would just have to be patient and wait until Zoe told him the results of Claude's meeting with his father.

Chapter 21

Viktor and Penny's new relationship blossomed very quickly. Once they had overcome the nervousness of moving on from being work colleagues and good friends to a closer relationship, they saw a great deal more of each other.

They enjoyed each other's company and, as well as art, they found other areas of mutual interest. Ludmilla, Viktor's mother, immediately liked Penny after their first meeting and she was confident that Viktor had made a good choice. Sergei, however, was less committal. Although he agreed Penny seemed to be a really nice young woman, he was just a little more reserved knowing that Penny worked with Ian Caxton!

Penny had recently told Viktor that she was now keen to move on from the apartment she had previously shared with her former boyfriend, who had moved out several months ago and had relocated to Paris. However, she also explained that this was difficult in the short term because there was still another 10 months until the rental agreement ran out. Viktor was similarly keen to move out from his parents' house. Neither, however, had yet got to the point where they were suggesting moving into just one property, together.

Life for Viktor certainly seemed to be 'on the up'. At work the gallery was working well, especially the website, and the agency was slowly improving too. This was especially so after Bob had emailed him a short list of clients now based in the UK who had completed business with Bob on the continent in the past. Viktor had followed up on these leads and was optimistic that they would produce more new business in the future.

Fortunately for Viktor, he did not have to wait too long. A man with a slight Midlands accent telephoned the gallery and announced that his name was George Jones and he wanted to discuss a particular painting with an expert. Mr Jones said his brother had recommended the 'Taylor Fine Art Gallery', because the brother lived in Monaco and had previously bought and sold paintings via Bob and Zoe Taylor's, *Les Roses Rouges'* gallery.

From his further discussions, Viktor established that the painting the man was talking about could be by Thomas Gainsborough! He agreed to visit Mr Jones the following evening at 7.30pm and jotted down the address. When Viktor finished the telephone call he opened his computer and accessed the internet. He wanted to find out as much information as he could about the renowned English artist, Thomas Gainsborough. This indeed, thought Viktor, could be a major find!

Viktor already knew that Gainsborough painted in the 18th century and was famous for both his portrait and landscape work. He was also aware that Gainsborough was an early exponent of printing his own pictures and along with his rival, Sir Joshua Reynolds, he is considered one of the most important British artists of that period.

For the rest of the day Viktor investigated many websites and catalogues. He made copious notes of his findings. Then, when he'd finally finished, he tried to summarise these results and typed them down on his computer:

Thomas Gainsborough (TG) painted quickly, with a light palette and easy flowing strokes. A prolific portrait painter, but gained greater satisfaction from his landscapes later in his career, sometimes merging the two together into one painting.

1727. TG was born in Sudbury, Suffolk, where he spent his childhood. He later resided there following the death of his father and before his move to Ipswich.

Early years. As a young boy he impressed his father with his drawing and painting skills, especially miniature portraits and small landscapes.

1740. TG was allowed to leave home to study art in London, where he trained under the respected engraver Hubert Gravelot. He also became associated with William Hogarth, the famous social critic and cartoonist.

1746. TG married Margaret Burr. His paintings at that time consisted mainly of landscape paintings, but these were not selling well.

1748. TG returned to Sudbury to concentrate on painting portraits. For the next few years he struggled financially.

1752. TG and his family, now including two daughters, moved to Ipswich. Commissions for portraits increased, his clientele included mainly local merchants and squires. Still struggling financially, he had to borrow against his wife's annuity.

1759. TG and his family move to Bath. There he studied portraits by van Dyck and was eventually able to attract a fashionable clientele. Bath had by now become a major art centre.

1761. TG started to send some of his work to the Society of Arts exhibition in London.

1769. TG submitted works to the Royal Academy's annual exhibitions. These exhibitions helped him enhance his reputation. TG was invited to become a founding member of the Royal Academy. He had a difficult relationship with the Academy.

1773. TG stopped exhibiting his paintings at the Royal Academy.

1774. TG and his family moved to London and three years later he began to exhibit his paintings at the Royal Academy again. Exhibitions of his work continued for the next six years.

1770s and 1780s. TG developed a type of portrait painting in which he merged the figures of his portraits into the landscape. Sometimes the sitter(s) are set to one side of the picture with the detailed distant landscape set to the other side. Also during this time he began to paint many famous people.

1780. TG painted portraits of King George III and Queen Charlotte and afterwards received further royal commissions. As a result of this high profile work TG's earnings increased substantially.

1788. TG died of cancer on 2nd August at the age of 61.

TG's most famous works include: Mr and Mrs Robert Andrews; The Blue Boy; Girl with Pigs; Portrait of Mrs. Graham; Mary and Margaret: The Painter's Daughters; William Hallett and His Wife Elizabeth, nee Stephen, known as The Morning Walk; and Cottage Girl with Dog and Pitcher.

1850s. TG's paintings became more popular with collectors. Lionel de Rothschild began buying his portraits. The subsequent rises in the value of TG's pictures were largely due to other members of the famous Rothschild family, including Ferdinand de Rothschild, collecting them.

20th Century. The complication of Thomas Barker of Bath!! A very competent late 18th Century artist, famous for his ability to closely emulate TG's techniques. Noted copier of TG's work.

Lasting legacy – the art world's major TG predicament of being able to correctly identify the true TG work to those painted by Thomas Barker!

2011. TG's portrait of Miss Read (Mrs Frances Villebois) was sold for a record price – £6.5 million!!

After Viktor had finished typing, he leaned back in his chair and decided he really liked Gainsborough's work. He liked the artist's ability to capture the likeness in the portraits, but also incorporate an interesting landscape setting. Mmm, he thought, this combination seemed to produce a warmer, softer, portrait than his competitors, who were still mainly painting a more austere and formal type.

Viktor's mind then began to focus on the record £6.5 million sale of the portrait of *'Miss Read'*. He smiled to himself and hoped that tomorrow evening he just might be viewing a similarly valued picture. He leaned forward and printed off a hard copy of his notes and then with his pen, manually wrote three extra details on the sheet. Yes, he thought, wouldn't it be brilliant if this picture turned out to be a true Gainsborough?

Later that evening Viktor and Penny were having a meal in a quiet restaurant in Covent Garden. Viktor explained that he was viewing a painting the next evening that might, he hoped, turn out to be by the artist, Thomas Gainsborough.

"I remember Ian saying that unless there was excellent provenance, it was very difficult to positively identify a Gainsborough painting," said Penny, hoping she would not deflate Viktor's enthusiasm, but at the same time, she was also trying to be realistic. "There are lots of copies and fakes about."

"Mmm, I know," replied Viktor. "There are some excellent paintings by a man called Thomas Barker. He was known as 'Barker of Bath' and he could capture Gainsborough's style and techniques back in the late 1700s. Over the years a number of once thought of as Gainsborough paintings, have since been reattributed to Barker. So, yes, I'm fully aware that this might be a waste of time, but... you just don't know. Remember the Turner paintings? The ones owned by John Baldwin?"

"Of course. You did an excellent job there, but you also had to put in a lot of time and effort to achieve that result. Do you still have that amount of time now?"

"I learnt a lot from that experience, Penny. Let's just see what I'll find out tomorrow. It's all a long shot, but nothing ventured is nothing gained! Isn't that what the English say?"

Chapter 22

Oscar was sitting on the patio at the rear of his villa. He was enjoying a cold beer and listening to the evening chatter of the tropical tree frogs in the background. He checked his watch. 10.30pm. He pondered on whether to have a cool shower before he went to bed.

Suddenly, he heard his mobile phone ring in the villa. He quickly got up from his lounger and jogged into the kitchen to answer the call.

"Hello?" said Oscar.

"Oscar? It's Ian Caxton. I wasn't sure whether you would still be up?"

"Ian! Hi. Just finishing my beer and listening to the frogs. Trying to keep cool and relaxed," replied Oscar, slowly walking back out onto the patio and picking up his can of beer from the table.

"Good. Glad you are still enjoying your Caribbean lifestyle. I was wondering if you could do me a favour?"

"Depends, old buddy. As long as it's nothing too energetic!" replied Oscar, with a smile on his face.

Ian laughed at the other end of the line. "No. I'm looking for some information and was wondering if you could put on your detective's hat!"

"Sounds mysterious. What do you want me to do?"

replied Oscar. He then sipped the remains of his beer and put the empty can back on the table.

"I have a name and an address. No need to make a note, I've sent you an email. I want you to use your local contacts and find out as much as you can about this person, please."

"Okay. But can you tell me why/"

"He could be someone who we might be able to do some business with in the future. Depends on what you're able to find out."

"When do you want to know?"

"It's not urgent. Just see what you can find out... when you can. Keep it low key. We don't want to alert or alarm anyone."

"Sounds easy enough. So how's things in the UK?"

"Actually, I'm not in the UK at the moment. The three of us are in Monaco for a few days, on holiday. Temperatures here are probably the same as in Antigua."

"It must be the middle of the night over there. Is Robert keeping you awake?"

"No, I'm just struggling to sleep tonight, so I thought I'd do something useful."

"Okay, Ian, enjoy your break. I'll be in touch. Cheers."

"Cheers, Oscar... and thanks."

Ian switched off his call and put his mobile phone into his dressing gown pocket. He leaned onto the balcony rail and looked down into the harbour below. It was now very quiet but the moonlight was still illuminating many of the large ships and yachts. The harbourside too was quiet. The outside restaurant tables and chairs had long since been moved inside the buildings, until later that morning when they'd all be returned.

Ian turned and left the balcony. He quietly crept through the apartment lounge area and back into the main bedroom. Emma was still sleeping in the same position she had been when Ian had earlier left the room. He removed his dressing gown, put his mobile phone on the bedside table and silently walked into the ensuite bathroom. After he'd flushed the toilet and washed his hands, he walked back into the bedroom. Emma stirred, but just as Ian thought she was going to wake up, she turned over and carried on sleeping. Ian carefully slipped back into his side of the bed and, five minutes later, he too was finally fast asleep.

After ending his phone call from Ian, Oscar went into his office and opened up his computer. There he found Ian's email. Oscar read the name and address and the few extra details that Ian had also included. I think I know that name, thought Oscar. I'm sure Wesley has mentioned him to me before. So, Mr Caxton, what are you up to this time?

Later that morning in Monaco, the first member of the Caxton family to be awake was Robert. After spending the first two days exploring all the rooms of the apartment, he now knew which room Mummy and Daddy slept in. He padded barefoot out of his own room, across the lounge area, and pushed on the slightly ajar door to his parents' bedroom. He ran over to the bed and pulled at Ian's left arm, which was hanging over the side of the bed.

"Daddy, Daddy," shouted Robert, which quickly woke both his parents up.

"Hello, little man, what are you doing here?" asked Ian, partly sitting up and then lifting Robert onto the bed.

"Wake up!" said Robert loudly.

"Well you've already achieved that," said Emma, also now sitting up.

"I need my breakfast," announced Robert.

"What's the time?" Ian asked Emma, moving Robert to a more comfortable position.

Emma glanced at the bedside clock. "It's a quarter to eight."

Ian lifted Robert off the bed and back onto the floor. "Give Daddy five minutes and I'll be in the kitchen."

Robert ran out of the bedroom and back to his own room. Ian climbed out of bed and went into the bathroom. Five minutes later he wandered into the kitchen in his dressing gown. He then proceeded to prepare the family's breakfast.

Ian had contacted Bob Taylor before he and Emma had arrived in Monaco and they had arranged a social get-together for the two families. Bob had suggested Sunday and a visit to a small adventure playground situated just off the main road to Nice. Ian said he and Emma would provide a picnic and Bob agreed to take them in his 'people carrier' car.

When Ian told Emma of the plans, she was pleased and said it would be good for Robert to mix with Bob and Zoe's children. It would also be an interesting challenge for Robert to understand the French language and try to communicate with them.

"It's going to be confusing though. If you remember, Bob's eldest is a Robert too!" said Ian.

"Oh that's right… and the little girl's name is Isobelle," replied Emma. "It should be a nice afternoon."

I hope it's going to be a productive afternoon as well, thought Ian. He wanted to try and get some information about Bob and his father-in-law's past business dealings with Andrei.

After they'd all arrived at the adventure park, the two ladies and the children made their way towards the adventure activities. Despite the concerns of the language barrier, Robert Taylor's spoken English was quite good and he managed to translate between Isobelle and younger Robert. Younger Robert also began to pick up some French words without any problems as well.

Ian and Bob walked together about 10 metres behind the

leading group. They chatted about the art world generally, Oscar's life in Antigua, the results of the new London gallery and Viktor's impressive start there. It was only when Bob started to mention the problems he was having with his father-in-law, that Ian began to see the opportunity of finding out more about the connections with Andrei.

"It must be difficult to get decisions sorted at the gallery and elsewhere?" said Ian, probing gently.

"Yes. The *Les Roses Rouges* gallery is the main problem, because, as you know, not only is the building our business premises, the apartment above is also our home. With the agency business I could just set up another account and gradually transfer the clients. However, I'm hopeful it won't come to that. Zoe's brother has been surprisingly good and Antoine does listen to him."

"This agency business, is that just in France?"

"No, no. We have clients and connections in a lot of European countries. Mind, I've given Viktor the small number in England and he is following those up."

"So do you think all these clients would be willing to transfer? Presumably they have been dealing with Antoine." Ian was now itching to delve deeper.

"The agency side has always been Antoine's domain. I've hardly ever been involved. However, over the last two years, Antoine has taken a less active role. He's still interested in the money side, but I deal with most of the clients now. Mind, without Antoine's day to day involvement, the number of clients has slowly reduced. I find splitting my time between the agency, the website and the gallery quite demanding."

"Didn't you mention to me about a Russian gentleman in 'Harbour Heights' that you dealt with?"

"Oh yes. Andrei. He and Antoine got on well together. Antoine did some good deals with him in the early days.

He was a likeable character, although I only met him once. I gather he died recently."

"So you might be looking for a new partner now?"

Bob suddenly stopped walking and so did Ian.

Bob looked directly at Ian. "Why? Are you interested then, Ian?" asked Bob, wondering what Ian was about to say.

"I might be, Bob. But I would need to know a lot more before actually committing. I've also got some ideas of my own."

Chapter 23

Park Street is situated in Highbury, North London and consists of a continuous line of upmarket three storey terraced properties on both sides of the road. Viktor arrived at number 22 at 7.28pm. He pressed the doorbell and within a handful of seconds the door was opened by a middle aged man, slightly overweight, with black hair, greying at the temples.

"Mr Jones? My name is Viktor Kuznetsov, from the Taylor Fine Art Gallery."

"Oh! I asked for an expert. You seem very young," replied Mr Jones, somewhat disappointed.

"I'm sorry, but I am the manager of the gallery. I was the person you spoke to on the telephone."

"You'd better come in."

Good start, thought Viktor as the two men walked along the corridor. Mr Jones then led Viktor into his study where, propped up on a dining chair, was an oil painting which looked exactly in Gainsborough's style.

"Well this is the picture I was telling you about. I've been told it's probably a Gainsborough," said Mr Jones, pointing in the general direction of the painting.

Viktor walked across to the painting and bent down and looked at it very closely. It was a landscape scene, with, in the foreground, a small clearing with a path leading off to the far right and disappearing into a dark wooded area. Standing in the clearing were three men obviously discussing some of the issues of the day. One man held the reins of a chestnut coloured horse. Above the trees, the sky was dominated by heavy, stormy looking, grey clouds.

Viktor reached into his pocket and removed a small torch. He switched it on and pointed the narrow beam at various sections of the picture. It looks old, he thought, a lot of aged cracks in the varnish, a nice piece of art. It would be even better if the old varnish was removed and generally given a good clean.

"It's a nice picture, Mr Jones," said Viktor, now resuming his normal standing height. "It would benefit from a good clean by an expert."

"So you think it's been painted by Gainsborough?"

"It's not that easy to say. It's certainly his style. Tell me how did you come to own it?"

"It's not mine. It's my uncle's."

"But do you know its history?"

"No. Other than that, my uncle inherited it from his father."

"Mmm. We would need to know its full provenance."

"What's that?"

"Provenance? That's the picture's history," replied Viktor. "It states who has owned the painting and when. It would tell us whether the experts have seen the painting before and reported on it. Has it been classified and authenticated to be a genuine Thomas Gainsborough painting? Basically, it's a paper record tracking the picture all the way back to when it was first painted."

"Authenticated? Isn't that what you are here for, young man?"

Viktor smiled and tried to keep his patience. "Partly, but

whatever I say to you now, this picture will still need to be supported by a good provenance."

"I see. So where do we go from here?"

"With your permission I would like to take some photographs so that I can see if the painting appears in the authorised Landscape Catalogue Raisonné, by John Hayes. That's the 'bible' of Gainsborough's landscape work. If this picture appears in that publication it means it could be a Gainsborough."

"Only could be?"

"I'm afraid so. This could also be a very clever copy. There are a lot of them around. That's why the provenance is so critical."

"I'll have to ask my uncle. But by all means, take your photographs."

Viktor removed his mobile phone from his pocket, set it to photo mode and took five photographs of the front artwork and two of the rear.

"Why do you need photographs of the back?"

Viktor pointed to a stencilled number on the frame, an auction house name and a faded scrap of paper glued to the canvas, which looked like it had a date of 1822. "These marks are all part of the picture's history. They may be useful as part of proving the provenance. Tell me, why is the painting in your possession?"

"It's my brother's idea. He lives in Monaco. My uncle is 82 and Charles, that's my brother, thinks we ought to get my uncle's belongings valued. We are his only heirs and my brother is concerned about paying UK inheritance tax. It's also likely that my uncle may have to go into a home soon, so we would then need to deal with his affairs. I was with my uncle a week ago and a neighbour was there. It was the neighbour who mentioned the Gainsborough name. I told Charles and he told me to get it valued, and quickly!"

"I see," said Viktor, "Well I don't think there is anything else I can do at the moment. I will make my enquiries and get back to you."

"Is there anything I should do in the meantime?"

Viktor put his phone back into his pocket. "You could speak to your uncle and try to find out any extra information he knows and ask him if he has any documentation relating to the picture and its history. Also, do you know if it's valued for insurance?"

"No. But what should it be insured for?"

"That's tricky. If it is a definite Gainsborough it could be worth between one to two million pounds at auction. If it's a copy, then much less, say 10,000 pounds, depending on the copier. The picture doesn't appear to have a signature, but it might be faded and hidden under the decades of accumulated dirt."

George Jones just stood and stared at Viktor. Both his eyes and mouth were wide open. He hadn't heard a word Viktor had said after 'one to two million pounds'. Finally he closed his mouth and swallowed.

"I'll be in touch in a couple of days. Thank you for the opportunity to view this picture. It is a lovely piece of artwork." Viktor put his hand in his side pocket and produced a business card which he handed over to the still shocked George Jones. "Please, look after this painting, it could be very valuable."

After Viktor left the house George returned back to his study and just stared at the painting. Wow, he thought, two million pounds!! I bet Charles will be pleased.

After Viktor had left Mr Jones's house he walked along Park Street and headed back towards the underground station. He weighed up in his mind the limited details he'd obtained from the viewing. He had some information and the photographs. At least that was a start for his investigation. He ruled out the possibility that the picture was definitely not by Gainsborough. The quality and style was too good. The composition followed the pattern of Gainsborough's work. The theme of people, trees and the wider landscape were typical Gainsborough, but of course, so were the many thousands of copies that currently existed in the art world. And then there was Mr Thomas Barker – the infamous, 'Barker of Bath'! Notorious for confusing the experts. Viktor wondered, was this a genuine Gainsborough, a Barker, or indeed, just a painting by the hand of yet another very clever copier? Time will tell!

Chapter 24

Ian and Emma were packing their cases. They were flying back to England later that afternoon. Emma was pleased that Robert had quickly adapted to his first flight in an aeroplane, his first trip abroad and the challenge of a foreign language. She thought he seemed to take everything in his stride. The benefit of being an innocent child!

"Ian?" said Emma. Ian looked up from folding his shirt. "I think we ought to come here more often. It's been a lovely few days, I get on really well with Zoe, and Robert's made a nice friend of Isobelle."

"The only problem there is that Robert starts school very soon, so if we want to include him on our trips it will have to be during the school holidays."

"I know. Maybe we could come on our own sometimes and with Robert at other times."

"That makes sense, although I will need to be able to contact work. It won't be all holidays for me."

"What about Sotheby's? Do you think you will be with them in the long term?"

Ian was stunned by Emma's question. It was an innocent and simple question, but Ian's immediate reaction was one of surprise. Not that long ago he knew Emma saw Ian working at Sotheby's all the way through to his retirement. "Wow," he replied. "What are you suggesting?"

"I'm not suggesting anything. It's just that I've been thinking how much Zoe enjoys her lifestyle here and Oscar has made the move to Antigua. I'm no longer working. Are we missing a big opportunity?"

"Emma, you astound me! This is not like you!"

"I know, but as I say, I've been thinking. Robert has adapted so well too."

"But what about our parents, our home in Esher?"

"I'm not suggesting we move out here permanently, just visit more often. Maybe invite our parents to join us occasionally."

Emma's comments were music to Ian's ears. His chat with Bob had been so positive and now, maybe, there was the opportunity to work closer with him and develop their business relationship. Maybe, there could be some very interesting times ahead!

"Good afternoon, Wesley," said Oscar, standing in the doorway to Wesley's office at the Shell gallery.

"Hey, Oscar, man, come in, come on in. What's your news?"

Oscar pushed the door wider and entered Wesley's office. He sat down opposite the big man.

"Just wanted to thank you for your information about Boscoe Holder and his paintings. My client bought my selections and he wants the two you have in store."

"Hey that's great news, so we're all winners! That's cool, man."

"I've just asked Worrell to pack them for me. I'll take them and deliver them tonight."

"That's really good."

"Wesley, didn't you once mention a man called Gladstone Clive?"

"Yea. I've bought and sold a few pictures from him over the years. I've got one of his paintings for sale in the showroom right now. Why do you ask?"

"Somebody mentioned to me that he had two William Blake sketches he wanted to sell... quietly and privately, so I was wondering if this guy was legit, could be trusted?"

"I've never had any problems with him. He usually buys and sells directly, but sometimes if he wants to sell to a wider audience, he will ask me. Mind, he does baulk about my fee. Must think I'm a charity!"

Oscar smiled. "Does he have his usual clients?"

"I think he has some people who he approaches first, but generally he will just take the highest bid. Mainly deals in the Caribbean, although... I think he said once that he did have an important connection in France. No, it's not France, er, somewhere nearby." Wesley tried to drag the information from the back of his brain.

Oscar tried to help by listing the countries he remembered surrounding France. "Belgium, Germany, Switzerland, Spain, er, Monaco, Italy..."

"That's it!" interrupted Wesley. "Yes I'm sure... it was Monaco!"

"Never been there, but I gather it's a nice place," responded Oscar. But his mind was wondering, why Monaco? Ian visits Monaco. Coincidence!?

"I've never been to Europe, full stop!" replied Wesley. "Been to a number of the other Caribbean countries and a couple of times to the US, but that's about it. Always on business though."

"Okay, Wesley, thanks for the information. I'll maybe contact him and see what he's got to say."

"No problems, man." Wesley looked at his watch. "Hey it's almost 5 o'clock do you fancy a beer? The bar across the road is open."

"Sounds like a great idea. I've got a couple of other bits to chat about so we can do it over there."

Chapter 25

Except for chatting to three potential customers who had come into the gallery just to browse, Viktor spent a large portion of the morning trying to track down information about George Jones's possible Gainsborough painting. Not having his own copy of the authorised Landscape Catalogue Raisonné, he'd asked Penny if she would help and look at Sotheby's copy in their library. Penny told him that he was in luck because Ian was not back from his holiday until tomorrow, so she would have a little bit of time this morning. Viktor emailed Penny copies of the photographs he'd taken and she promised to email him back her findings as soon as possible.

Viktor searched for more information on a number of websites, but without any luck. He found three pictures that were similar but quickly established that each one of these paintings were owned by national galleries around Europe. Another dead end.

It was just after 11.30am when Penny's email arrived in his inbox. He quickly opened it and began to read:

Vic. Not the best of news I'm afraid. I couldn't find your painting. The nearest I got to compare it with was Gainsborough's 'Road from Market'. Similar layout, so your picture might have been painted about the same time(?) – if it is a G at all!!

Sorry, See you this evening.
Penny x

Mmm, pondered Viktor, another dead end. Oh well, another couple of websites still to visit. You never know.

By lunchtime, however, Viktor was no further forward. He decided to put together his report for Mr Jones and not to spend any more time on this exercise, at least not for the time being. He gathered all his notes together and started to draft his email:

Dear Mr Jones,

Thank you for inviting me to examine your painting last evening. It is very much in the style of Thomas Gainsborough and the theme of the subject matter is typical of his work. However, without full and detailed provenance it is very difficult to prove, without much deeper and expensive investigations, whether it is a genuine Gainsborough or not.

I have spent most of this morning researching your picture, but unfortunately, I have not been able to identify it as being accredited to Thomas Gainsborough. It is not listed in the 'Landscape Catalogue Raisonné', by John Hayes. As I mentioned last evening, this catalogue is the 'bible' of Gainsborough's landscape work. All authorised pictures of Gainsborough's work appear in this catalogue. This exclusion, on its own, does not mean your picture is not by Gainsborough, it means that, to date, it has not been authenticated as being a genuine Gainsborough.

It is at this point that a decision has to be taken. There are several options:

1. *A possibly lengthy and expensive investigation can be carried out to establish the painting's provenance. This would include forensic tests, infrared cameras, x-ray technology*

on the painting, trying to obtain expert opinion and investigating the painting's full history, prior to it being owned by your family.

2. The painting could be professionally cleaned to identify the painting's original colours, a better look at the style of the artist and hopefully, a signature.

3. The painting could be investigated to establish if it was painted by Thomas Barker or, indeed, any other artist or copier.

4. None of the above and the painting remains in your family in its current condition. At least until further evidence comes to light that would make it more financially viable to pay for the full investigations I have mentioned in number 1 above.

Please do not hesitate to contact me to discuss this matter further.

Yours Sincerely,

Viktor Kuznetsov.

Manager,

Taylor Fine Arts Gallery.

Viktor read through and checked the details of the email. He amended a couple of words and pressed the 'send' button. He sat back in his chair and wondered whether he would ever hear again from Mr Jones.

That same evening Viktor met up with Penny at their favourite restaurant in Covent Garden. Viktor thanked Penny for her time in checking Sotheby's copy of the Gainsborough Catalogue Raisonné. He told her about the lack of any further evidence he had managed to find and also the contents of the report he had sent to George Jones. He concluded by saying that he didn't really expect to hear from Mr Jones again.

"Oh well," sighed Penny. "At least you had a go. I hope Mr Jones appreciates that at least. It sounds as though he really has little understanding of what is involved in establishing the true identity of an old painting."

"Yes, I know. He had no idea about what, or how important, a provenance was! He thought that just because his uncle's neighbour had said that the painting was maybe by Gainsborough, that would be sufficient!"

Penny laughed. "The neighbour is obviously a Gainsborough expert!" she said sarcastically. "You tried your best."

"So how's your quiet time been without Ian?"

"Not as quiet as I had hoped it would be. Michael Hopkins's PA went down with the flu, so I was drafted across to help. Actually it was quite interesting. A lot more high level company business and less specific on art issues. Maybe if Ian moves on, that's what I'll try to do."

"Do you think Ian will be moving on soon?" asked Viktor, a little surprised with Penny's comment.

"Well, from his career to date, he has not been in any one place for very long. He's well thought of at Sotheby's, so I'm just assuming he would be moving on soon. I don't know anything for definite though."

"Ian likes you and has a high opinion of you, Pen. What would happen if he did move on and he wanted you to join him?"

"Oh! I'd never really thought about that! If he was staying in London, well I guess, that would be fine. But I don't think I would want to go to New York or Hong Kong… at least, not on my own."

"I don't think Ian would want to go back to Hong Kong or New York. These days he's married and has a child to consider. No, I think Ian's next move is more likely to be away from Sotheby's."

"Well isn't that interesting, because I was thinking the same thing. He's ambitious, but I don't think that ambition would be limited only to the world of Sotheby's," said Penny, thinking of how much of a coincidence it was that they both had a similar opinion of Ian's future!

Viktor decided to change the subject. "I enjoyed the Dover sole the last time we were here, so I think that's what I'm going to have again this evening."

Penny picked up her menu, which she had not really looked at so far. Her mind was still on the discussion about Ian and how his next move may, or may not, affect her future… and of course, how that would have an impact on her relationship with Viktor!

Chapter 26

It was a week later when Viktor received a surprise visitor to the gallery. He was just making himself a cup of coffee, when he heard the entrance doorbell ring. He walked back into the main display area where he found Mr Jones standing at the front of his desk. He had a parcel under his arm.

"Hello, Mr Jones, what can I do for you today?" asked Viktor, walking back to his desk. "Please sit down."

Mr Jones sat down on the sofa chair and placed his parcel on the floor next to him, leaning it against his chair.

"Thank you. I thought I would come into your gallery to discuss our picture. After your visit and your email report, I telephoned my brother, Charles, in Monaco. He has a much better understanding of the art world than I do. I explained to him what you'd told me and his reply was that he wasn't surprised. He said your response seemed very professional, fair and reasonable... in the circumstances. He then told me to speak to you again and bring in the painting. We would like a quotation for the painting to be thoroughly cleaned."

"I see," said Viktor. He was pleased with Charles Jones's comments but still very surprised to see George Jones again. "We use two very competent firms for this particular cleaning work. One is more expensive and tends to work on multi-million pound paintings. The other is still very good and I would recommend their services in this case. Their premises are not too far away so I could take your painting to them sometime tomorrow."

Viktor went on to explain the gallery's charges for these services and an approximate cost for the professional cleaning.

"That is in keeping with what my brother was thinking, so yes that's fine. It's okay for the cleaning to go ahead on those figures too. Can I leave the picture with you?"

"Of course," replied Viktor.

Mr Jones lifted up his parcel and handed it to Viktor.

Viktor unwrapped the paper covering and the inner plastic bubble wrap. He removed the picture and gave it a thorough inspection, both front and rear. Satisfied that it was the same picture he'd examined just over a week ago, he placed it on the side of his desk. "I'll telephone you if the definitive quotation is different to the figures I've just indicated. We can then decide where we go from there. Is that okay?"

"Yes, that seems fine," replied Mr Jones.

"By the way, have you obtained any more information or documents that would be useful towards establishing the provenance?"

"I mentioned the provenance to my brother and he suggested I speak to my uncle. I did that two days ago and my uncle said he would look in the attic. He keeps all his old files up there in a large box. I am visiting him this weekend so I will see what he's been able to find."

Viktor nodded to acknowledge his understanding and then said, "Let me give you a receipt for the picture. It's just to say the painting is temporarily in my and the professional cleaner's possession."

Viktor completed the paperwork and handed a copy to Mr Jones.

"Thank you, Mr Kuznetsov. I look forward to hearing from you in due course." Mr Jones got up from his seat, shook Viktor's hand and left the premises.

Well, well, well, thought Viktor, now that was a real surprise!

The next morning Viktor took the painting to the restorers for the quotation. They confirmed a similar figure to what Viktor had indicated. Viktor gave them authorisation to carry out the cleaning work. The restorers said it would be ready in three days.

As Viktor walked slowly back to the gallery he was excited that he would finally have the opportunity to see this possible Gainsborough painting in all its original glory. He would then be better able to understand and see the artist's style. He hoped he would now witness the famous Gainsborough subtle and flowing confident brush strokes. But even with all this extra information, he knew it would still not be enough. He still needed proof, the expert opinion and, especially, sound provenance!

When Viktor arrived back at the gallery, he stood outside and looked at the existing pictures being exhibited through the two large front windows. He wondered if the display needed refreshing. Were the current paintings displayed attracting enough attention, or should he change the layout?

"Looking for a good picture, mister?" said a female voice behind him in a London cockney accent.

Viktor turned quickly and looked at the source of the comment. It was Penny. When he saw her face he smiled. "You made me jump and what's with the funny accent?"

"Just a bit of fun," replied Penny, still smiling. "I've brought you a sandwich."

"Oh good. Come on in." Viktor opened the door, switched off the burglar alarm and held the door open for Penny to pass through.

"So where have you been skiving off to? I called here 10 minutes ago."

Viktor explained about George Jones returning yesterday and him taking the painting to the cleaners that morning.

"So are you more hopeful that it is a Gainsborough picture after all?"

"No, not really, but I might have a slightly better opinion once I see it again… when it's been properly cleaned up. When that's all done I'd love Ian to have a look at it."

"Do you want me to ask him?"

"Yes please. I know the 18th century is not really his forte, but he does have a good eye and I do rate his opinions. I've been promised that the picture will be ready to collect on Friday."

"Okay, I'll ask him. Now then the sandwiches, do you want tuna or cheese?"

The restorers telephoned Viktor first thing on Friday morning to say the painting was ready for collection. As soon as Viktor had put down the phone, he got up from his desk and put the temporary 'closed' sign in the door's window. He set the alarm, locked the door and walked quickly to the restorer's premises. He was anxious to see the results of the cleaning and the original colours of the picture.

Thirty minutes later he had returned to the gallery with the painting, which was protected by a canvas picture case. He unzipped the case and removed the picture. He had minutely inspected the painting at the restorer's and was certainly pleased with the result. Now he was anxious to display it properly in one of the gallery's front windows. He hoped it would encourage inquisitive and possibly knowledgeable passers-by to call in and enquire about it. He'd already set up a vacant easel and he now placed the painting so that it took centre stage in the window display. He adjusted a soft spotlight to focus attention on the picture and stood back. Yes, it looked good. He adjusted the spotlight just slightly again, this time to emphasise the newly revealed signature in the bottom right hand corner. He then went back outside to view the display from the pavement area.

Yes, he thought, that should certainly attract some attention.

As Viktor stared through the window, he was suddenly conscious of someone looking at the same view, over his shoulder. He turned around and looked at his former boss's face.

"It looks very impressive, Vic. I gather you think it's been painted by Gainsborough?"

"Hello, Ian. Good of you to come. Have a closer look inside."

Ian followed Viktor into the gallery and they walked over to have a closer look at the painting together.

Viktor gave Ian a few minutes to make a closer inspection of the picture's features and also to look at the details on its rear.

"So what do you think?" asked Viktor, anxious to hear Ian's opinion.

"It's good, Vic. A very nice piece of work. The signature looks authentic. Yes, I like it. Does it have a good provenance?" asked Ian, rubbing his sweaty palm.

"Let's just say that that's a 'work in progress' at the moment."

Ian smiled. "What sale price are you going to put on it?"

"Well, it's er, not actually for sale at the moment. The client just wanted it to be cleaned at this stage. I've just collected it from the restorers. The client hasn't even seen it yet."

"I see," replied Ian, still focusing his attention on the painting. "Would he accept £250,000?"

"What!? Are you serious?" replied Viktor. He was shocked at Ian's comment.

"It's a good piece of work. Everything about it says Gainsborough, but…"

"I was waiting for the 'but'," interrupted Viktor.

"…But, it has no provenance! It could be a Barker of Bath! I've seen similar work that confounded the experts. It could be worth, say two million or it might be worth just five to ten thousand pounds! Costly exercise to subject the painting to forensic tests, imagery techniques, infrared and x rays, pigment analysis, etcetera."

"I know, I've told the client all this. All he's asked for at the moment is for the painting to be cleaned."

"Okay. Put the offer to him, see what he says. A bird in the hand and all that!" replied Ian, now standing back up to his full height again.

"You're prepared to take the gamble and the extra costs?" said Viktor. This was a side of Ian that Viktor hadn't seen before.

Ian smiled and then said, "Let's just see what your client thinks of my offer. Sorry, Vic, I must go. I've a meeting with Michael Hopkins in twenty minutes."

"Okay, Ian… and thanks," said Viktor, still somewhat baffled by Ian's offer.

As Ian opened the door to leave the gallery he shouted back, "It's a nice piece of work, Vic! Bye." Ian smiled again and scratched his itchy scalp.

Chapter 27

Viktor sat in his chair and watched Ian slowly disappear into the crowd of people walking along the pavement. I don't believe that!! he said to himself. I really don't believe that has just happened!

After a couple of minutes wondering what exactly Ian was up to, Viktor decided to email Mr Jones. He wrote:

Dear Mr Jones,

I am pleased to tell you that the restorer's quotation for cleaning your picture was within £10 of what I had indicated at our last meeting. Therefore, as per our agreement, I instructed them to carry out the work.

This has now been completed and it has made a tremendous improvement to the painting's appearance. The original colours have been restored and this has resulted in the painting being brought back to life! The signature is now clearer too.

I have put your picture on show in our window display area and already it has generated an inquiry. We can talk about the details of this inquiry when we next meet.

Could you please let me know when you intend to come into the gallery again so that we can discuss the painting's future?

Were you able to find out any information from your uncle which could improve the painting's provenance?

Yours Sincerely,
Viktor Kuznetsov.
Manager,
Taylor Fine Arts Gallery.

Viktor read through his email for a second time and then pressed the 'send' button. So we'll just have to wait now, thought Viktor, and see what Mr Jones has found out... if anything!

Viktor went to his small kitchen area situated in the rear storeroom. This room also doubled up as the gallery's office and packing area. He switched on the kettle to make himself a mug of coffee. Once his coffee was made he carried the mug into the display area. He walked over to look again at the 'possible' Gainsborough picture. He sipped his drink and stared at the painting again, taking in all its fine details. After a few minutes he thought, this painting definitely needs a name. We can't keep calling it a 'possible Gainsborough'. Maybe Mr Jones will have that answer when he returns later.

Viktor, once again, thought about Ian. Why, he wondered, did his former boss make an offer knowing there was no provenance? Not even a name! It didn't make any sense! Did he spot something that he was not willing to tell me? Has he seen this picture before? Mmm... what is it that I'm missing?

After Ian's meeting with his boss, Michael Hopkins, he went directly to Sotheby's library and sifted through a number of old catalogues relating to Thomas Gainsborough and his paintings. He also searched Sotheby's auction records for the end of the 19th century. If he was right, he would definitely find the answer to what he was looking for in one of these publications.

For over two hours he searched and searched, but then

suddenly, he finally found the article he was looking for. Bingo! He exclaimed to himself. I thought I was right! So, now we have a section of the provenance and also, just as important, the name of the picture. Ian rubbed his sweaty palm and slowly a broad grin spread across his happy face.

It was a day later when Viktor received the email from George Jones. Mr Jones stated that his brother was visiting from Monaco for seven days and they would visit the gallery on the following Tuesday. They should arrive at about 11 o'clock. Could Viktor confirm if the date and time were convenient for him?

Viktor quickly typed a brief email reply confirming both the date and time were agreeable. He also emphasised how important it was that they should bring with them any information that could help build up the composition of the painting's provenance. He'd become increasingly frustrated that Mr Jones seemed to ignore the urgency of helping to build up the painting's provenance. After all, a solid provenance could be the difference between the value being just a few thousand pounds or possibly into the millions!

On the following Tuesday, at 10.55am, George Jones entered the gallery with another man. Viktor quickly walked over to greet Mr Jones, who then introduced his brother, Charles. Viktor could immediately see the likeness. The main difference was that Charles had a much darker skin tone, acquired, Viktor guessed, through many years of residing next to the Mediterranean Sea. Viktor said he was pleased to meet Charles and directed both men to where their painting was being displayed in the window.

"Wow, what a difference," announced George. "It doesn't look like the same painting."

Viktor explained the technical details of what had happened to the painting and, whilst George still seemed to be amazed, Charles was far more relaxed.

"I cannot remember seeing this painting at my uncle's over the years," announced Charles. "I've been living in Monaco for the last 12 years and don't get back to Britain very often."

Viktor pulled out some photographs from the folder he was holding. "Here," Viktor passed the photographs to Charles and both brothers looked at them. "I took these photographs when I first visited Park Street."

"I agree with George, it certainly doesn't look like the same painting! The restorers have done an amazing job," said Charles.

Viktor was keen to move the men on to the more serious point of the meeting. He suggested they sat down next to his desk. "So, gentlemen, the key questions now are what is the next step for this picture's future and what information have you obtained to help build up the provenance?"

Charles seemed to want to take charge at this point. "I understand how frustrated you must feel because of the lack of information my brother has provided to date. However, you will be pleased to know that we have spoken to our uncle and we now have some additional details relating to the history of this picture."

At last! thought Viktor. Maybe we can finally get the ball rolling! "That's good," he said. "What do you have?"

Charles pulled out of his inside jacket pocket three pieces of paper. "Our uncle has lent us these documents to show to you, Mr Kutzetsov. This first paper shows a receipt from Giles and Co in Birmingham. They sold the painting to my uncle's father in 1902. The picture is called *Meeting on the way to market*. Unfortunately, as you can see, there is no reference to Gainsborough." Charles handed the sheet to Viktor to inspect.

"This next document shows a valuation dated 1912. Again no reference to Gainsborough." This too was handed to Viktor. "The third paper is a photocopy of the last will and testament of my uncle's father. It shows that all property was passed on to my uncle following the death of his father. Again it's lacking in detail, but does specify two paintings, one of which is the '*Meeting on the way to market*'."

Viktor looked at all three pieces of paper. "Do you mind if I take photocopies of these?"

"No, no," said Charles. "Please, carry on."

Viktor went into the office at the back of the gallery and made his photocopies. He then returned and handed back the originals to Charles. He put his own copies into his folder. "Please keep those documents safe. On their own they have little value because much more information is still required. Nevertheless it is a good start and they do show the history of the painting since 1902. So, gentlemen, what do you want to do next?"

"Well, we were hoping you may have some suggestions," replied George, speaking for the first time for a few minutes.

"Well, the options are still as I stated in my email. A much more detailed and technical investigation is going to be very expensive and nothing you have given me so far, even suggests that your picture was painted by Gainsborough. Yes, the painting is very similar to Gainsborough's style. The subject matter is very typical of Gainsborough's work and it has a possible Gainsborough signature, but of course, that could still mean it's just a very good copy!"

"You said in your last email to George," interrupted Charles, "that you have already received an inquiry?"

"Yes, the first day the painting was on display, after it was cleaned, a man came into the gallery and after inspecting it for a few minutes, he offered £250,000!"

"What!" exclaimed George, who looked straight across to his brother.

Charles just gave a relaxed smile and said, "Why would

he do that? You told him, I presume, that there was no provenance?"

"Indeed I did. I told him that I was waiting for further information from you."

"And he still offered £250,000, despite knowing there was no provenance at that moment?" asked Charles. "The man is either a complete idiot or a Gainsborough expert!"

"I have dealt with him before and I know he is not an idiot."

George and Charles looked at each other.

It was George who spoke first. "I think we should snap his hand off!"

"Tempting, I must admit," replied Charles. "We don't have any evidence that it was actually painted by Gainsborough and, as Mr Kuznetsov says, it could well be a good copy, worth what, maybe £10,000 at the most!"

Viktor nodded his head.

Charles continued, "But it still could have been painted by Thomas Gainsborough... and probably worth several millions. Tricky situation."

"Charles, Mr Kutnetsov has told us that we could spend many thousands of pounds trying to prove our case and we could still fall short, or even find it's just a copy after all. I say we take the man's money."

Charles ignored his brother's comment for a moment and asked Viktor, "Do you happen to know, Mr Kuznetsov, if this man is a Gainsborough expert?"

"All I do know, gentlemen, is his occupation. He is employed by one of the major art auction houses."

George and Charles looked at each other once again. Charles just smiled and said, "Why am I not surprised."

"I still say we should take the man's offer," repeated George.

Charles shifted uneasily in his chair. He then stood

up and walked over to look at the painting that was now known as *'Meeting on the way to market'*. He looked long and hard at the picture and then more closely at the signature. He also turned the painting over and looked at the back. "Okay," he said finally. "We'll take the man's offer! £250,000 will be extremely useful to our uncle. When do we get paid?"

Chapter 28

After George and Charles had left the gallery, Viktor emailed Ian setting out a summary of the discussions he'd had with the Jones brothers. He deliberately didn't mention the three documents he'd seen and had photocopied, or, the name of the painting. He wanted Ian to tell him his own thinking before offering him any of this extra information.

Ten minutes later Ian replied and when Viktor read Ian's note he was astonished! The email read:

Hi Vic,
Well done. I will call in to the gallery later this afternoon for a chat about your painting
'Meeting on the way to market'.
Ian.

How the hell did Ian know the name of the painting? Viktor wondered. I need to get to the bottom of all this!

It was just before 5.00pm when Ian arrived at the Taylor Fine Art Gallery. When he saw Viktor, he gave him a knowing smile.

"Hello, Vic. Had a good day?"

"Certainly a different one… thanks to you! What's going on, Ian?"

The two men sat down next to Viktor's desk.

"I'll tell you, Vic… once I own the painting! Mr Jones may yet decide not to proceed and I will have opened my hand."

"I won't tell anyone, Ian. You know you can trust me."

"I know that, Vic, but I just want to keep my findings to myself for the time being. So what's going to happen next?"

"The brothers are going to inform their uncle and sort out the legal paperwork at their end. Apparently the uncle has already told his nephews that they can have the painting, but they obviously want and need legal proof of ownership first. Also I want to make sure everything is legal and above board too."

"Well done. You are coming along nicely. What commission have you agreed to?"

"15%. They have accepted that."

"Okay you can tell them they do not need to pay you. On completion I'll give you £40,000 instead. You can tell them you have been able to negotiate a special deal!"

"That's very generous of you, Ian, but why would you do that?" replied Viktor, becoming more suspicious and confused by the minute.

"Let's just call it your 'finder's fee'."

I've still got a lot to learn, thought Viktor. "So what are you going to do with the painting?"

"Put it on the wall at home, of course! It will look nice in the dining room," said Ian, but then he produced a broad smile.

"You're not going to tell me!" said Viktor, responding to Ian's smile with his own disappointment.

Ian laughed. "Well, I'll be hanging it at home, in the short term!" Ian enjoyed teasing Viktor. "You and Penny can come round for dinner one evening and you'll see it hanging on the dining room wall."

It was Viktor's time to smile. "You know who you remind me of, Ian? Andrei Petrov!"

Ian laughed again. "You think that, do you. Well that's very interesting. Do you fancy a quick pint at 'The Grapes', there are some other things I want to discuss with you. One of which is, how are you and Penny getting on? She seems very happy at work."

Viktor smiled and agreed to the drink. As he prepared to close the gallery for the day, he wondered what other surprises Ian would be revealing during the next hour!

Ian's chat with Viktor in 'The Grapes' was very productive. Ian explained a few of his future ideas and Viktor agreed that he would like to play his part in the UK. Ian asked Viktor to keep all this information to himself and not even to tell Penny… for the moment, as nothing was absolutely certain… just yet! Again, Viktor agreed. Nevertheless, he was definitely intrigued and very surprised with this new Ian Caxton.

When the two men finally left the pub, they walked away in different directions. Ian headed towards the Underground station, whilst Viktor decided to walk the 20 minute journey to his home. He also wanted some quiet thinking time. Time to ponder on Ian's ideas. Yes, he thought, there could certainly be some exciting times ahead! Risky? Probably. But he had a high opinion of Ian's abilities and also knew this could well be the sort of exhilarating opportunity he had been hoping for when he'd decided to leave Sotheby's. Suddenly he had a skip in his step and exciting thoughts in his mind!

On his train journey home, Ian pondered on his conversation with Viktor. He had not wanted to inform Vic of all his plans, but he was pleased with Vic's initial reaction and comments to the few ideas he had mentioned. He'd used Vic as a sounding board and now he was convinced of his long term plan. It could really work... and be a huge success! There was, however, one serious problem that needed to be solved first. He needed a large fund of money, a 'war chest'! A far bigger fund than he could put his own hands on, or indeed, would be prepared to lose if everything went wrong. What he needed was some like-minded investors. Investors, or partners, who were prepared to join him on his venture. Viktor could see the positives, now he needed other people who were brave enough to risk millions of pounds on this, a once in a lifetime 'risk and reward' massive gamble!

Chapter 29

In Monaco, Zoe had just replaced the telephone receiver after a long discussion with her mother. The main topic of conversation being her father. Zoe made a long sigh and then a broad grin appeared on her face. At last, she said to herself, we can finally get on with the rest of our lives! She decided to immediately go downstairs to the gallery, where she hoped she would find her husband.

When Zoe arrived in the gallery, Bob was looking at some paintings on the internet. He immediately looked up when she walked over. "Hi, Zoe. To what do I deserve this visit?"

"I've just been speaking to my mother and she says that father has agreed to legally hand over the running of the business without the need for him to sign documents or you needing to get his general permission any more. He still wants to keep his share of the business, but he is going to leave all the everyday issues to you and me."

"Well that is great news! How has your mum managed to persuade him?"

"She didn't. It was all Claude's doing. He's been a revelation."

"Wow, he certainly has. I must give him a call to say thank you."

"I'm sure he would like that. Are you coming up for lunch?"

"Give me 10 minutes, I just need to finish this investigation first."

Zoe left Bob still looking at his computer. She walked towards the elevator, stepped inside and pressed the button for the top floor. As the elevator ascended she started to consider the possibility of getting back to and being more involved in the business once again. She knew the children were both settled in their schools and now she had a lot more free time, at last. Mmm, she pondered, I'll mention it to Bob over lunch.

Not too far away from the Monaco art gallery, Julian was just locking his apartment door. He was leaving to carry out his weekly appointment to transport Mrs Bisset to her business premises on the outskirts of Nice.

Mrs Bisset had, two years ago, on her sixtieth birthday, handed over the daily running of the veterinary surgery and animal parlour business to her competent three members of staff. However, she still liked to pop into the premises once a week to get an update on the current business matters and sort out any problems. She and Julian had become very good friends over the months and during the three hours of their two car journeys, she had been helping Julian to gradually get over the loss of Andrei. More than anything else, Julian found Mrs Bisset's wise and comforting words very therapeutic. His outlook on life had gradually improved and he now felt much happier in himself and more ambitious about his future. He also knew that Andrei would definitely not want him to continue to suffer as a result of his death.

As Julian entered the elevator to travel down to the car park, he thought again about Mrs Bisset and wondered what and when he was going to tell her. How would he explain his position? She had been so good to him and he now felt that she might see his decision as letting her down. However, he also knew that one of the main reasons why he was now going to change his outlook on life was due to her inspiring him to make such positive decisions. It was definitely going to be a difficult car journey this time!

Julian collected Mrs Bisset at the usual time and they spent the next 30 minutes telling each other what they had been up to since their last journey. Julian was desperately looking for an opportunity to tell her of his decision, but by the time they'd arrived at the surgery, he had failed to find the right moment. He decided he would definitely tell her on the return journey. In the meantime he went to his usual local cafe and ordered a salad lunch and a mug of coffee. He then waited for the telephone call from Mrs Bisset to say that she was ready to be taken home. Sometimes the surgery visit lasted for about an hour, sometimes much longer. It all depended on whether there were issues to be dealt with.

When the phone call finally arrived Julian looked at his watch. Mmm, 68 minutes this time. One of the quicker visits.

It took Julian just two minutes to drive the short distance to the surgery. He turned into the small car park next to the surgery. Mrs Bisset was waiting and she opened the front passenger door and stepped in. As she sat down she made a long sigh.

"No problems I hope?" asked Julian, with genuine concern.

"Not exactly a problem, more of a decision I've got to make, Julian. The three people I leave in charge of the surgery want to buy me out."

"Oh! How do you feel about that?" Julian started up the car and they moved out of the car park and on to the main road. He then headed back in the direction of Monaco.

"My husband and I started the business nearly 40 years ago, but as you know, he died five years ago. Initially, I carried on on my own, but with the help of some very good staff. Just over two years ago I decided to hand over the day to day running to this competent team. Now, the next natural step is, that they take over completely and I get out altogether."

"But is that what you really want to do?"

"The girls have made me a very attractive offer and I told them that I would think about it."

"Difficult. What would you do without the business? You still go there each week."

"Yes, and to be honest, it's no longer something I enjoy, or really look forward to anymore. I have been wondering for a while if I should take some time out to visit my sister in England. She's always asking when I'm going to visit her. It really would be nice to see her and her family again. The two boys are now at university!"

"Sounds as though you have made up your mind," said Julian. It all seemed to make sense to him.

"But I will certainly miss the chats and discussions we've always had during this journey."

"You have been wonderful to me, Mrs Bisset. You have changed my outlook on life completely. I now have some plans to do some travelling. I've already booked my first trip, it starts in a month's time. When I get back we could still meet up, every now and then, and continue to have our chats if you would like that."

"I would definitely like that, Julian. My world is surrounded by women, it's so refreshing to be able to have a sensible discussion with a man occasionally."

Julian laughed. "It sounds as though we are both very good for each other. When have you got to make your decision?"

"The business's financial year ends in six weeks time. The girls would like to start afresh from then. So I really need to give them my answer in the next few days. That way all the legal paperwork can be done in good time. Today could be our last trip!"

Julian looked across to Mrs Bisset. He noticed a tear slowly appearing in her left eye.

"As I say, I really would like to stay in touch with you. Your kind words have really inspired me," replied Julian. He too was beginning to feel emotional.

Mrs Bisset wiped away the tear and looked across at Julian. "So would I, Julian. So would I."

Chapter 30

Ian sat in his home office and was once again reading the list of contacts that Andrei had left him. He'd now scribbled some more notes in the end column. These comments were based on his interpretation of Andrei's dealings with these people and their geographical location. With just seven exceptions, all the others seemed to have some potential for his plan. However, he was certainly not going to rush and try to deal with all of them at once. To start the ball rolling he had selected just five names.

The first was Bob Taylor in Monaco. Ian's initial discussions with Bob at the small adventure playground had gone well. Now it was Ian's turn to be proactive, although he was concerned about Bob's current conflict with his father-in-law. Would that jeopardise his position?

Three of the five selected names were based either in Japan or Southeast Asia. Chosen because he thought this was an area he knew quite well. The fifth was May Ling in Beijing. He had added her name to Andrei's list as Andrei had not mentioned any mainland Chinese representation.

In addition, he had initially selected Gladstone Clive who was based in Antigua. However, he subsequently decided to let Oscar follow up and deal with that option himself. After all, Oscar had already completed the local investigations and was also on Gladstone's doorstep.

So, thought Ian, the plan is set. With Emma taking Robert to visit her parents on Thursday and Friday, this will give me the time and opportunity in the evenings to concentrate on my next step. However, for now, he returned the papers back into his safe and then wandered into the kitchen where he found Emma preparing their evening drinks.

In Monaco, Bob Taylor was drafting his email to Ian. He was now able to update Ian with the latest developments on his father-in-law's decision to step down from his everyday involvement in the gallery's business decisions. Bob knew that this particular issue was a major concern for Ian and he quickly wanted to allay Ian's fears. He checked through the wording of his email before finally pressing the 'send' button. He hoped Ian would now be fully on board with his suggestions and plans.

The following afternoon, Ian had returned from a business meeting and had just sat down in his Sotheby's office. He finally had a chance to read Bob Taylor's email. He was pleased to read that the father-in-law issue had now been resolved and he replied saying he was pleased to hear this news and would be in touch again very shortly.

Also in his inbox, Ian had received a very unexpected email. Well, well, well, he thought. What a coincidence, what a surprise! The email was from Yuki Tanaka in Tokyo. Yuki was one of the names mentioned on Andrei's listed contacts in Japan. The big surprise was that Yuki was number four on Ian's list of five people to contact, but he hadn't had a chance to contact Mr Tanaka yet! So, Ian wondered, how had he obtained my name and email address? However, after finally reading Yuki's email the picture became a little clearer:

Apologies for contacting you like this, Mr Caxton. Our mutual friend Andrei Petrov recommended that if I came to England, then I should contact you. I am arriving in London on the 21st of this month and will be staying for three nights at The Waldorf Hilton hotel. If you are available it would be a great honour for me to meet with you. Would you be available for dinner one evening?
Thank you,
Yuki Tanaka.

What an interesting coincidence, thought Ian. He tried to recall the information about Mr Tanaka on Andrei's list. He remembered that Yuki was a very big player in the Japanese art market. Mmm, he thought, this could be a very timely and interesting meeting!

Later that same evening Ian looked at Andrei's report and he re-checked his information on Mr Tanaka. It was all positive and so he replied to Yuki's email confirming he would be pleased to have a meeting with him. He suggested the 22nd at 7.30pm in the Waldorf's Homage Grand Salon. Ian had eaten there once before and remembered he'd enjoyed an excellent meal.

Almost immediately, Ian received an email reply from Mr Tanaka. Ian looked at the time of the email, 5.57am Japanese time. Mmm, he thought, obviously one of the early risers in the land of the rising sun! The email confirmed Ian's suggestion and Mr Tanaka informed him that he would book a table.

Ian's thoughts were now interrupted when Robert entered his office. "Mummy says it's time for my bath."

"Okay, little man. Let's go." Ian switched off his computer and followed Robert out of the office. "If you are a good boy in the bath, I'll tell you a bedtime story later."

Robert stopped half way up the stairs. "Another story about the dragon?" he said, hopefully.

"Okay," replied Ian. He would have to think quickly of another adventure as Robert didn't like the same story twice!

Two evenings later Ian was at home alone. As planned, Emma had taken Robert to visit her parents for two days. After preparing and eating his meal in the kitchen, he relocated to his home office. There he switched on his computer and also retrieved Andrei's listing from the safe. On the listing he ticked Bob Taylor and Yuki Tanaka's names as being contacted, although neither had yet been fully informed of his plans. He then began to draft an email that would be sent to each of the two Southeast Asian contacts, one based in Malaysia and one in Singapore.

Dear (name inserted),

We have a mutual friend, Andrei Petrov. I am not sure if you are aware, but I am sorry to report that Andrei died recently. Before he died he gave me your name as a possible business contact.

Because he both enjoyed, and greatly respected, his business dealings with you, he suggested I should contact you to inquire whether you would be interested in continuing a similar business relationship with me in the future.

I look forward to hearing from you in due course.

Yours Sincerely,

Ian Caxton.

For May Ling, Ian decided that a separate, more personalised, message was more appropriate having met her previously with Oscar in Hong Kong. He drafted the following email:

Dear May,

I hope this email finds you in good health and your business is still prospering well.

I am in the process of setting up a partnership consisting of a select number of art dealers, who will be based throughout the world. The main objective is to identify and connect your local clients' needs with other art markets around the world.

The partnership will be able to borrow and trade paintings from within the group, thus giving extra opportunities to grow your business.

You would be the partnership's sole representative for China and Hong Kong.

I hope you agree that this could be an exciting opportunity.

I look forward to hearing from you soon.

Kind regards,

Ian.

When he was finally happy with the three draft wordings, Ian pressed the 'send' button. He continued to watch the computer screen until a message confirmed the three emails had all been sent. He checked his watch for the time, 11.42pm. He closed down the computer and put Andrei's listing back in his safe. He suddenly felt quite tired and alone. No Robert to read a story to tonight and no Emma to cuddle up to in bed. The house seemed so unusually quiet. Mmm, he thought, I don't think I would like to exist like this full time. It obviously suited Andrei, but of course, we didn't always agree on everything.

Chapter 31

It was two weeks following Viktor's meeting with the Jones brothers, that he received an email from George Jones. The email confirmed that the brothers had told their uncle the selling price of '*Meeting on the way to market*'. The uncle was pleased and immediately instructed them to arrange for the transfer papers to be drawn up as quickly as possible. They all agreed that the sooner the painting was transferred to the brothers' names, the less of an issue it would become when the uncle eventually died. Charles also informed his uncle that the money would be deposited into a special investment account, where it would be used to top up his current income and, if necessary, to pay for a better care home if their uncle's health deteriorated sometime in the future.

In his reply Viktor informed George Jones that he had been able to negotiate a special arrangement with the buyer over his commission. Viktor did ask, however, that once the transfer had been completed between the brothers and uncle, a copy of the agreement should be emailed, or posted to him, as quickly as possible. Once this was in his possession he could then proceed with the sale. On receipt of the buyer's money he would transfer to the Jones brothers the £250,000, less the costs already incurred for the picture's cleaning.

To Viktor's surprise, it was only three days later when George Jones arrived at the gallery with the signed transfer document. Viktor checked it thoroughly and confirmed that all seemed to be correct, but he said he would still need to show it to the gallery's solicitor for confirmation. He emphasised that this was usually just a formality and no time would be lost because the same solicitor would also be drawing up the documents for the sale from the Jones brothers to the buyer. Viktor estimated this should all take about a week to complete.

George Jones seemed pleased with Viktor's comments and, after he'd taken the opportunity of looking at his picture, still on display, for probably one last time, he left the gallery a very happy man.

Immediately after George Jones had left the gallery, Viktor composed an email to Ian and informed him that the Jones family transfer of the painting had now been completed and he would get the gallery's solicitor to draw up the new transfer paperwork. Viktor also attached an invoice for the sale plus the agreed commission costs. After he finally pressed the 'send' button he strolled over to where the painting was still being displayed and bent down to scrutinise the picture thoroughly. A few minutes later he stood back up to his full height and gently shook his head from side to side. He still couldn't understand why Ian was so keen to buy the painting with such a poor provenance. Viktor, my boy, he said to himself. You are obviously still missing something that Ian has spotted, but exactly what!? That was the big question!

Later that same day Ian received two separate emails from the two Southeast Asia contacts on Andrei's list. Unfortunately, the contents of each email were very similar. The potential partners in Malaysia and Singapore both said that they were very sorry to hear about the sad news of Andrei, but no, they were not looking to set up a new business arrangement.

Ian was disappointed, but not totally surprised. He was still waiting for a reply from May Ling and was hopeful that Oscar would make some progress with Gladstone Clive. In the meantime he had been doing some calculations trying to establish the level of 'war chest' he thought the partnership would need to start the venture off on a positive note. He eventually decided that £50 million would be the minimum required! He pondered on this amount of money. Could the plan work on a lower amount if the partnership was not willing, or even able, to find this level of investment capital?

Other than Viktor, Oscar and May Ling, Ian had not yet shown his hand to the other prospective partners. He had discussed the possibility of working with Bob Taylor, but he only intended to give details of his own plan to Bob once he had received some positive news from May and Yuki Tanaka. If these people did not agree, then he would have to revisit Andrei's list and decide on the next group of contacts to approach. Indeed, he began to think that he may have to do this anyway if the commitment was not there for the £50 million.

The Waldorf Hilton, London hotel, formerly known as the Waldorf Hotel, is situated in the Aldwych district of London. It is now part of the Hilton Hotels & Resorts chain but has a history dating back to 1908. The hotel was originally established by William Waldorf Astor, who was the 1st Viscount Astor and a member of the famous Astor family. The hotel is located in the Covent Garden area and within walking distance of The Royal Opera House.

Yuki had emailed Ian to confirm he had reserved a table in the hotel's Homage Restaurant, but suggested they meet beforehand in The Parrot cocktail bar at 7 o'clock. Ian had never been in this bar before so decided to investigate its details on the hotel's website. He discovered that, as well as offering cocktail drinks, The Parrot venue also provided music, light meals and entertainment in an intimate, tropical environment. The venue seemed to combine old world sophistication with contemporary details. Okay, he thought, that should be a nice start to the evening.

Two days later, Ian walked into The Parrot cocktail bar just after 7pm. He asked the barman if he knew Mr Tanaka and the barman pointed to a smartly dressed Japanese man sitting at a nearby table listening to the live music. Ian walked over to join his host.

"Mr Tanaka?" asked Ian, and the Japanese man stood up and slowly bowed his head. "I'm Ian Caxton," Ian also bowed his head then held out his hand.

"Good evening, Mr Caxton, it is an honour to meet you," said Yuki, shaking Ian's hand and bowing again. "Please call me Yuki, much less formal… and please sit down. Would you like a cocktail?"

"Thank you, Yuki. Please call me Ian," he said, sitting opposite Yuki. "But I would prefer a glass of chablis please."

A waiter arrived at their table and Yuki ordered two glasses of chablis.

Ian guessed Yuki was probably in his early fifties. He looked very fit and seemed to have a constant small smile on his face.

"Is this your first visit to London, Yuki?" asked Ian, keen to break the ice.

"No. I come here about every one or two years. I have some Japanese clients in London and I also like to attend some of the better auctions. But it has been about three years since I was last here," replied Yuki.

"Have you been to any of Sotheby's auctions?" Ian was curious to hear Yuki's answer.

"Only once. It really depends on the quality of the

paintings in the auction. I usually bid for only the paintings my clients, or I, need."

Ian nodded. "We have a mutual colleague, Andrei Petrov. Did you know he had recently died?"

Yuki looked surprised. "No I didn't. Oh that is a real shame. I had not spoken to him for a while. I'm sorry. A really nice man."

"Yes. Have you dealt with him for some time?"

"Yes, some time. Probably, 10 years, I think."

The waiter brought their glasses of wine and put them on their table. Both Ian and Yuki picked up their drinks.

"Kanpai!" said Ian.

"Kanpai, Ian. You speak Japanese?" asked Yuki, a little surprised. Both men touched glasses.

"No. I just know one or two phrases."

The two men spent the next twenty minutes talking about their involvement and experiences in the art world. The waiter then informed them that their table was ready for dinner. The two men picked up their drinks and followed the waiter to the Homage Restaurant.

"Have you eaten here before, Ian?" asked Yuki.

"Yes, just once. Mind it was about four years ago. I remember the food was very good."

"I ate here last evening, before going to the Opera. The lobster was excellent."

Both men looked at the options on the menu. Ian decided on the Dover sole and Yuki, the lightly grilled shark.

After the waiter had taken their orders and walked away, Ian asked, "So why have you come to London this time, Yuki?"

"I have three customers to see and want to go to the auction at Christie's tomorrow. There are two paintings that I am particularly interested in. One I already have a buyer for in Tokyo… as long as I can obtain it at the right price."

Ian smiled. He would have loved to have known which two pictures Yuki was interested in, but he always thought it was bad manners to ask before the auction. If Yuki wanted to volunteer the information, well, that was fine. But he didn't.

Ian decided now would be a good time to find out whether Yuki would be interested in Ian's plan. "Yuki." Yuki put down his menu and looked up at Ian. "I was wondering what your immediate thoughts were now that Andrei is no longer in your business future?"

"I have been thinking about that question since you mentioned his sad death earlier this evening. I am not really sure. I would like to retire in about five years time, so I was wondering if I should take this opportunity as the first step towards that retirement. Mind, I would still like to 'keep my hand in'. Is that the correct English phrase?" Ian nodded. "But maybe concentrate just in Japan and avoid all the international travelling. That bit has become very tedious and tiring. Why? Do you have an idea?"

Ian smiled. "Let me explain my plans and you can then decide if you are interested in my little adventure."

For the next ten minutes Ian explained his idea about the proposed partnership. However, when he was interrupted because their meals had arrived, Yuki insisted Ian continue whilst they ate. He was very interested in everything Ian had to say.

The conversation went well. Yuki had his own suggestions, which Ian thought were interesting and constructive. Yuki also mentioned a business colleague who had illegal access to some of the free port records in Singapore. Ian was aware that a lot of owners of paintings rented space in these buildings because of their tax and security advantages. These tax advantages were different in each individual country and were dependent upon where each free port was located. However, Ian was also aware that in recent years, the free port system, especially in Switzerland and Singapore, had been accused of facilitating international art crime, allowing stolen artworks to remain undetected in storage for decades.

Yuki explained that this colleague was able to keep a record of a lot of the paintings stored there, who the owners were and both the comings and goings of all the artwork. Yuki also said that, as a result of this valuable information, he had been able to facilitate a number of purchases for his clients which he would not normally have been able to do without this inside knowledge.

Ian was impressed with Yuki's enterprise and business acumen, although he sounded a bit like Andrei with his illegal inside knowledge of the free port records. Ignoring that for the time being, Yuki still seemed to work very hard and was obviously achieving the just rewards from his efforts.

When Ian left the hotel he knew he could do business with Yuki. Yuki too was pleased and when he returned to his room the first thing he did was to telephone a colleague in Japan.

Chapter 32

Oscar had been invited to an art exhibition at the Shell Gallery. The exhibition opened at 6pm and after an hour the gallery was quite busy. Just after 7.15, whilst Wesley was talking to Oscar, he spotted Gladstone Clive arriving at the gallery. Wesley called Gladstone over and introduced him to Oscar. After a few minutes Wesley was called away and Oscar and Gladstone chatted together. The two men discussed various pictures that were on display, but eventually decided not to buy any of them. Afterwards, Oscar invited Gladstone for a drink at the bar across the road. It was the bar that Oscar and Wesley often frequented. Gladstone thought it was an excellent idea and they left the gallery and crossed the road.

The two men ordered cold lagers. It was still a warm evening, despite the earlier heavy shower and they sat outside on the veranda talking and people watching.

"I love this climate," said Oscar. It never gets cold here does it?"

"I've never been anywhere else outside of the Caribbean," replied Gladstone. "The only cold I know is my fridge and freezer back at home!" Gladstone laughed at his own joke.

Oscar smiled. "You know, Gladstone, I really feel lucky living here. It's less frenetic and more laid back than Hong Kong, but there's still some business to be done."

"It used to be more difficult. Most of the local people cannot afford some of the prices of good art. Now we have more foreigners residing here and they have the money. It's made a big difference to my income."

"So what are your plans, Gladstone? Are you ready to retire yet?"

"No, man. I still need to work for a few more years, yet. I'm still in my mid fifties."

Oscar nodded. "You know, I've a friend in England. We used to work together in Hong Kong. He's got big plans and wants me to join him," said Oscar, trying to raise Gladstone's curiosity.

"What, in the art world?"

Oscar nodded. "He says he's looking to set up some sort of a partnership. Looking to have a representative here in the Caribbean."

"Sounds interesting. Just in the Caribbean?"

"No, I think he's been talking to people and galleries from about six places in the world. He's mentioned Europe and China amongst others."

"So what's involved?" said Gladstone, eager now for more details.

Hooked! said Oscar to himself, and then to Gladstone. "Let me get you another beer and I'll tell you what I know. It would be great to get an opinion from such an expert as yourself." Oscar picked up the two empty glasses and walked inside and across to the bar. He left Gladstone to think about the bait he'd left dangling!

Later that evening, back in his villa, Oscar opened up his laptop computer and started to type an email to Ian:

Hi Buddy,
Made contact with our man this evening. He thinks your

*scheme has possibilities and wants more information. Nice guy,
we could work together over here.*

*Say hello to Emma and Robert for me. How's Robert's cricket
progressing?*

Cheers,

Oscar.

Ian read Oscar's email with a smile on his face. Okay, he
thought, we are beginning to build up a solid group. He
was, however, a little concerned that Oscar had made no
mention of Gladstone's previous involvement with Andrei,
but he eventually decided that was probably not critical
as Oscar seemed to be establishing a good start to their
relationship.

All I want now, thought Ian, is for May Ling and Bob
Taylor to come on board and we will then be able to
identify what our final 'fighting fund' is likely to be. He
still hoped that the £50 million target could be achieved,
because at that level of money, they would certainly be able
to be involved in multi-million pound deals as well as some
smaller options of up to just a few million.

Ian sent Oscar a holding reply. He said he was pleased
with Oscar's work and would be in touch again shortly.
After the email had disappeared he looked in his inbox. Ah!
he exclaimed to himself. A reply from May, at last! Although
he was slowly getting used to the long pauses between sending an email to May and receiving a reply, it was, nevertheless, still frustrating. He opened up the message and read:

Hello Ian,

*Once again sorry for the long delay before my reply. Been in
Beijing for a few days and like to reply to emails when I'm back
in Hong Kong.*

Your partnership plan sounds interesting. Obviously I would

need more details, but at this stage, yes, I would like to be involved.
May.

Excellent, thought Ian. Another tick to add to my list. Now for Bob. My plan may cut across his present thinking, but hopefully he will see the bigger benefit in my idea. Ian began to type his email to Bob Taylor. He hoped this would be the final piece in his jigsaw.

If Bob does come on board, thought Ian, as he was typing, then we can get down to the basics of money and trading procedures. Also we'll need to agree and establish the right strategy and mechanism, so we can achieve my ambition of doubling our money within the first year!

The next day Viktor emailed Ian to tell him that all the transfer paperwork was now ready for his signature and his payment. George Jones had already signed his copy. Ian replied to say the money would be transferred to the gallery's account later that afternoon and he would call in on Friday to collect his new painting, *'Meeting on the way to market'.*

Viktor, meanwhile, was still trying to work out what he was missing. He knew Ian sometimes had a sixth sense, a gut feeling, a tingling or, however people wanted to describe this extra awareness or intuition. But he definitely sensed that Ian knew something more tangible, something extra this time! He also knew that the 'something extra' was going to mean the painting WAS a genuine Gainsborough! Well good luck to him if he could prove that satisfactorily to the art market. However, he was determined to get Ian to answer this conundrum. It was driving him mad!

Bob Taylor was quick to respond to Ian's email. He told him that he was surprised with Ian's plan, but agreed it could just work. Whilst he still wanted to expand his own plans, he was prepared to put that on hold and join in on the partnership in the short term. Privately, Bob saw Ian's plans as a great opportunity for him and his gallery. Especially with the more wealthy art buyers in Monaco who, to date, he hadn't been able to attract... so far!

Okay, thought Ian, we are now there! The moment of truth! Can we get to the £50 million commitment?

Ian started to draft his email. This was going to be sent to each potential partner. He listed the main areas that he thought were key to achieving the partnership's success:

• The £50 million investment fund.
• All the suggested trading procedures, strategy and mechanisms to be employed.
• The aim – to double our investment within the first year!

He concluded by asking for a continued commitment and the amount of money each partner was prepared to put into the fund. Finally he asked for any suggestions, amendments or improvements that anybody might have.

Ian read his draft three times and each time made minor alterations. Finally he was happy. He held his breath and his finger hovered over the 'send' button. Under his breath he said, 'I hope you approve, Andrei!' He then pressed the button and watched the computer screen until the message came up, 'all sent'. He smiled to himself. A mixture of excitement, apprehension and relief swirled through his brain. He closed the computer down and went to pour himself his first glass of whisky of the year!

On Friday, at 3pm, Ian arrived at the Taylor Fine Art Gallery to collect his newly purchased painting. He found that Viktor had been very organised and had already parcelled up his picture ready for collection.

After Ian had signed the transfer papers, Viktor was

itching to ask Ian the big question. "Right then, Ian, you now own this painting and you promised to tell me WHY you think this picture was painted by Gainsborough."

"Okay. But now you've wrapped it up I can't actually show you, but I checked it out on Sotheby's records and found it all tied up with my thinking," replied Ian, still teasing Viktor a little.

Viktor folded his arms. He was waiting quietly and patiently. He wanted the whole story. "And!?"

"It was the repair work that's still in evidence on the rear of the canvas. I remember Bill Travers, it was during my trainee years, he explained the different types of repair work that could be carried out on various types of damaged pictures. Using Sotheby's records he showed me, and the other three trainees in our group, photographs of a few repair examples. One of the photographs I remembered looked very much like our friend over there." Ian pointed to the wrapped parcel. "After you let me view the picture, I knew I'd seen something similar before. I also had a strong feeling about its authenticity. When I went back to the office I searched our records. I went through all our library records on Gainsborough's work, sifted through a number of old catalogues and accessed Sotheby's old auction records for the end of the 19th century. For over two hours I searched and searched. I was just about to give up when... there it was!"

"There was what!?" Viktor asked excitedly.

"Patience, young Vic."

Viktor grimaced with frustration.

Ian continued. "I found in our auction records dated 1891, I think it was, a catalogue record of a painting called 'Meeting on the way to market' by Thomas Gainsborough. The painting had been previously authenticated as a genuine Gainsborough and had now been entered for sale by auction. However, separate Sotheby's documents recorded that about a week before the auction, the same painting was on display at one of the nearby galleries. Apparently, a man went into this gallery and as he stood in front of the painting, he suddenly shouted that he was a relative of Gainsborough, pulled out a knife from the inside of his jacket and slashed the top right hand corner of the canvas. He was about to strike again but was apprehended by two guards. He then shouted that the painting was not real but a fake! Somehow he managed to escape from the guards' clutches and ran out of the gallery, never to be seen again. It transpired that the man was not actually a relative of Gainsborough after all! There were some conspiracy theories, but nothing was ever proven. However, the painting was now both damaged and tainted. It was withdrawn from Sotheby's auction and about a year later it was officially delisted from the authorised records of Gainsborough's landscape paintings."

"Wow!" exclaimed Viktor. "And you knew all this?"

"Not quite, Vic. It was the scar on the back of the painting that prompted my further research. With the more modern investigation techniques now available I'm fairly sure that I can convince the experts that it is, and was, a genuine Gainsborough all along. It was only that idiot who damaged the picture that introduced any doubt. Without him I'm sure it would never have been challenged, or even considered to be delisted. It would have stayed in the auction and been purchased by somebody completely different!"

Viktor was still staring at Ian in awe. "That's brilliant, Ian. Absolutely brilliant! So, now you are the owner of a two million pound painting!"

Ian leaned closer to Viktor and whispered, "Between you and me, Vic, I'm hoping it's going to sell for nearer £3 million!"

Chapter 33

It was nearly 7.30pm when Ian arrived home with the parcel under his arm. The days of Robert running up to greet him had long passed. He was growing up far too quickly, thought Ian. Emma, however, did walk into the hallway from the kitchen to give him a kiss.

"A present for me?" she asked, spotting the parcel under his arm.

"Could be, I'll explain later when Robert has gone to bed," replied Ian. He changed his shoes and walked through to the office where he placed the parcel on his desk.

Later that evening, once Robert had been put to bed, Ian took Emma into the office. He slowly unwrapped the painting, stood it on his desk and leaned it against the back wall.

"Well, what do you think?" asked Ian, switching on his desk lamp and pointing the light directly onto the picture.

"It's lovely, Ian." Emma walked towards the painting and began to examine it much closer. Then she noticed the signature. "Gainsborough!? she exclaimed. "Thomas Gainsborough! But that's got to be worth, what, millions! Is it real!?"

Ian summarised the story from how Viktor had answered the initial telephone call from George Jones right the way through to Ian collecting the picture from the gallery earlier that day.

"Oh, wow, Ian. So you think it is a real Gainsborough?"

"Well it's cost me nearly £300,000 so far, so I hope so. If I'm right, well, it could be worth maybe ten times that!"

"So what are you going to do with it now?"

"I thought it would look nice hanging on the far wall in the dining room."

"Ian! We can't keep it. What about security and insurance?"

"I've already insured it for £400,000, so until I can get the technical people to look at it, I thought we ought to have the benefit of it here in our home. Besides, I've invited Vic and Penny for dinner and I promised them it would be on the dining room wall when they came."

"When have you invited them for?" asked Emma. She was alarmed that this was the first she'd heard of this arrangement!

"Oh, don't worry. I haven't suggested a date yet. I thought you'd want us to discuss it first."

"Mmm, okay. We shall have to look at the calendar."

Ian wanted to get back to the subject of the painting. "So you like the picture then?"

"It's wonderful, Ian. I would love to own something like that. So much history and just think about when it was painted!"

"If it is by Gainsborough, then it was painted about 1785."

"Really! Wow. Well over 200 years ago! It still looks wonderful. I love the moody setting of the sky and the three men, they could be talking about the latest football results!"

Ian laughed. "More like the price of corn, or cattle, at the market."

Emma calmed down and was quiet. She just stared at the painting. Ian wondered what she was thinking.

"Do you know, Ian," said Emma, jokingly, "you could

probably make more money from buying and selling pictures than from working at Sotheby's!"

Ian knew that Emma was not serious, but he decided to respond in a similarly light hearted manner to see where the conversation went. "What would you say if I did this as a career move?"

"I was only joking, Ian."

"I know you were, but what would you think?"

"I don't know. It would be a drastic change. We would lose a secure income."

"We have several million Swiss francs in the account in Switzerland that Andrei set up and I've made quite a bit of money from the Isaac Tobar paintings. I haven't touched any of that money so far and then there's the value in the apartment in Monaco. That's worth a few millions too."

Emma went quiet again. Eventually she asked, "Is this all to do with Andrei?"

"Andrei's dead, Emma. This is to do with us, our future and Robert's future."

"Since you met Andrei, you've changed, Ian."

"I hope for the better. We are certainly a lot wealthier and I don't feel so trapped as far as work is concerned. My career at Sotheby's is no longer the 'be all and end all'! We can now afford to send Robert to the private school you've always admired."

Emma looked away from Ian and back to the painting.

"That picture alone, Emma, will probably be worth three million pounds in a few months' time," said Ian. "Also there are the paintings in the apartment and the vault in Monaco. They are probably worth a further five, maybe six, million pounds." He was desperately trying to persuade Emma to at least consider this option.

"I need to think about it, Ian. It is a massive decision."

"I agree. But so was your decision to vote for the sale

of your accountancy partnership! It was the right decision then and it would be the right decision now."

Emma turned and looked seriously at Ian. "I need to think about it."

"Okay," said Ian.

Over the next few days Ian struggled to concentrate at work. His mind was far away from Sotheby's. He had received two positive responses to his partnership email and wondered whether the others would give a similar positive reply or now decide to back out. He was also waiting on Emma's answer about his thoughts on a career change. Also he'd now approached the Tate and the London Courtauld Institute, to arrange for the forensic testing of his painting, 'Meeting on the way to market'. It was a seriously busy time.

Viktor and Penny were invited to Ian and Emma's home for dinner on the following Friday evening. It was the first time either of them had been to Ian and Emma's house. They all gathered in the lounge and Ian served them drinks. Emma had not met Viktor before and it was only the second time she had spoken with Penny face to face. They all chatted until Emma said she was going to check on the meal. When she returned she announced that the food was on the table.

As Viktor walked into the dining room, he immediately spotted the painting 'Meeting on the way to market' on the far wall. He laughed and pointed to the picture and told Penny, "That's the Gainsborough I was telling you about. Ian said he was going to hang it on the dining room wall… and he has!"

Ian smiled at Viktor. Penny's chair was just in front of the painting, so she took a closer look and said, "It's a lovely painting, especially now it's been professionally cleaned."

After they'd all sat down, Viktor removed some papers from the inside pocket of his jacket and offered them to Ian.

"You had better have these. The originals are still with the Jones family."

Ian took the papers. There were three sheets of photocopies. He looked at each copy in turn.

Viktor explained, "That first sheet is a receipt from Giles and Co, in Birmingham. They sold the painting to the uncle's father in 1902. You can see the picture is actually named *'Meeting on the way to market'*."

Ian smiled and nodded.

"The second sheet," Viktor continued, "is a valuation dated 1912 and the third is a photocopy of part of the last will and testament of the uncle's father. It shows that all property was passed on to the uncle following the death of his father. It's not overly significant, except that it does specify two paintings, one of which is the *'Meeting on the way to market'*."

"Thank you very much, Vic. I owe you," responded Ian. He had a broad smile on his face. "This information fills in one of the gaps in the painting's provenance. Excellent, well done."

Viktor smiled back and Penny tapped Viktor lightly on his thigh. "I'll get the original papers from George Jones for you."

"I think we had better get started before the food gets cold," said Emma, breaking the silence and picking up her knife and fork.

Chapter 34

Emma's auditing work and overseeing the accounts at Clinton and Beck until the takeover was completed, had now finally finished. The takeover had gone through smoothly and Emma had worked temporarily with the new owners, RB Hutchins, part of the Li Fong empire in Hong Kong. She was able to answer most of their questions and queries and iron out any remaining wrinkles.

David Gould was impressed with Emma's commitment and had personally delivered to her home a cheque for her fees and costs that had been agreed some time ago. He also presented her with a lovely bouquet of mixed coloured roses with a card of thanks signed by all of the former board members. Emma was surprised by the visit, the flowers and the card. David explained that it was the least they could do, because without all her help and her true professionalism, the company would not have benefitted from the takeover and certainly it would have faced much heavier fines for the previous years' accounting errors.

After David had left, Emma put the flowers in a large glass vase. She stood them, pride of place, on the sideboard in the lounge. She placed the thank you card just in front of the vase... and continued to hold the cheque in her hand. After adjusting two of the roses to a better position in the vase, she stood back and looked at the display. Suddenly it occurred to her – it was all over! She and Susan had worked hard together to sort out Clinton and Beck's accounting issues. Now Susan was stepping back from accountancy work altogether. She'd told Emma that she now just wanted to spend most of her time looking after her family. After all, she reminded Emma, she'd only agreed to come back to help for a short period... and part-time!

Emma sat down on the sette and reflected on the last few years and also considered what she personally wanted to do in the future. She'd already told Ian that she didn't intend to take on any more new clients after Clinton and Beck. Indeed she now accepted that returning to work, after being out of the 'workplace' for the extended break after Robert was born, had been far more difficult to adjust to than she had expected. To re-establish her career and also juggle the needs of Robert and Ian, meant that often she felt stressed and shattered, despite all Ian's help. She also realised that it was not the accountancy work that she had been missing, but the people. The everyday interaction with her staff, colleagues and clients. Accountancy work, she'd decided, was definitely now less relevant to her future life.

She stood up and wandered over to the french windows and looked out into the garden. Her mind, however, was not focusing on the view, she was thinking about her husband. I've had my career change, but what about Ian? He's now the main breadwinner, but is that the main criteria? He obviously wants to move on and to do something different. Is it a midlife crisis? I don't think so. Obviously the relationship with Andrei has changed his outlook. He says his life at Sotheby's is now just a job, it doesn't excite him so much as it once did. But what about security of income? As Ian says, the world has moved on. There are no secure jobs anymore and as he also pointed out we are financially secure anyway.

Emma continued to ponder on the financial implications. My share of the partnership sale and this cheque from David, plus all the assets Ian listed the other evening, well yes, we are certainly in a far better position than most people. Am I worrying far too much?

Ian was finding his concentration on Sotheby's work becoming more difficult by the day. He had been checking his personal email inbox twice a day for the last few days, looking for the replies on the partnership funding. He'd received four positive responses and was now awaiting May Ling's reply. Viktor had also confirmed that he was keen to invest too. He didn't just want to help the group in the UK, he now wanted to have a financial stake in the partnership as well. When he had told Ian about his idea he also mentioned that he was going to speak to his father and try to get a loan against his inheritance due to him soon from Andrei's will.

Without Viktor and May Ling, but including himself, Ian had a total of £38 million committed so far. He still wondered if he would reach the £50 million target. He had already taken the optimistic step of contacting his Swiss bank and asking them to set up a second bank account. The bank had agreed and, as a temporary measure, Ian had immediately transferred one million Swiss Francs from his existing account. This new bank account was where the partners would deposit their committed funds and it would also operate for all the future partner money transactions.

As well as confirming his commitment, Yuki had also sent Ian a list of many of the paintings currently stored in the Singapore free port. He suggested that Ian kept these details to himself as they were not for public distribution. However, Yuki did say that Ian could use them to help identify possible purchase targets and for coordinating with the partners' future needs and requirements.

Ian was now itching to 'get the show on the road'. It had been a long journey and he still felt frustrated by the delay in May Ling's reply. He hoped it would be worth the wait when her email finally arrived!

In Monaco, Bob had agreed to Zoe's request that she now wanted to be involved again in the day to day running of the gallery. When she'd first made the proposal, Bob had been initially worried that they might be 'stepping on each other's toes'. However, after giving the matter a lot more thought, he could see a number of positives. Zoe was still very attractive and before the children had come along, a lot of the male customers specifically asked to deal with her. Not only was she popular, but she was also a good sales-woman. In addition, Bob thought that her father would also probably be happier knowing his daughter was more directly involved in the business once again. He, himself, he decided, would have a lot more time to allocate to the new partnership that Ian was in the process of setting up. So, all in all, he concluded, it was a win-win situation.

Zoe was understandably surprised when Bob had been so easily persuaded, but now that he had agreed, she intended to show both Bob and her father that she'd not lost any of her sales abilities. To prove this point, on the second day during her turn in the gallery, she had convinced a possible new customer that 'her' gallery had the specialist connections that would enable her to discover possible sellers of any Stubbs painting that he was hoping to buy.

Just before the gallery's closing time, Bob came downstairs to the gallery floor. Zoe told Bob about the conversation she'd had with the possible new customer. Bob was impressed, but did tease Zoe when he said, "So, who are these specialist connections you are going to ask?"

"Well, I was going to ask you! Who would you

recommend?" replied Zoe, with a slightly sheepish grin on her face.

Bob laughed. "Okay, let me have a think," he replied, but privately he knew this was a prime case for the partnership. "Stubbs, you say?"

Zoe nodded. "We've certainly not sold one of his paintings before, have we?"

When Ian next accessed his email inbox there was a surprise waiting for him. Still no reply from May Ling, but Bob Taylor had emailed to ask, if through the partnership, anybody knew of any Stubbs paintings currently for sale? He said he had a possible buyer in Monaco, who was prepared to pay up to 12 million euros for a really good painting? Ian felt even more frustrated now, as this was exactly the sort of transaction the partnership should be involved in. Nevertheless, he took this opportunity to search the Singapore free port listing that Yuki had provided for him. After checking every item, he had identified two Stubbs paintings that were being stored there, but obviously he had no knowledge as to whether either of these pictures were, or would be, for sale! He pondered on contacting Yuki to ask him how he could find out, but then decided to wait for May's reply first. He could see that it would not be proper, or appropriate, to proceed without the £50 million being in the bank account first, or before all the partners had finally indicated they were fully committed.

In response to Bob's request, Ian decided to send him a holding email stating that he had identified two possible Stubbs paintings, but needed to check to see if either were for sale and, if so, at what price. After Ian had pressed the 'send' button, he noticed that Viktor had emailed him. The email read:

Hello, Ian,

Good news! My father has agreed to give me a loan of £2 million against my inheritance. He also says that he is prepared to invest a further £2 million himself, so put the Kuznetsov family down for a total of £4 million.

Hope that helps.

Viktor.

Ian was pleased with Viktor's £2 million, but was very surprised and a little suspicious with regards to Sergei wanting to be involved. He had deliberately avoided any Russian connection with the scheme after his own close call with the Russian Mafia in the past. At least Sergei was not based in Russia and very unlikely to ever be so again. Nevertheless, Sergei still had his Russian contacts. Mmm, okay, but this is one area that I must keep a very close eye on!

Chapter 35

Emma was waiting for Ian to come home from work. He'd told her early that morning that he wasn't sure what time he would be home as he had an appointment that afternoon with a potential new client for Sotheby's. She'd thought long and hard about their current situation and finally she'd made her decision. To help set a relaxing atmosphere for what she had to tell him, Emma had cooked one of his favourite meals, beef stroganoff. She'd also put one of the better bottles of burgundy on the worktop in the kitchen to reach room temperature.

It was 8.15pm when Emma heard Ian's car pull into the driveway. He had telephoned her to say he was just leaving the client's property and, subject to the vagaries of the M25, he hoped to be home before 8.30. Robert was in his pyjamas ready for bed, but wanted Daddy to tell him a story before he went to sleep. The last thing Emma wanted was a strained atmosphere when Ian walked in, so she'd agreed that he could stay up later than normal, just this once!

When Ian entered through the front door he was immediately greeted by Robert and his demands for a story.

"Okay, okay, little man. Let Daddy get into the house first. Go and get your book and I'll be upstairs in a few minutes," replied Ian, finally able to put his briefcase near the office door and change his shoes.

Emma appeared from the kitchen and met Ian in the hallway with a kiss. "He insisted you should tell him a story, so why don't you follow him up and I'll finish off preparing our dinner?"

"Okay," said Ian, "I thought he preferred reading on his own nowadays."

Emma spoke in a whisper, "I think it's just an excuse for him to stay up a bit longer."

Ian nodded and made his way upstairs to Robert's bedroom. Emma went back into the kitchen and checked on the meal.

Twenty minutes later, Ian returned to the kitchen and poured two glasses of the burgundy wine. Mmm, he thought, this is a rare treat. A red wine he knew they usually only drank on a special occasion.

Emma was finishing serving up the meal and then put the two plates of food on the table. They both sat down.

"Oh, great, stroganoff! We've not had this for ages," said Ian, looking at his meal.

Emma picked up her glass and said, "Cheers", to Ian.

Ian did likewise and then said, "Okay then, what's happened!?"

"What do you mean?"

"Come on, Emma, Robert up late waiting for me, stroganoff and our special bottle of burgundy. I know you, you're up to something!"

"Emma smiled. "Well, actually, I wanted to have a relaxing chat."

"Sounds intriguing," replied Ian, putting some of the food into his mouth.

"I've been thinking about what you said the other day, about a possible career change."

Ian put his fork down on his plate and looked at Emma with raised eyebrows. He waited anxiously for her next words.

"What you said, about our financial situation. I now realise, it does make sense. Anyway, if you seriously want a career change then yes, I agree."

Ian was staggered. What had Emma just said? "Wow, Emma, I didn't expect that! Are you sure?" He reached for his glass of wine and took a sip.

"We've supported each other's decisions on different issues throughout our marriage. If this is what you really want, then yes, you have my support."

"Well I'm not going to suddenly resign from Sotheby's tomorrow. But now I know you do support me, it will help tremendously with my thoughts, plans and timescales. What I will say, Emma, is whatever I do in the future, I promise you, it will have to make both financial sense and give us a much improved quality of life."

Emma smiled at Ian and a tear started to appear in her right eye. She quickly brushed it away and said, "Eat up your meal before it gets cold."

For the next few minutes they both ate their meals in silence. Both minds were whirling and thinking about what each other had just said. However, what they didn't know was that Ian and Emma were not actually thinking about the same things! For the rest of the evening and, despite Emma's attempts to have a relaxing discussion, somehow the atmosphere had just become a little more strained.

The next morning, being a Saturday, Ian was up early. When Robert was much younger and awake at the crack of dawn, Ian took the responsibility to get up at the same time as he usually did on a work day. Thus giving Emma a chance for a lie in. Now that Robert was older and almost needed dragging out of bed in the morning, Ian still got up at the old time and went into his home office and took advantage of the peace and quiet. After first tidying up some files that he'd been looking through earlier that week, he opened up his computer and checked on his incoming emails.

Immediately he spotted the email from May Ling! At last! he said to himself. He started to read the long and detailed message and when he'd finished he was relieved. In summary, May had said yes she still wanted to join the partnership, and subject to the listed provisos, she was prepared to invest the equivalent of £10 million!

Ian was very happy with May's provisos. They did make some sense and he decided to include these changes into the email he now proposed to send to each of the partners. However, before starting to type his draft he checked on the maths of each partner's financial commitment. After a few seconds, he leaned back in his chair and a broad grin appeared on his face. Excellent! he thought. Including both Vic's and Sergei's contributions, the partnership now had a revised total 'fighting fund' equivalent to about £52 million! Right, he said to himself… let's get the show on the road!

Ian started to draft the detailed email that would be sent to each of the partners. He confirmed the total fund now available, each individual's own percentage contribution and the details of the Swiss bank account. Finally he set out the instructions as to how and when their monetary share should be deposited into the new bank account.

In a second email solely to Yuki, Ian told him about the possibility of a buyer for one of the two Stubbs paintings currently stored in the Singapore free port. He asked Yuki if he could find out if either of these paintings might be available for sale and, if either were, what would be the likely sale price. Ian was still not sure of the procedures of trying to buy pictures from 'clients' storing their paintings at the

Singapore free port, so he asked Yuki what was the routine that he normally followed?

After sending out all the emails, Ian leaned back in his chair. Another broad grin slowly re-appeared on his face as he wondered how Andrei would have reacted to this new, big adventure. He hoped it would have been with one of his usual booming loud laughs!

Chapter 36

It was two weeks later when Ian checked the new Swiss bank account and noted all of the £52 million had now been deposited. Yuki had also approached the owners of the two Stubbs paintings and had established that one was for sale and the other was just a possibility... at the right price! After some toing and froing, Yuki finally established that the oil painting, *'High Spirits and Brown Mac'*, would be available for eight million euros. When Yuki asked if he could borrow the painting, the seller was firm. "You can see the painting at the free port, but it does not leave there until it is finally sold... and for cash or a banker's draft."

Yuki had already planned to visit two of his usual clients in Singapore and so agreed to view the painting whilst he was there. The date and time of the viewing was agreed and Yuki arrived at the high security Singapore free port building in his hire car.

Yuki was greeted by the seller's representative, Mr Johnson, who took him to a small secure room just along the corridor from the reception area. There Yuki was able to inspect the painting in great detail. He measured the exact picture size and also took several photographs of both the front and the rear. He was generally happy with the painting's condition and was reasonably certain that it was not a copy or a fake. Mr Johnson also produced papers and documents proving the provenance. Yes, all looked in good order, thought Yuki.

Two days later, Ian received a detailed report from Yuki, who'd signed off by saying that he would await Ian's further instructions. Yuki also mentioned that he valued the painting closer to seven million euros rather than the seller's required price of eight million.

Ian had already started to check out the history and provenance of *'High Spirits and Brown Mac'* himself, and now added Yuki's report findings into the painting's file. Once he was satisfied with all his investigations, he too, put a buying valuation in the region of seven million euros. The report was emailed to Bob Taylor in Monaco. There Bob and Zoe read through all the file's information and inspected Yuki's photographs. Happy with Ian's report, Bob suggested that Zoe should contact their client, Mr Linton, and show him their findings. This Zoe did and an appointment was arranged for Mr Linton to visit the gallery at 10 o'clock the next day.

When Mr Linton arrived, Zoe was waiting for him with the *'High Spirits and Brown Mac'* file. Mr Linton was a large man, in his late sixties with a strong American accent. Zoe offered him a cup of coffee, but Mr Linton declined. After a brief general chat they both sat down at a nearby table.

"Right," said Mr Linton. "Let's get down to business."

"As I mentioned on the telephone yesterday," said Zoe, in her best business voice. "I have been able to identify a George Stubbs painting that could possibly be for sale," said Zoe.

"Only 'could possibly' be for sale?" replied Mr Linton, a little concerned.

"The painting is not currently being advertised on the market for sale. However, our local representative in Singapore has been able to contact the owner to see if he would be interested in selling. The owner implied that the painting could be for sale as it was currently in storage and potentially surplus to his future requirements. However, he also indicated that if he was going to sell, then it would only be after receiving an acceptable offer."

"Okay, so how much are we talking about? What's this guy willing to take?"

"Our representative thinks the owner might accept an offer of over 10 million euros."

"Mmm. How much over 10 million?"

"I'm not sure, but obviously we will negotiate the best deal possible."

"So what's the picture?"

Zoe opened up her file and explained that the painting was named, *'High Spirits and Brown Mac'*. She showed him the eight photographs that Yuki had taken.

"It's a nice painting. I like the quality of the two horses," said Mr Linton, looking closely at the photographs.

Zoe continued. "It was painted in 1775 using oil on a wooden panel. It measures 82.5 centimetres high by 102.2 centimetres wide. As you can see, it depicts two very early racing horses relaxing in an English field. One is grazing whilst the other is watching his colleague. The arrangement of the two horses is centred in the foreground. In the distance there is a tranquil lake, trees to both sides and a blue sky with gentle, wispy strands of cirrus clouds. It all gives a lovely calm and peaceful picture of the English countryside that existed in the 18th century. A really nice composition."

Mr Linton still stared at the photographs. "When can I see the real deal?"

"At the moment the picture is in store in Singapore. For us to transport it to Monaco, it will mean we will be incurring a significant cost. We are prepared to do that, if you can show a similar commitment."

"You mean you want a deposit?"

"That's correct. In the event that you decide not to buy, then we would refund the deposit less our costs. But first we need to go back to the seller and present him with a serious offer."

Mr Linton pondered on this point. "Okay, if it really is the real deal and it is in great condition, then I will offer 10.5 million euros. That would be a take it or leave it final offer."

"I will put your offer to the seller and see how he responds. I am hopeful that he will take this offer. If he does, I think you'll have a good painting and a solid investment. Now Mr Linton, we need the deposit of one million euros."

"Take a cheque?"

"Yes, of course."

After Mr Linton had left the premises, Bob joined Zoe in the gallery. Zoe explained what had happened, but finished off by saying, "The problem now, Bob, is that in order for us to get the painting to Monaco the gallery would need to buy the picture in the first place. Do we have that amount of money?"

Whilst Bob did not want to explain the full details of the partnership to Zoe just yet, he did tell her that if it was necessary to buy the painting from the seller, then the Singapore connection would buy the painting first, but they would then charge a commission.

That afternoon Bob emailed Ian and relayed the story about Mr Linton and Zoe's concerns. Ian immediately wrote back to say he would contact Yuki to sort out the purchase. Ian hoped Yuki could complete the deal for nearer the seven million euros than the eight million that the seller said he wanted. After all expenses it would then be a profit to the partnership of just over two million euros! A great start for the team.

Of course, thought Ian, there was always the possibility that once Mr Linton saw the picture 'live' he may decide not to proceed after all! The partnership would then have a seven million euro painting on its hands. However, having the funds already in the bank, gave the partnership the protection and also the contingency it needed. Even in this worst case scenario, he was still convinced that the painting would sell for at least nine million euros at auction, given the right marketing.

In Antigua, Oscar was getting used to meeting on a regular basis with Gladstone Clive. He'd decided that Gladstone was an interesting character and certainly knew his way around the art market in Antigua and in a number of the other nearby Caribbean islands as well. Once Gladstone had heard the full story about the partnership, he'd been keen to explore the proposition in more detail as he instantly saw lots of benefits. Eventually he and Oscar decided to have their own sub partnership and Oscar informed Ian that they intended to make a joint investment totalling US$12 million.

Oscar's latest meeting with Gladstone was due in a few minutes' time. Oscar had already arrived at their usual bar and purchased two glasses of lager. As he sat down at their now regular table situated on the outside veranda, Gladstone arrived and spotted him and wandered over.

"Hi, Gladstone," said Oscar, looking up at his new business partner. "I've bought you a cold lager."

"Excellent, man. I need that, thank you. Still a warm day," replied Gladstone, sitting down at the side of Oscar and taking a long drink. Both men had a good view of the passing people in the street and also glimpses of the beach area to their left hand side. The sun, however, was already beginning to set and very soon it would be too dark for them to see the beach properly.

"Have you been busy today?" asked Oscar, sipping his own beer.

"Been to see a client on the other side of the island. He's an American and we've done some business together in the past. He now wants to sell his Whistler painting and has asked me for a valuation."

"Whistler, you say. I've not seen many of his pictures."

"He was an American, but spent most of his life in the UK. Not a big demand for his work on this island. Thought maybe the partnership might be interested."

"What a good idea. Let me have all the details and I will email Ian. What sort of valuation did you say?"

"Told him that, in the Caribbean, he might get two million US, but elsewhere it could be upwards of nearer five. He seemed quite pleased because he said he'd paid 1.2 million US, about six years ago."

"Interesting. Let's get the other partners working. We could all be on a winner with this one."

Chapter 37

When Yuki received Ian's email about the '*High Spirits and Brown Mac*' painting, he contacted the seller and relayed his opinion that the market value for the picture was nearer seven million euros. The seller initially baulked at this figure, but then calmed down as he wanted to get rid of the painting as quickly as possible. He already had plans for the money. After more toing and froing, they finally agreed on 7.55 million euros. Yuki thought this was a good deal against the prospect of a 10.5 million euros onward sale. The seller said that as soon as the money and paperwork were cleared, Yuki could collect the painting from the free port. Yuki was not expecting this but the seller said it was not a problem, as he would send the release authorisation as soon as the money was in his account. Yuki was still nervous with this development, but although he'd done something similar before, with a client he already knew, he was unsure that this man could be trusted to fulfil his side of the bargain. Eventually, however, he persuaded the seller to accept a bankers draft.

Yuki emailed Ian with the details of the proposed purchase and after reading and then copying the papers to his computer, Ian emailed the same report on to Bob Taylor. Zoe then contacted Mr Linton and told him they hoped to have the painting in the gallery within the next 10 days. She would be in touch with him again when the painting had arrived at their gallery.

Ian was pleased with this first result for the partnership. Obviously the deal was not going to be fully completed until Mr Linton's money was in the partners' bank account, but nevertheless, he was pleased that the system seemed to be working well.

Ian was just about to close his computer down when he heard the 'ping' of another incoming email. He accessed his inbox to find out who had written to him. He was pleased when he saw it was from Oscar. Ian smiled as he read the communication:

Hi Buddy,

This is from the 'dynamic duo' in the Caribbean!

Gladstone has just come up with an interesting proposition. He has a client who wants to sell his Whistler painting. This is not an artist that I am very familiar with, but Gladstone thinks it could be worth US$5 million outside the Caribbean. I have attached Gladstone's report and photographs. Let me know what you think? Is this a picture that one of the partners might be interested in?

Hope Emma and Robert are well.

Cheers,

Oscar.

Ian opened the attachment which contained Gladstone's report and photographs. He wrote some separate notes on his notepad and started to investigate the history of the picture entitled, *'Arrangement in Red, Purple and White – Elizabeth'*, by James Abbott McNeill Whistler.

Ian knew a little about Whistler's work, but had not heard of this particular painting. His initial reading of

Gladstone's report revealed that the picture was painted using oil on canvas and also known by the name of '*Elizabeth in the salon*'. It measures 78cms x 52cms and was painted in 1873. The picture depicts a woman in a full length red dress standing by a large window and looking out into the garden. Covering her shoulders is a white lace shawl. The curtains, behind her and partly to her right hand side, are of a shade of purple. The painting was last sold six years ago, by private sale to Mr Raymond Bryson in Antigua, for US$1.2 million.

Okay, thought Ian, so Gladstone's report seems to stack up nicely. Now let's check a bit deeper into the painting's history and provenance.

Accessing the internet and his two books on Whistler's works, Ian was able to trace most of the various owners of the painting for the past 150 years. It was all looking good. The only complication left though, thought Ian, was whether the picture that Mr Bryson was offering was the real painting and not a copy or a fake. At the moment he was relying on the talents of Gladstone Clive, who he assumed was the only person in the partnership who had actually seen the picture so far.

When Ian replied to Oscar, he told him of the investigation and his findings. He also emphasised to Oscar that he should see the picture for himself and appraise it thoroughly.

In the meantime, Ian decided that it could be an interesting challenge for Viktor to try and find a possible buyer. Therefore when he sent an email to all the partners informing them of this new development he also added at the end of the email, specifically to Viktor, three names and contact details. These people, Ian told Viktor, all lived in England and were avid collectors of Whistler's work.

Viktor responded immediately and said he would contact all three potential buyers by the end of the day.

Emma, meanwhile, was following up on Ian's arrangements to deliver the '*Meeting on the way to market*' painting for forensic analysis. She was amazed to see the various techniques that the Courtauld Institute were now employing to examine and prove the authenticity of the 'old master' paintings. The signs were positive and Courtauld's had promised their final report would be mailed to her in the next few days.

True to their word, Emma spotted their letter amongst the morning mail just three days later. She immediately telephoned Ian to tell him the results. "Ian, I've just received a detailed report from the Courtauld Institute. In summary they confirm that the painting really could be by Gainsborough!"

"Hey, that's great news," replied Ian. "Now all we need to do is convince the Gainsborough experts and get it reinstated as a genuine work by Thomas Gainsborough."

"What time will you be home tonight?" asked Emma, changing the subject.

"Should be about 7.30. Why?"

"I thought we should celebrate this good news!" replied Emma, excited at the thought of owning a genuine Gainsborough painting.

"We are not there yet, Emma. There's still a few more hurdles to clear before it is fully authenticated. Sorry to spoil your excitement."

Emma was a little deflated. She accepted that there were still some more people to convince, but at least, she thought, the Courtauld Institute appeared to be on their side. Surely, that's got to be a big positive!

Yuki arrived at the Singapore free port to meet with Mr Johnson for a second time. As he walked towards the security reception area, the building still reminded him of photographs he had seen of Fort Knox in America.

Yuki knew the free port building was opened in May 2010 and had a reputation as a top secure storage vault. It was built for the sole purpose of the safekeeping of high value collectibles. Ultra modern and copied on the Swiss free port model, the building provides wealthy collectors with a facility for long term storage and a trading ability for their valuable collections. Crucially, there are no customs duties or any goods and services taxes to pay.

When Yuki entered the reception area, he looked around for Mr Johnson and then spotted him standing next to the reception desk. The seller had told Yuki to expect Mr Johnson to be waiting for him in the reception area.

Yuki walked over to join him. They shook hands, exchanged pleasantries and started to walk alongside each other towards the seller's storage vault.

Except for their footsteps and the slight background humming noise from the air conditioning unit, there was no other sound or indeed, any other people about. Along the corridors the walls and doors were all constructed of shining stainless steel. The ceiling lighting emitted a subdued purple hue.

Eventually they both stopped outside a large stainless steel door displaying, at eye level, the engraved number 'M45'. Mr Johnson removed a set of keys from his pocket and inserted one into the lock. He turned the key twice until he heard a click. The door slowly opened electronically and the two men walked inside. It was not a large room but had stainless steel cladding on three sides. The fourth wall had a bank of locked safes and metal cabinets.

Mr Johnson went over to the large cabinet numbered '12', bent down and inserted another key into the lock. Once unlocked he pulled the door open and gently rolled out a wooden case which was secured to a wooden platform. Under the platform were a set of four rubber wheels. The case was also secured by its own padlock.

During this activity, Yuki stood back and watched quietly. He had seen this level of security here several times before.

Mr Johnson now unlocked the padlock, removed the wooden cover and eased away the protective inner packaging. He then lifted the painting out from the case for Yuki to view. Yuki carefully examined the picture and then the rear side. He was particularly looking for the worn black paint mark on the rear of the canvas and the small mark he had scratched on the back of the frame during the visit when he viewed the painting for the first time. To his relief, both were still visible, so he was happy that this was the same picture that he had seen before. He passed it back to Mr Johnson offering a smile and a small bow.

Mr Johnson returned the smile and gently re-covered the painting with the packaging and placed it back inside the wooden case. The case was once again padlocked and Yuki was given the padlock's key. He placed the key into his pocket. Again he smiled and made a small bow. The contract had almost been completed.

Mr Johnson produced from his briefcase a cardboard folder containing several papers and documents. He passed the folder over to Yuki. Yuki checked each sheet slowly and carefully.

Yes, he thought, these were the same papers he had seen before. He put them all back inside the folder and from the inside pocket of his jacket he removed a banker's draft for 7.55 million euros. He handed the draft to Mr Johnson.

Satisfied the draft was correct he then gave Yuki a receipt already signed by the seller. The contract had been completed. The partnership was now up and running!

Mr Johnson relocked the now empty cabinet and the two men exited the vault. They walked back together towards the reception area. Because the wooden case was secured to the wooden platform on the four rubber wheels, Yuki was able to push it along the corridors without too much effort. When they arrived back in the reception area, the two men shook hands again and Mr Johnson left the building. They were never to meet again.

Yuki remained at the reception desk and produced from his inside jacket pocket a separate set of papers which he handed to the guard. These papers authorised the free port to release the wooden case containing the *'High Spirits and Brown Mac'* painting to a firm of international carriers who would be collecting the package tomorrow at 10 o'clock. Yuki had already given the Singapore carrier Bob Taylor's name and the gallery's address in Monaco, the shipment's final destination.

Yuki signed and finalised all the paperwork and the guard gave him a receipt. The guard then picked up an empty clear plastic folder, inserted Yuki's paperwork inside and took charge of the wooden case. Both men then walked along the corridor and entered a separate secure unit. This was the transit storage room for items that were due to be collected during the next 24 hours. The guard unlocked a large cabinet, pushed the wooden case inside and re-secured the lock. He made a note of the cabinet number on the paperwork and inserted the key into a small plastic zipped pouch on the front of the plastic folder. Yuki watched carefully and, once he was satisfied, both men walked back to the reception desk. However, instead of leaving the free port building at that moment, Yuki had another business issue to attend to. He signed yet another document for the guard and this then enabled him to visit his own personal secure vault in the building!

About an hour later Yuki arrived back at his parked hire car and unlocked the car's boot. He then gently placed a different wooden case onto the boot's floor. After closing the lid he opened the driver's side door and climbed in. Using his mobile phone he sent a brief email to Ian confirming that the Stubbs painting, *'High Spirits and Brown Mac'*, was now the property of the partnership and would be collected by the international carriers tomorrow morning. He also added that Bob should expect delivery within the next seven to ten days.

Yuki then drafted a second email to his business partner in Japan, Yoshihiro Tsuzuki. The message simply said:

Yoshi,

The Stubbs painting for the partnership deal is now complete.

I have collected our own Stubbs painting and will deliver it to our client this afternoon.

I should be back in Tokyo tomorrow evening.

Yuki.

Chapter 38

It was becoming more and more apparent to Penny that her boss was spending a surprising amount of time away from the office. Even when he was at Sotheby's his mind seemed to be elsewhere. Several times she had protected him from colleagues and even his boss, Michael Hopkins. However, she was now weary and concerned about having to keep making up excuses or stories for his absence. Finally she decided it was time to confront Ian and tell him her problem.

"Ian?" asked Penny, standing in the doorway to his office. "Can I speak to you?" Ian had only been in the office for about 30 minutes and it was obvious to Penny that he was packing his papers ready to disappear again very shortly.

"Of course, Penny, what's on your mind?" said Ian, standing at his desk and closing his briefcase.

Penny walked into his office and sat down in her usual seat on the opposite side of his desk.

"Ian," said Penny, almost embarrassed to look at Ian directly in the face. "Over the last ten days you have hardly been in the office and I've not known where you were or when you would be back. I know this is not my business, but what certainly is my business, is answering your telephone calls and having to make up stories for your absence, particularly to Michael Hopkins."

Ian's face suddenly became serious. He placed the briefcase on the floor, sat down on his chair and looked across directly at Penny. "Yes, you are right, Penny, you should not have to be doing that for me. I'm sorry. I'm not too sure what to say, especially in this office." Ian was then silent for a few moments, obviously struggling to decide what to say. Penny sat patiently waiting for his answer.

Finally Ian said, "I've got a meeting in 20 minutes. What about a drink at 'The Grapes' at 6 o'clock. Can you do that?"

Penny now looked directly at Ian. Okay, she thought, if we can get to the bottom of this issue then, well fine, it will be worthwhile. "Alright, Ian, but I do not want to tell any more lies to clients, or to Michael Hopkins, either. I'm sure he's already suspicious!"

"Please don't do that, Penny. I'll explain later… promise. Now I must go, see you at 6 o'clock." Ian picked up his briefcase and left the office. Penny was still sitting on her chair, her eyes followed Ian as he disappeared out of the room.

It was at that moment that Ian's desk telephone began to ring again. Penny ignored it and walked back to her own desk.

When Penny walked into 'The Grapes' at five minutes after six, she spotted Ian at the bar talking to the barman. When she joined him, he immediately stopped his conversation and said, "Hello, Penny. What would you like to drink?"

Penny was not in a drinking mood, so she asked for a tonic water with ice. The barman prepared and poured her drink. He handed it across to her and Ian paid for the two drinks. Ian picked up his pint of beer and they both walked over to an empty table and sat down.

"So, Penny, how are you and Vic doing nowadays?" asked Ian, then taking a sip of his beer.

Penny ignored Ian's question as she wanted him to explain his absenteeism. "Ian, you were going to explain your reasons for your repeated absences."

"Okay, Penny." Ian looked around the room and when he was satisfied that nobody could overhear their conversation, he continued. "I know I can trust you, Penny, but this is between us two only. Is that okay?"

Penny tentatively nodded her head and waited for Ian to carry on.

"I'm in the process of setting up a new venture. It's very early days so far, so I've been involved in a number of meetings. Most of the groundwork has been completed and if all works out well, then I will be leaving Sotheby's at some stage soon. But that's in the future, not yet."

Penny just stared at her boss, a number of questions sprung to mind, but she decided not to interrupt Ian's flow.

"In the meantime," continued Ian, "there are two things I want to achieve. Firstly, I intend, as of tomorrow, to be back in the office on a more regular basis and concentrate on Sotheby's business. When I am out of the office, you will know where I shall be. There will be no more embarrassing situations for you, I promise. Secondly, you have a good profile at Sotheby's, Penny, and between now and when I leave, I want to promote your career development and entrust you with bigger challenges. Then I will recommend that you are formally promoted to my role."

Penny was speechless! She tried to say some words. "But... er... Ian," was all she could offer immediately.

Ian continued, "Tomorrow is the first day of the rest of our lives! If I do not make a move soon, I will never do it and then my career would stagnate and it would be at the whims of Michael Hopkins and the Sotheby's board. I've always tried to be in control of my career and have pushed, when necessary, to achieve my ambitions. I recommend you spend the next few months pushing your own career. You are much better than you think you are. Get in front of Michael Hopkins as much as you can. I aim to leave my department in your excellent and capable hands."

"Wow, Ian! This is all such a surprise," replied Penny, finally being able to speak properly again.

"As I say, Penny, this is just between you and me, okay? Not even, Vic, at this moment, please." Ian knew Vic was in on his plans, but, at this stage, he'd told Vic to keep that to himself as well.

Penny nodded and sipped the last of her drink. Ian similarly finished the last drops of his beer and stood up. Penny followed suit.

"Come on, let's both go home. I'll see you bright and early tomorrow morning."

Penny was not really sure what to say, but finished by simply responding with, "Thank you... I think."

Ian smiled. "It's me that needs to thank you and I really do apologise for putting you in such a difficult and embarrassing position. It won't happen again... promise."

They both then left 'The Grapes' together, but Penny turned to the left and Ian to the right when they exited the pub. They said their goodnights and both disappeared into the throng of London's commuter pedestrians also heading for their homes.

As Penny walked towards the Underground station, one phrase of Ian's still dominated her thinking – 'Tomorrow is the first day of the rest of our lives'!

When she finally sat down on the London underground train, she realised that Ian had not told her what he'd actually been doing during his absences. She now knew he was trying to set up a separate business, but doing what? In the art world? Who else knew? Maybe it was not really her business, but what about Ian's promise of his role when he left? He could only recommend her for his job, but was that what she really wanted to do when Ian did finally leave Sotheby's? Then there was Vic. Should she tell him? No, she decided, after all she had promised Ian she would not tell anyone – in the short term.

As the train pulled into her station, Penny rose from her seat and waited for the train to stop and the doors to open. She had finally decided, at least for the time being, to play along with Ian's game. That would then really give her the time to consider all her own options going forward. Yes, 'Tomorrow REALLY is the first day of the rest of **my** life'!

Chapter 39

It was two days after his discussion with Penny, that Ian was experiencing a very anxious day at Sotheby's. He had back to back meetings and was struggling to focus his attention for most of the time. His full day had meant that he could not attend the appointment with two of the most recognised experts on Thomas Gainsborough's landscape paintings. Therefore it was agreed that Emma would attend on her own and now he was desperately waiting on Emma's text message.

The previous evening he and Emma had discussed at length, the painting *'Meeting on the way to market'* and how best she should present their information to the experts. Ian was still not sure if he had acquired enough information to guarantee the painting would be reinstated. Nevertheless, he was optimistic that the experts would not refuse its reinstatement completely out of hand and that they might just get lucky! It was going to be a close call.

Emma attended the agreed 2 o'clock appointment complete with the painting, the detailed report from the Courtauld Institute and a collection of papers and documents which catalogued the painting's history of ownership – the provenance. She was going to follow Ian's suggested strategy exactly and was determined to give it her best shot!

At 3.53pm Ian finished his last but one meeting of the day. His final meeting was with his boss, Michael Hopkins, in his boss's office at 4pm. He quickly looked at his mobile phone whilst he was walking along a corridor and checked his emails and text messages but still no answer from Emma. Damn! he thought. He was just about to put his phone back into his pocket when it 'pinged', indicating a text message. He stopped and quickly read the brief note Emma had sent:

Ian, Just left the meeting. No verdict. They are going to discuss and decide their decision over the next two days. Tell you more this evening. Love Emma x.

Okay, he thought, at least they have not declined the proposal. I guess that must be the good news. I'll just have to wait to hear the full story this evening. At least all is not lost. He checked his watch and quickly jogged the last short distance to his boss's office. He arrived at 3.59pm.

When Ian arrived home that same evening, he had a thumping headache. It had been a stressful day what with the back to back meetings and the extra pressure of waiting for Emma's message. To cap it all, Michael Hopkins was in a bad mood so Ian felt he'd been battered from all sides.

Emma heard Ian come in through the front door and joined him in the hallway. "Are you okay?" she asked. "You look absolutely shattered."

Ian changed his shoes and whilst taking off his coat said, "It's been a tough day. Too many meetings, and now, I've got a rotten headache! Have we got any aspirin or paracetamol in the house?"

Emma and Ian both walked into the kitchen. Robert ran up to him, but Emma asked Robert to leave his father for a minute because he had a headache. Robert did not know what his mummy was talking about, but he quickly saw from Ian's face that he was looking 'a little bit poorly'.

Emma removed a medicine bottle from a kitchen cupboard and removed two white tablets and gave them to Ian. Separately she poured and handed him a glass of water. Ian quickly swallowed both tablets and drank the water in three gulps. He handed the empty glass back to his wife and sat down on one of the breakfast bar chairs. Emma gently stroked his head.

"Emma, I've just about had it at work," he said, resting his head on his right hand with his right elbow perched on the table.

Emma continued to gently stroke the back of Ian's head. Robert just looked on. He had never seen his daddy look like this before.

"We'll talk about it later, Ian, I'll get Robert ready for bed and we can then chat after dinner. Come on, Robert, let's leave Daddy to have a few minutes' peace and quiet."

As Emma and Robert left the kitchen, Ian heard Robert ask, "Is Daddy poorly?"

To which Emma responded, "Yes, he's got a headache, but he'll be alright in the morning. Come on, let's get you bathed and then we can all have dinner."

By the end of dinner, Ian's headache had eased. The tablets were obviously doing their job. He even felt well enough to take Robert upstairs to supervise him cleaning his teeth and getting him into bed. Fortunately for Ian, Robert decided he would read to himself that evening, so Ian gave him a kiss and said Mummy would be up later to switch off his light. Robert smiled and said goodnight. He wanted to carry on reading the exciting book he had borrowed from his nursery school.

When Ian returned, Emma was in the lounge. She had made two cups of coffee.

Ian joined her on the settee. He decided too much coffee would not do his headache much good so only took a few sips.

"So, tell me," said Ian, "how did the meeting go? Tell me all the details. Did you enjoy the experience?" asked Ian. He was pleased that his headache had almost disappeared.

"I was very nervous meeting the two Gainsborough experts, but they were very kind and not over technical. I followed your suggestions and gradually began to relax. It was an interesting meeting. Yes, I enjoyed it too."

"So what did they say?" asked Ian. He wanted to get to the nitty-gritty.

"They listened to what I had to say, examined the painting thoroughly and then discussed their thoughts. They particularly focused on the repair mark on the back of the canvas and read through the report and documents. There was no shaking of heads or any negative comments. They said they wanted to spend some time reviewing the period around the time the painting was delisted as a genuine Gainsborough. They mentioned Barker of Bath, but only as a consideration, not suggesting the painting was by him. I got the distinct impression that they were erring towards accepting the picture, but, as I say, they wanted to fully review the circumstances as to why the painting was delisted in the first place."

"When did they say they would make their final decision?"

"In about a week's time. Do you think I did okay?"

"It sounds like you did brilliantly. Let's hope they agree with your argument. The painting will then probably be worth... about three million pounds!"

"Oh my goodness. I'm not sure I'm going to be able to sleep until we get an answer!"

Ian smiled. He knew Emma would be her usual self and

sleep like a log! "I told Robert you would pop up and switch off his light."

Emma finished the last of her coffee, stood up and walked towards the door. However, she suddenly stopped and turned around to face Ian. "You know, Ian, I think I like the art world. It's fun, isn't it?"

Ian smiled as Emma went upstairs. He thought to himself for a minute. Yes, Emma, it certainly USED to be really great fun!

In Monaco, Zoe had received an email from the shipment company confirming that the delivery of the Stubbs painting, '*High Spirits and Brown Mac*', would be delivered the next day at about 10 o'clock. Zoe immediately got up from sitting next to the kitchen table and went downstairs to the gallery. There she found Bob talking to a customer and standing in front of a painting by a local artist. She didn't want to interrupt their discussion so she walked into the small kitchen area and made two cups of coffee. When she heard the gallery's doorbell ring she peered out from the kitchen doorway and noticed that Bob was now on his own and back sitting at his desk. She picked up the two cups of coffee and went to join him.

"Oh great, Zoe, you were obviously reading my mind. Thank you."

Zoe put both cups on the desk and asked, "Another client?"

"He could be. He liked the Pierre Mocan painting of the collie dog. He said he wanted to bring his wife into the gallery to view it."

"I've just received an email. The shipment company is delivering '*High Spirits and Brown Mac*' here tomorrow. Do you think I should ring Mr Linton and let him know?"

Bob thought about the question for a few moments.

"Mmm. Let's just make sure it does arrive here tomorrow first. I also think we ought to check to see what condition it is in too. It should be okay… but let's wait and see. We need to make sure everything is fine."

Chapter 40

It was just after 9.30am when Emma returned home from dropping Robert off at his nursery school. Located next to the front door was their postbox. She unlocked the metal door and removed two letters. On the top envelope she immediately noticed the name of the school she and Ian were hoping to get Robert into. She excitedly opened the front door, switched off the burglar alarm, and walked into the kitchen. Putting her handbag and the second letter on the table, she quickly ripped open the envelope that had the school's name printed in the top left hand corner. She put on her reading glasses, unfolded the letter, and read the contents:

Dear Mr and Mrs Caxton,

We have pleasure in advising you that Robert has been accepted...

Emma ignored the rest of the letter and cheered out loud. "Yes, yes, well done, Robert. I must tell Ian!"

Emma quickly removed her mobile phone from her handbag and telephoned Ian's mobile. When he answered she immediately recognised from the background traffic noise that he was in his car. "Ian, great news, Robert has been accepted by Brookfield school!"

"Well that's great news, Emma. Thanks for telling me. Must go, I'm just turning into the client's driveway. See you tonight." The line went dead.

Emma switched off her phone and placed it on the table, part covering the envelope of the second letter. She picked up the school's letter once again and read the rest of its contents. It mainly listed the school's requirements, school fees and payment options, plus Robert's starting date. Emma then read the letter for a second time, this time more slowly and with a huge smile on her face. She then laid it next to the landline telephone, where Ian normally placed his keys and wallet when he came in. Suddenly the landline telephone rang which gave her a start. When she answered the call, she discovered it was her mother who was ringing. For the next twenty minutes, Emma explained every tiny detail about the new school that Robert was soon to be attending.

When Ian returned home and walked into the driveway, he was surprised to see Emma helping Robert out of the car.

"So, you've been out celebrating have you?" teased Ian.

"Sorry, Ian, but after picking Robert up from nursery school I called at Jane's house to tell her the good news."

"What, and you have only just got home. You must have had a lot to talk about with your sister!"

"Can you take care of Robert please, I'll pop in and switch off the slow cooker. I managed to set that up before I left," said Emma. She then entered the house and switched off the burglar alarm. Robert and Ian followed behind her and Ian closed the door.

"The school's letter is next to the phone in the kitchen," shouted Emma, who was now examining the slow cooker.

Ian changed his shoes and helped Robert do the same. They both then walked into the kitchen. Robert ran off to the far end, which was his play area and Ian placed his house keys and wallet next to the phone. He then picked up the school's letter and sat down next to the breakfast bar where he read the details.

"That's really good," said Ian, after he'd finished reading. "All we have to do now is find the money for the school fees!"

"Come on, Ian, you know we have that all sorted out."

"Just joking." Ian then spotted the unopened letter also on the breakfast bar. "What's this other letter over here? It's addressed to you," said Ian.

"Oh yes," said Emma, chopping some potatoes to boil. "It also came this morning. I forgot about that in all the excitement. Why don't you open it?"

Ian looked at both the front and the back of the envelope but it gave no clue as to who had sent it. He tore the top of the envelope and removed and unfolded the single sheet of A4 paper. He quietly read the contents to himself. After about a minute he stood up, his heart was now racing and his brow was slightly moist from perspiration. He walked slowly over to where Emma was putting the potatoes into a saucepan.

"Emma, I think you had better read this," he said, holding the letter out towards her.

Emma wiped her hands and looked at Ian. "Is it bad news? You look serious."

"Just read it!" insisted Ian.

Emma picked up her reading glasses and collected the letter from Ian and began to read.

Dear Mrs Caxton,

Thank you for giving us the opportunity to view your painting 'Meeting on the way to market'. As promised we have reviewed the details and circumstances surrounding the delisting of this painting and have come to the conclusion that it should never have been delisted.

After also examining the painting thoroughly, reading the detailed report from the Courtauld Institute and the collection of papers and documents proving the painting's provenance, we *confirm that we believe the painting was indeed painted by Thomas Gainsborough. It will be entered in the next publication of the authorised Landscape Catalogue Raisonné, by John Hayes.*

Yours Sincerely,
Charles Baydon-Smythe.

Emma slowly took off her spectacles and looked at Ian with both her mouth and eyes wide open. "Oh, my God!!" she exclaimed.

Ian looked at her with a big smile on his face and nodded his head. "Well done, you."

"Well done, me!? It's well done, you! You were the genius that spotted it."

"Okay, well done to both of us. I think we'll remember this day forever, don't you!?"

Chapter 41

Oscar was waiting for Ian to give him feed-back about the Whistler painting, *'Arrangement in Red, Purple and White – Elizabeth'*. It had been a few days since he'd emailed Ian and he wondered why there was a delay. Certainly it was not like Ian to be so tardy. May Ling, yes, but not Ian. He began to worry that his old buddy was probably trying to juggle too many balls at the same time.

What Oscar didn't know, however, was that Ian had emailed Yuki, Bob Taylor and May Lee about the Whistler and he was still waiting for their replies. In addition, he had given Viktor the names and email addresses of three known keen collectors of Whistler's work. He suggested that Viktor should contact them.

James Abbott McNeill Whistler was a new artist to Viktor, so as well as contacting the three possible buyers, he was also trying to learn everything possible about this American artist. He started his investigations by reading up on the details and history of the present picture. After all, if he was trying to sell it, he ought to know more about it!

He made the following notes:

'Arrangement in Red, Purple and White – Elizabeth'.
- Picture was painted using oil on canvas and was also known by the name of *'Elizabeth in the salon'.*
- Size is 78cms x 52cms and was painted in 1873.
- Picture shows a woman in a full length red dress standing by a large window. She is looking out into the garden. Covering her shoulders is a white lace shawl. The curtains are a deep purple colour. Hence the name of the painting.
- Painting was last sold six years ago, by private sale to Mr Raymond Bryson in Antigua, for US$1.2 million.

Viktor then widened his investigations to research Whistler's career. He noted that many of Whistler's paintings were either full length figure portraits, or moody landscapes, mainly painted in the UK, but also some were painted in Paris. His most famous work was completed in 1891, known simply as *'Whistler's Mother'.* It became the first painting ever to be purchased by the French state and it represented the peak of Whistler's radical work of modulating tones of single colours.

He also discovered that Whistler, in addition to his art, was also strangely famous for many quotations, two in particular he decided he really liked: *'An artist is not paid for his labour but for his vision'* and *'I am not arguing with you – I am telling you!'*

After completing his analysis, Viktor concluded that although he had smiled at some of Whistler's quotations, he found the man's art work not really to his own taste. Nevertheless, he now accepted that there was a market for this sort of work, but mainly with the more specialist Whistler collectors.

In Monaco, a few minutes after 10am, Zoe and Bob had just taken delivery of the Stubbs painting. Yuki had posted the key to unlock the inner protective case earlier with the file containing a copy of the painting's provenance. Zoe now retrieved this key from the gallery desk whilst Bob started to carefully unpack the outer packing. Both he and Zoe were excited, but also a little anxious, to be able to see this Stubbs picture for real. Bob, in particular, just hoped nothing had been damaged during the journey from Singapore. Mind, even he had to admit that the parcel had been very professionally packed.

Gradually they got down to the wooden case and Zoe then used the key to unlock the padlock. The top lid was lifted off and the front wooden panel slowly lowered to reveal some more packing and the rear of the painting. Whilst Bob held the picture's wooden frame, Zoe removed some of the inner packing and then eased the picture from its casing. She carried it across to the gallery desk and laid it down gently on its back. For the first time Bob and Zoe could see the actual picture. They both stood quietly and stared in awe at the wonderful talent of George Stubbs.

"Do you know, Zoe," said Bob, breaking the silence. "This picture was painted about 250 years ago. We are looking at serious history here."

Zoe nodded her head gently in acknowledgement, but she just wanted to spend every second concentrating her attention on the painting. She particularly marvelled at the skill of the artist in painting the two horses' heads and especially their eyes. "It's one of the most wonderful pictures I've ever seen. Pity we can't keep it for ourselves."

Bob smiled. "It looks in good condition, probably needs a careful dusting, but we'd better check it thoroughly before we telephone your client."

Whilst Bob had a closer look at the front, sides and the

rear of the picture, Zoe went to collect a duster and a can of low pressurised air for the corners of the painting. Bob said all seemed to be fine and Zoe gently sprayed into the corners and gave the whole picture a gentle dusting. Bob set up a display easel and the picture was lifted into place. Zoe finally rubbed the brass plate on the bottom of the frame until the name *'High Spirits and Brown Mac'* stood out and was shining brightly. Bob then switched on two spotlights above the picture and adjusted each setting until they projected their diffused light exactly in the right place on the painting.

"Right then," said Bob, standing back and admiring the painting from about two metres away, "I think it is ready for Mr Linton's eyes. Let's hope he'll be just as impressed."

Later that afternoon, Mr Linton arrived at the gallery. He'd told Zoe, when she had telephoned him, that he had hardly slept at all the previous night in anticipation of this moment. Zoe was sitting at the gallery desk when Mr Linton walked in through the door. She quickly rose from her seat and walked over to welcome him with a handshake. She then guided him over to the spotlit painting of *'High Spirits and Brown Mac'*.

When Mr Linton stood in front of the painting his first words were, "Gee, this is better than I had hoped." He then stepped closer and looked at both the horses. "The guy sure had a talent!"

"So you are happy with it, Mr Linton?"

"Oh, I sure am. When can you get it delivered?"

"Firstly we need to deal with all the paperwork. Make sure you are completely happy with the provenance and then there is the matter of the balance of payment."

"Okay, little lady, let's get started!"

Chapter 42

Viktor arrived at the 'Taylor Fine Art Gallery' just after 8.30am. He wanted to complete a couple of administration jobs before he opened the gallery properly at 9 o'clock.

By 9.15 the gallery was open and his jobs were completed. He sat behind the gallery's desk and switched on his computer. In his email inbox he found five new entries, but one in particular caught his immediate attention. It was from Brian Cooper, one of the people recommended by Ian to contact about the Whistler painting. He opened up the email with hopeful anticipation and read the contents. After he'd finished reading, however, he sat back in his chair and considered the points being raised by Mr Cooper. Now that is interesting, he thought. I wonder if Ian is aware of all this!?

Viktor spent the next few minutes writing a separate email to Ian. He also attached a copy of Mr Cooper's email. He pressed the 'send' button and expected a telephone call later that day.

When Ian read Viktor's email he smiled. He knew Brian Cooper very well and also knew he was quite an aficionado of Whistler's work. Someone whose judgement and comments Ian always took seriously. He immediately forwarded Viktor's email to Oscar for his views.

In the meantime, Ian telephoned Viktor and explained Brian Cooper's background in the art market. He told Viktor, "Brian is an expert on Whistler's work and a well respected authority when it comes to Whistler's paintings. He is also a member of a small, worldwide group of enthusiastic collectors who call themselves 'The Whistlers'. 'The Whistlers' hold half yearly on-line meetings and they also publish a quarterly on-line newsletter. Both communications are dedicated solely to Whistler's work."

"That sounds a bit weird!" said Viktor. He was staggered that such enthusiasm really existed for Whistler's work! He was still not totally convinced about the quality of the artist's work and wondered what exactly could all these aficionados really see!? What was so special about Whistler's work that he was missing?

Ian continued, "In addition several auction houses, and some galleries, sometimes use 'The Whistlers'' expertise."

"Okay," acknowledged Viktor. "So the guy knows his Whistlers. Is there anything I should be doing in the meantime?"

"I've sent Brian's comments and the file notes on to Oscar for his comments. It will be interesting to hear what he and Gladstone have got to say! In the meantime can you chase up on the other emails you sent out? It'll be interesting to see what the other two have to say. Maybe, they will have different thoughts and opinions."

"I'll do that straight away. By the way, how is your Gainsborough investigation going?"

"Didn't I tell you? The authorities have agreed to reinstate it. It will be included in the next publication of the authorised Gainsborough Landscape Catalogue Raisonné."

"You're kidding me aren't you, Ian? Seriously!?"

"All agreed and documented. About a week ago."

"Wow, I do have a lot to learn. Well done you."

"Thanks, Vic. But it was Emma who did most of the legwork."

"Tell her from me, well done. What are you going to do with the painting now?"

Ian smiled when he told Viktor his reply. "It still looks good in the dining room!"

"Come on, it's worth a few million pounds now, surely you are going to sell it? Do you need the services of a good gallery?"

Ian laughed down the line. "Thanks for the offer, Vic, but it will probably go to auction."

"Well, one can only try."

"Must go, Vic. I'll speak to you when I get a reply from Oscar. Would you drop Brian Cooper a note, please. Tell him thanks from me and that I will be in touch."

"Will do, bye," said Viktor, but Ian had already gone.

It was the following morning when Oscar read the email from Ian complete with the attachments from Viktor and Brian Cooper. He was staggered! What was going on!? He immediately telephoned Gladstone. Gladstone was similarly astonished and the two men agreed to meet at 6 o'clock at their usual bar.

After Oscar had finished his conversation with Gladstone, he opened up his computer and decided to find out everything he could about Mr James Abbott McNeill Whistler and his work. He was annoyed with himself because he didn't normally get involved with artists he knew little or nothing about. Now he felt he might have just put his 'foot in it' with Ian.

After two hours of investigation Oscar was beginning to get a better feel for Whistler's work. However, something in the back of his mind was now telling him that there might be a problem with this Mr Bryson, so he decided to now look for the evidence highlighted by Mr Cooper. In particular, the details of a certain sale that had occurred in New York... only two years ago!

Gladstone Clive was a worried man. He thought long and hard about what Oscar had just told him about Mr Bryson's painting. Whilst he was the first to accept that he was not an expert when it came to Whistler's work, he had seen the painting and it had looked good to him. The provenance had all stacked up, so why now, suddenly, the big issue? The more he pondered the more worried he became. Had Mr Bryson pulled a fast one? If so, had he done it before and I didn't spot it? Holy shit! Have I bought fakes from him in the past!?

At 5.50pm Gladstone sat at his and Oscar's customary table in their usual bar. Two pints of cold lager were already sitting on the table. One partly consumed and the second one waiting for his drinking partner.

Oscar arrived five minutes later, spotted Gladstone and walked over to join him.

Gladstone saw Oscar strolling towards him and said, "Hi, man, got you a drink."

"Thanks," said Oscar. Both men had serious looks on their faces. Oscar sat down and took a sip of his beer.

"This is a mess, man," said Gladstone, watching Oscar drinking his beer. "I think Bryson has tried to take us for suckers."

"Mmm, I know," replied Oscar. "I don't think this is the first time either. I've done some research today and I think I've found some other examples where he's bought a genuine picture, had it copied, and then sold off the copy as the real deal."

"But he's still got the good provenance!"

"All part of the con. This Whistler, which Bryson says he wants us to buy, he bought originally six years ago. For US$1.2 million." Gladstone nodded and Oscar continued. "That's all true. However, just two years ago, he sold the original painting to a gallery in New York for US$3.5 million! I know, because the gallery he sold it to, subsequently sold it for US$4.2 million… to a buyer in Switzerland. The gallery had all the correct provenance papers and the painting had been checked for authenticity."

"So are you saying there are two sets of provenance?"

"Exactly! Well not quite. There is the original set that the New York gallery passed on to their buyer and a second set that has been very cleverly forged."

"I don't feel very well!"

"Come on, Gladstone, we have not lost any money, but gained quite a lot of experience."

"I have bought four paintings from him in the past."

"For a lot of money?"

"About US$2 million, in total. All except for one, I've already sold on."

"Oh dear. The question now is what are we going to do about it?"

"It's not really your problem, Oscar. It's me that he's screwed. He's taken me for an idiot."

"Finish that beer and I'll buy you another. Then I'll tell you about my little idea."

When Oscar arrived back at their table, he handed the new pint of lager to Gladstone.

"Hey, Oscar, this is all good of you, but…"

"No buts, Gladstone. This guy needs sorting. He's the sort of person who gives the art world a bad name."

"I'll owe you for this, man."

"You've not heard my idea yet!"

Over the next 30 minutes Oscar explained his idea.

Gladstone listened carefully and as the plan slowly unfolded, he liked it more and more… and, just as importantly, he thought it just might work! "Man, that's brilliant!" he replied. "Let's screw him… real good!"

Chapter 43

Yoshihiro (Yoshi – to his friends) Tsuzuki is the junior partner in the art partnership with Yuki Tanaka. The business is based in Tokyo and Yoshi is mainly responsible for overseeing the partnership's three art galleries in the city. Yuki, however, spends most of his time travelling throughout wider Japan and abroad, visiting clients and buying and selling quality art.

Although they usually keep in touch on a daily basis by the wonders of modern technology, Yoshi and Yuki usually only meet 'face to face', about once a month. Today was one of those once in a month days. They sat together in their company's main office, located on the first floor, above the 'Cherry Blossom' art gallery. They were discussing the previous month's activities.

Yoshi was explaining the sales figures for all their three galleries, whilst Yuki was telling Yoshi about the purchases and sales he had recently made. He also updated Yoshi on the progress of the new Ian Caxton partnership he had entered into.

"It's still early days," said Yuki, refilling his coffee cup, "but I think Ian Caxton's idea will bear much fruit over the coming years. Hopefully, that will mean I won't need to travel abroad quite so often."

"I understand the Stubbs painting, '*High Spirits and Brown Mac*', sold for a nice profit in Monaco," said Yoshi, taking a sip from his glass of mineral water. He did not drink coffee or tea.

"Yes, it was a good start and I also managed to unearth that second Stubbs painting from the Singapore free port at the same time. That was a bonus. Of course, that picture has nothing to do with the Caxton partnership."

"You were also able to deliver it to the client whilst you were in Singapore," said Yoshi. "That was a convenient move."

Yuki nodded. "I calculate we made 140 million yen, after expenses. A nice profit. Have you any new requests for me to follow up on?"

"No, not at the moment."

Yuki sipped his refreshed cup of coffee and then said, "The Caxton partnership is looking for a home for a Whistler painting, but I'm not really interested in that one."

"Okay. Whilst you've been away I've been reviewing our current surplus stock. We have some nice pictures, but they are not so popular in Tokyo. I suggest we should offer them to the Caxton partnership. See if he can find them a new home."

"That's a great idea. Which ones are you suggesting?"

In Sotheby's office in London, Penny was briefing Ian about a forthcoming auction. Following Ian's suggestion, she was currently managing two other colleagues, who, between them, were in the process of obtaining the pictures from their owners and arranging for them to be properly cleaned. Penny was also responsible for putting together the draft catalogue and she wanted to get Ian's agreement before she presented the final draft to Michael Hopkins for his approval.

"I like it, Penny," said Ian, flicking through the pages for the third time. "It's got a good balance and feel. It should interest a number of different types of buyers. Maybe look at the front cover again, though. I would change the Dali picture, only because most of the paintings being auctioned were painted before Dali's modern art era."

"That's a good point. At first glance, some people might be put off thinking it was all just modern art, when of course there are only four modern art paintings in the auction. What if we swapped it for the Reynolds portrait?"

"That would be much better. More representative of the majority of paintings being auctioned. I think you'll also find that Michael is much more likely to approve that idea."

"Thank you, Ian."

"When are you seeing him?"

"This afternoon, at 2 o'clock."

Ian nodded. "Good. Remember what I said, be confident and assertive. Michael respects those qualities."

"I'll try, but as you know, that is not my normal style."

"Come on, Penny, you're always assertive with me!"

"Well that's different," said Penny, with a smile.

Ian laughed. "Seriously, Penny, Michael likes slightly pushy people. Feels they have something to say and need to be listened to. Just don't go over the top though!"

This time Penny laughed. "I don't think there is any danger that I will be doing that!"

Oscar and Gladstone were in a meeting at Oscar's villa. They had got together to discuss the Raymond Bryson / Whistler issue.

"Who are Bryson's favourite artists?" asked Oscar. He had a plan to help Gladstone out of his tricky predicament.

Gladstone thought for a few minutes and then listed four names.

"Is there any one of these that is more special than the others? An artist that would really grab his attention?"

Gladstone pondered again, and then he said, "Picasso, I think. I know he doesn't own any of his work."

Oscar nodded, "Okay, this is what we'll do to start with. Would you contact Bryson and tell him that you may have found a buyer for his Whistler. Then tell him that you might also be able to obtain a small Picasso. Ask him if he would be interested in buying it. We need to keep him focused."

The next day Gladstone telephoned Raymond Bryson. He followed Oscar's suggestions and explained the position with the Whistler painting. He also introduced the possible sale of a Picasso. Immediately after the call he telephoned Oscar and told him the results of his conversation with Bryson. Oscar was pleased to hear that Gladstone had obviously captured Bryson's attention.

In the meantime, Oscar proceeded to the next stage of the plan. He emailed May Ling and asked her if she still owned Picasso's 'Woman with her green mandolin'? If she did, he asked her if he could borrow it and also get Lee Son, the talented forger in Hong Kong, to paint one of his magic copies for him. Could he also provide a copy of the painting's provenance as well? Oscar finished the message by confirming that he would pay for all the incurred costs.

When May Ling received Oscar's email she was curious and wondered what exactly Oscar was up to. She immediately responded and confirmed she still did own the Picasso painting and asked him why he needed it and what he was doing.

In his next email, Oscar explained to May the full details of his colleague's situation and that he and Gladstone intended to get their own back on Mr Bryson. Oscar said he wanted to follow the same method May had seen in action in Beijing a few years ago.

May emailed back promising Oscar he would receive the two paintings by the end of the month. True to her word, both paintings duly arrived at Oscar's villa.

After Oscar had taken delivery of the two paintings he telephoned Gladstone and asked him to come to his villa that evening. When Gladstone arrived, Oscar explained what he was going to do next. Gladstone was curious and listened intently.

"Right, Gladstone, I now need you to help me with these two paintings," said Oscar. He placed the original painting on his table and the copy on a nearby chair.

"You got it, man. What do you want me to do?"

Firstly Gladstone was asked to hold the original painting whilst Oscar gently prized off the existing frame. Gladstone then placed the frame on Oscar's sofa. Next Oscar placed the original painting into a similar and exact same size frame. He then secured it with the same pins and in similar positions.

Oscar then picked up and handed the original picture in its new frame to Gladstone and asked him to hold the picture steady whilst he took several close-up photographs of the picture in its new frame. Oscar particularly focused on both the front and the back of the frame.

"Why do you need the photos?" asked Gladstone. He then passed the picture back to Oscar.

"When Bryson sees this original and decides he wants to buy it, my guess is that he will mark the frame. Probably with a ring or his finger nail. Especially when we tell him that 'our seller' won't release it until the payment is in their account. Whilst he gets his money together that's when we'll swap the original painting back into its correct frame and the forgery will be inserted into the marked frame. The forgery will then be delivered to Bryson. Complete with the copy of the provenance."

Gladstone nodded, but was now wondering if it really would all work out!

Oscar now walked over to the chair and picked up the forgery. He then showed it to Gladstone. "May Ling knows an excellent specialist copier in Hong Kong. His name is Lee Son. A great artist and a wonderful copier!"

"Wow!" said Gladstone. He was astonished and immediately compared it to the original painting. "I can't see any difference! The guy's a genius. It really is a Picasso!"

"Let's hope Bryson thinks the same way," replied Oscar. But he then pointed to a tiny blue speck of paint in the top right hand corner of the copy.

Gladstone had to use Oscar's magnifying glass to see it.

"Once the frame is in place that speck will be hidden. We don't want to get the pictures mixed up, do we!?"

"This is brilliant! Have you done this stunt before?"

"No. But May Ling, our partner in Beijing, told me about a similar case she'd seen," said Oscar. He placed the original picture out of the way on the nearby chair.

Gladstone shook his head gently in surprise. "What's the original painting worth?"

"I think about US$8 million, so we had better take good care of it! Bryson will know this value, so we'll offer it to him for seven million and compromise at say six million. Three million for me and three million for you!"

"Wow, man. You think he's going to bite?"

"Let's just see. Send him an email and attach the photos. Tell him the client lives in Beijing and is looking for US$7 million. You can also tell him that I know the client."

Ten minutes later Gladstone had used Oscar's computer and sent Bryson an email with five photographs attached. He also mentioned that the painting was currently residing in Beijing.

Chapter 44

Ian was sitting in his home office and pondering on the early results of the partnership. He decided it was progressing very nicely. Probably better than he'd expected... or even hoped. It was now the end of the first six months and he had arranged a video conference with Yuki, May Ling, Viktor, Bob, Oscar and Gladstone. It would be the first time that the partners could put a face to the name. Ian switched on his computer and waited for the link to connect.

It was a nervous start to the meeting, but Ian eventually broke the ice by informing the team that, subject to two paintings in the last stages of a sale being finalised, they were making a profit of £14 million to date. A little short of Ian's target of doubling their money in the first year, but nevertheless very acceptable. He brought smiles to everyone's faces when he commented, "Where else can you get an investment return of 53% in six months... tax free!?"

They all generally agreed this was an acceptable start and each partner then highlighted their own individual contributions. The meeting ended after it was agreed to adopt May and Yuki's suggested changes which they said would both increase turnover and improve the business model. The result – even bigger potential profits in the future!

When Ian closed down the connection, he sat back in

his chair with a small smile on his face. He was extremely pleased with the positive buzz and enthusiasm generated by the team at the meeting... and the new ideas! His conclusion? 'It's definitely a case of WHEN he would be leaving Sotheby's... not if'!

In Antigua, Oscar also closed down his computer. He was sitting in his home office with Gladstone.

"Well, what do you think?" asked Oscar. It was the first time Gladstone had seen Ian and the rest of the partners.

"Seemed to go well. Interesting to see all those different faces. Somehow, I just assumed they would all be white Europeans!" replied Gladstone. "A nice surprise."

"Yes, a bit like a meeting at the United Nations!" Both men laughed.

"So, Gladstone, where are we now with our 'friend', Mr Bryson?"

"As you know, he came back to me after I'd sent that email. Said he wanted to see the Picasso painting for himself. I reminded him the painting was still in Beijing and the seller was not going to release it without some insurance."

"Okay. That's a good start. What did he say to that?"

"He asked what the insurance amount was. I told him that US$2 million would be required and deposited with the seller's legal people in Hong Kong. If he eventually bought the painting, then that would be deducted from the total cost. If he decided not to buy, then all costs to date would be deducted and the balance returned to him."

"I bet he didn't like that!"

"He went quiet on the other end of the telephone. I thought he'd closed the call, but he then said that it was okay, but he wanted to agree to a new price of US$6 million... if he bought it. I told him that the client was unlikely to accept that, but I would relay his offer. That's where we are at the moment!"

"Okay, so we're making good progress. We're right not to be too pushy. Let's tell him the client still wants a minimum of seven million and try to get his two million in the bank. I've already got a separate business bank account in Hong Kong so we can tell him that's where the US$2 million dollars needs to be transferred. We'll say that once he accepts this agreement, we will arrange for the painting to be shipped to Antigua. My guess is that we'll still finish on the six million we wanted."

"That would be brilliant!"

"Yes it would, but there's still a long way to go."

A week later a final sale price of US$6 million had been agreed and Bryson had transferred US$2 million into, what he thought was, the seller's lawyer's bank account in Hong Kong. Oscar immediately faked an 'official' receipt and emailed it to Bryson. He used the name and address of a firm of lawyers he had previously dealt with in Hong Kong. He knew Bryson would check up to make sure this firm of lawyers really existed and was legit.

Gladstone emailed Bryson and informed him that the seller's lawyers had confirmed to their client that the money was now in their bank account. The client would therefore be now arranging shipment of the painting to Oscar's address. Gladstone concluded by saying he would contact Bryson again once Oscar had informed him that the picture had safely arrived in Antigua.

Ten days later Gladstone collected Bryson and took him to Oscar's villa. There Bryson was shown the original painting, but still in its changed frame. He was also shown copies of the provenance papers, which Oscar explained, were completely accurate, with the exception of the current owner's name. He then said that once the painting was sold and the balance of money was in the lawyer's account, the full provenance, including the current owner's name and details would be given to him.

Bryson examined the picture thoroughly and then the frame and the rear. Eventually, he agreed that he would pay the balance of US$4 million. He wanted to take the painting away with him there and then, but Oscar said he had strict instructions not to release the painting until all the money had been received into the lawyer's bank account. Bryson argued about trust, how unethical this all was, but Oscar reiterated that he was only following the client's instructions and promised he would personally keep the painting safe and secure in the meantime.

Bryson reluctantly accepted the situation and said he would be back on Friday to collect the picture. The balance of US$4 million would be in the lawyer's account by then.

After Bryson left the villa, Oscar and Gladstone removed the original painting from the frame shown to Bryson. Oscar pointed to a new scratch on the back of the frame. He told Gladstone that he noticed Bryson making that mark with his ring.

"I didn't see him do that!"

"Sneaky, but I noticed the scratch when he handed the painting back to me. If we look at the photos I took last week, it won't be there."

"Gladstone shook his head slowly. "I seriously owe you, man."

"No you don't. Come on let's get the pictures properly swapped and into their correct frames. I want to get the original painting, and its original frame, shipped back to May Ling well before Friday arrives."

On the Thursday afternoon Oscar accessed his alias lawyer's bank account. There sat the balance of US$4 million. He once again created an invoice confirming receipt of the money and emailed it to Bryson. He telephoned Gladstone and Gladstone then emailed Bryson. This time Gladstone told Bryson that the client had been informed that the balance of money was now in her lawyer's bank account and had given permission for the painting now to be released.

On Friday evening at 6 o'clock, Bryson arrived at Oscar's villa. Oscar and Gladstone were waiting for him. The forgery was sitting on the table. Bryson spotted it and picked it up. He inspected it thoroughly, including the rear, where he ran his finger over the scratch on the frame. Oscar and Gladstone briefly exchanged glances.

"All okay?" queried Oscar.

Bryson was still examining every square centimetre. "It's a bit cleaner than when I saw it last."

"I thought it was a little dusty, from the journey from Beijing, so I gave it a gentle blow with a can of pressurised air. It wouldn't have done any damage."

"No, no. Seems fine. Okay gents. What about my Whistler painting?"

"Still working on it, Raymond," replied Gladstone. "The guy I thought was keen has backed out."

Bryson nodded, shook hands with both Oscar and Gladstone and walked towards the door with his painting. He stopped, looked back at Oscar and Gladstone and said, "Picasso is my favourite artist. This is the first one that I've ever been able to own."

At this Bryson left the villa and both Oscar and Gladstone gave a great sigh of relief.

"I owe you, man. Seriously owe you," said Gladstone. "That was pure genius!"

Oscar smiled. "No, Gladstone, I owe you... US$3 million!"

Chapter 45

The auction Penny had organised had been a success. Ian said it was a great first effort and he praised the presentation that had been published on Sotheby's website. He also pointed to the increase in the number of 'hits' the on-line catalogue had generated.

Penny was a little embarrassed, but pleased that everyone thought it had been a success. She thanked Ian for his support and told him that Michael Hopkins had telephoned and had asked her to come to his office so that he could congratulate her personally.

"That's great, Penny. That's what I want to hear. I will push your name to Michael at every opportunity I get. Remember, I want you to take over from me."

"Do you really think that will happen? I've got nowhere near the level of experience you have."

"You are building up your experience right now. Plus we've got the makings of another auction in about three months' time. I want you to manage that one. I'll email you the listing I've got so far. There is also an extra Thomas Gainsborough painting that I want to be included!"

Penny smiled. Although Ian had not actually said so, she assumed it was going to be the lovely picture she had seen hanging on Ian and Emma's dining room wall. Viktor had told her that Emma had been able to persuade the experts that the picture was, after all, an original Thomas Gainsborough painting. Mmm, she thought, it will be interesting to see what reserve price Ian finally puts on it!

In Monaco, Zoe was enjoying the return to her part-time role in the *'Les Roses Rouges'* art gallery. Following her success selling the Stubbs painting, *'High Spirits and Brown Mac'*, she was now very keen to prove to her husband that this was not just a 'one off' fluke. Since the completion of the Stubbs sale she had achieved two further sales from their own stock and had bought in, and then sold on, a further painting, all just in the space of three weeks!

Bob Taylor was extremely pleased with Zoe's enthusiasm and her successes. It reminded him of the early days before the children had come along. Now with the added bonus of Ian's group partnership, the business had really improved and the turnover had just over doubled in the last 14 months. When Bob and Zoe had shown the new turnover figures to Zoe's father, Antoine, he said he was also really pleased. He even went as far as to praise his daughter's contribution, something he'd never ever done before!

After Bob and Zoe left their meeting with Antoine and had climbed into their car, suddenly Zoe burst into tears.

"Hey," said Bob, putting his arm around his wife's shoulder. "What's this all about?"

"That's the first time, ever, that my father has praised me. Why has he had to wait all this time?"

Bob shook his head in frustration and squeezed her shoulders tightly. "I don't know, I really don't. He's had lots of opportunities in the past. Maybe he'll try to catch up on lost time."

Zoe sat up and looked at Bob. "I'm not going to hold my

breath." She leaned across and gave Bob a big kiss on his cheek, and then said, "Come on, let's go home."

Bob started the car's engine and drove out of Zoe's parents' driveway. He really did hope that, finally, this was the start of a better relationship between Antoine and his daughter – before, of course, it was all too late! He knew that Antoine's health was slowly deteriorating.

During the next twenty minutes of the journey, on their way back towards Monaco, they passed by some lovely parts of the French countryside. Zoe had calmed down and had wiped her eyes. She looked out of the passenger side window, but her mind was elsewhere.

Bob glanced across at his wife and wondered what she was thinking. After a few minutes he decided now was the time to tell her about the partnership.

"Zoe." Zoe looked across at her husband. "There's something I want to tell you."

Zoe sat up in her seat and waited for Bob to continue.

"Remember, Ian Caxton?"

"Yes, of course." What a strange question, thought Zoe.

"Well he's set up a partnership. It's a group of art dealers based in various locations throughout the world and they help each other to buy and sell paintings for their clients."

"Okay, that sounds good," said Zoe, still none the wiser as to what this was leading to.

"Mmm, that's what I thought, so I've joined the partnership." Bob held his breath waiting for Zoe's new response.

Zoe remained quiet for a few seconds as she pondered on this development. "I see. So what does this actually mean?"

Bob started breathing again. "It means that I have put a large part of my own savings into the partnership. The partnership has created a special fund of money for buying and selling paintings. None of the gallery's money is involved, it's just my own money at the moment."

"Why have you not told me before?"

"Well, it's been difficult, what with the problems and your worry with your father. I just decided to put it off, temporarily. Now things have settled down with Antoine, well I decided to tell you now."

"I see. So when did this partnership start?"

"The first painting was your Stubbs, '*High Spirits and Brown Mac*'. It was the partnership that bought the painting in the first place, borrowing money out of the partnership's funds."

"So we don't get all of the profit from that sale?"

"Not in this case, no, but of course the deal would not have occurred at all without the partnership funding the purchase in the first place. Neither would we have had your Mr Linton as a new client. We've also had a share of the other partnership deals too."

"I see." Zoe pondered on these points. She then asked, "Have you been involved in any other similar deals?"

"Just two. Remember I sold the Thomas Lawrence portrait and the John Martin moody landscape that we've had for ages? Well they were bought by clients of the partnership. We've been able to get rid of two sticking paintings and the gallery gains some extra profit."

"So how much profit have you made?"

"I've not made any profit, I've put the profit into the gallery. We now have an extra 1.3 million euros to date."

"But if you've invested your own money, then surely you should get that profit."

"That's not why I decided to join the partnership. I saw it as a small risk, but mainly as another source of income for the gallery. All profits from these paintings will still be going through the gallery's books. And, of course, anything we do on our own, well, the profit from those is still all ours."

Zoe was beginning to see the benefits.

Bob continued, "It also means we are now able to buy more valuable paintings than was previously possible. We can also offer a better service for more people and also the wealthier potential clients of Monaco – something we could only do in our dreams before."

"Mmm," replied Zoe. "I need to think about this."

Bob breathed a quiet sigh of relief. He decided not to continue the conversation. He wanted Zoe to consider all the points he had made without potentially adding any further possible confusion.

Zoe turned her head away from Bob and returned to watching the passing countryside. She had mixed thoughts about what Bob had just told her. She could see the extra financial gains that could be made from this partnership arrangement, however, she was also wondering what, potentially, the downsides were likely to be.

Chapter 46

Robert's first few weeks at his 'big' school had resulted in a mixed report from his form teacher, Mrs Barnsdale. She'd told Emma that Robert was a bright boy and had made two good friends. However, he seemed to occasionally become bored too easily which would then result in him becoming disruptive. Nothing too concerning at the moment, but it needed to be addressed before it became a more serious matter.

When Emma told Ian what the teacher had said, his immediate reaction was, "Well, maybe the teacher needs to do more to stop him getting bored in the first place!"

"I think that's a little unfair, Ian. Robert is just one of the pupils in the class."

"Look, Emma, we sent Robert to this school for the more personal attention he is supposed to be getting. They advertise that one of the school's strengths is that they develop each child at their ideal pace. Being bored is the last comment I thought we would hear!"

"Mmm. Well it is still early days. I'll have a chat with Robert and see if we can get to the bottom of it."

"Okay. But be gentle. Being bored is, in one way, a good thing, because it does show he wants to be challenged more, which is far better than being accused of being disinterested!"

Emma pondered on Ian's comments. Maybe he's right, she thought. I'll see what Robert has to say.

The next evening, when Robert had just finished his homework, Emma looked briefly at his answers. She was impressed and decided to take that moment to have a chat about school.

"How do you like your new school?"

"It's really good, but sometimes it can get a bit boring," replied Robert, packing his papers into his school bag.

"When does it get boring?"

"Painting. We usually get silly things to paint."

Emma was quite surprised, she knew Robert usually enjoyed drawing. "What silly things do you have to paint?"

"Flowers and leaves… and things. They're boring!"

Emma tried hard to keep a straight face. "Would you like to paint some other things instead?"

"Jimmy Parker says his teacher lets them paint animals and dinosaurs."

Again, Emma was surprised. "Oh! Would you like me to speak to your teacher?"

"I don't want to paint flowers, they're just girls' things."

"What about any other subjects, are they boring too?"

"No. The rest are alright. I like reading and writing best."

Emma decided to leave it at that and helped Robert finish packing his bag. "Come on then, young man, let's get you bathed before Daddy gets home. We can then all have dinner together."

Later that evening Emma explained to Ian what Robert had told her.

"I can't say I blame him. I'd find painting flowers and leaves boring too!" said Ian, smiling at the thought.

"I'll speak to Mrs Barnsdale after school tomorrow," said Emma.

Gladstone sat in his small office area at the back of his villa. He was still feeling severely in debt to his colleague, Oscar, because, the very next morning, after Raymond Bryson had departed Oscar's villa with his 'new Picasso', Oscar had transferred the US$3 million into Gladstone's bank account. He knew he owed Oscar a big favour, but also he wanted to use this windfall to correct possible errors he might have committed in the past.

For the last two days he'd been trying to locate the buyers of three of the four paintings he'd bought from Bryson and subsequently sold on. He was now convinced that these three paintings were probably fakes!

Unfortunately, two of the buyers no longer lived on the island and the third agreed to have a meeting with Gladstone. Gladstone explained that he had received information that threw some doubt on the authenticity of the painting that he had sold to the client. The client was initially surprised, and then annoyed, but Gladstone said he was prepared to reimburse him and give him an extra 10% by way of an apology. This seemed to calm the client and Gladstone gave him a cheque and took away the possible 'tainted' painting. He hoped this gesture would help to restore any damage to his reputation. Gladstone was well aware that Antigua is a small island and any bad news travels very quickly!

Later that same day, Gladstone and Oscar sat at their usual table in their regular evening bar. They had just started their first glass of lager.

"You know, Oscar, you have probably saved my career. Without you, man, my reputation would now be in tatters," said Gladstone, peering into his beer and shaking his head.

"We needed to kick that Bryson where it hurts most… in his wallet! You've built up a nice business and a good reputation, I wasn't going to allow that to be damaged. Besides,

I've gained a few extra dollars myself and sent May Ling some money too… by way of a thank you."

"Do you think he'll come back to us when he discovers his painting's just a copy?"

"What copy? May Ling's painting was the real deal."

"But…"

"No buts, Gladstone. If he contacts May Ling she will tell him that she sent both the authenticated painting and the correct provenance, to me, which she did. If he then accuses us we'll ask him how he thought we could have produced an exact copy of the painting in just the four days that the painting was in our possession? We just stick to that story… and make sure we never do any business with him again!"

"I've already put the word out that the guy is bad news."

"Great! Keep a lookout for a 'for sale' sign appearing at his house sometime soon!"

Gladstone smiled at Oscar. "Thanks, man."

It was the first smile Oscar had seen on his colleague's face for several days.

"Gladstone, we need to get back to the honest art market. Any thoughts or suggestions?"

Chapter 47

Over the last month Penny had spent quite a lot of her work time putting together the new auction catalogue and also preparing for it to be uploaded onto Sotheby's website. As Ian had requested, she had also included his Gainsborough painting, *'Meeting on the way to market'*. Now she was awaiting Ian's final decision on what he was going to set the reserve price at.

Penny and Viktor had tried to guess what the reserve price was likely to be. In the end they decided to have a wager on who would be the nearest to Ian's final decision. The loser would pay for a meal at their favourite restaurant. Penny guessed it might be about £2.5 million, Viktor thought it would be nearer £2.75 million.

Penny was still awaiting Ian's answer when she received a telephone call from Michael Hopkins' PA asking when Mr Hopkins could see the catalogue's final draft? Penny explained that she had not received all the reserve prices and also Ian still needed to see the document to add his comments as well. Nevertheless, Penny did agree to see Mr Hopkins in two days' time.

After the telephone call she stood up and walked to the door between her area and Ian's office.

"Ian, can I have a word with you about the auction?"

Ian was sitting at his desk and looking at two separate computer screens. "Yes, come in, Penny. Sit down."

Penny sat on her usual seat directly opposite him. "Ginny, Mr Hopkins' PA, has just telephoned and I've had to make an appointment to see Mr Hopkins on Thursday at 3pm. That's in just two days time. I need to get your approval on the catalogue first."

"Okay, should we talk about it now?"

"The problem is, it's not quite finished. I'm still waiting for both Paul Hardy's and your reserve price."

"Ah, right." Ian sat up and then leaned forward slightly, putting his arms on his desk. "Give Paul a ring, he's probably just forgotten. Now, for my Gainsborough, I've decided at £2.5 million for the reserve price."

Penny jotted Ian's figure down on her notepad and tried to hide her smile. Wait till Vic hears! she thought to herself. "I'll ring Mr Hardy right now and then get the draft uploaded. Can we meet tomorrow morning please?"

"Sounds good. Should we say about 10 o'clock?"

Penny rose from her seat. "Thank you, Ian."

When Penny got back to her desk she typed a brief email to Vic telling him to book their usual restaurant. She wanted the expensive menu!

One month later Ian and Penny arrived at Sotheby's auction room and stood at the back. All the seats were occupied and other people were standing at the back and down the sides as well. Penny glanced at her catalogue and reminded herself which Lot number Ian's Gainsborough painting was assigned to. She looked at the index and it read: "Lot 15. *Meeting on the way to market*. Thomas Gainsborough."

Penny listened to the auctioneer and established that he was currently auctioning Lot 11.

When the auctioneer's gavel came down on Lot 11, both

Ian and Penny looked at each other, smiled and nodded. Paul Hardy's painting had been sold for 20% above the reserve price!

Ian looked back towards the auctioneer but then he noticed that Emma was sitting in the audience, four rows from the front. He smiled and was pleased with the increased interest Emma had recently shown in the art world.

Lots 12, 13 and 14 were duly processed.

The auctioneer then announced, "Now, ladies and gentlemen we come to Lot 15. *'Meeting on the way to market'* by Thomas Gainsborough. This painting was recently re-evaluated and reinstated as being a genuine piece of work by this celebrated British artist. It's a landscape scene showing two early 18th century race horses resting in an English country field. Can I have an opening bid of one million pounds? One million, I hear. Do I hear one million, five hundred thousand pounds? Thank you, sir…"

The bidding quickly moved up to £2.7 million, but a number of the early bidders now declined further bids and shook their heads. The auctioneer tried to encourage the audience by reaffirming the quality of the painting and the name of the artist. £2.8 million was then bid from the audience.

Ian's heart was now beating faster and he was beginning to perspire a little. He kept his arms folded, but his fingers were firmly crossed. He was also watching Emma and wondered how fast her heart was racing?

Penny was also excited and kept stepping up and down on her toes with each subsequent bid.

"2.9 million? Thank you, madam," said the auctioneer. He continued to look around the room for possible bidders. Some of the audience followed the direction the auctioneer was looking, hoping to catch a view of the next bidder. Suddenly, there was a wave from a man holding a telephone receiver at the side of the room. Here there was a bank of six telephones and they were all in use.

"Three million pounds I have… on the telephone," announced the auctioneer.

There were some gasps of breath from the audience now that the £3 million level had been achieved.

"Now, ladies and gentlemen, we are seeing the real value of this lovely painting. Ah…" The auctioneer stopped, cupped his ear with his left hand and leaned forward. He was trying to hear better over the rising murmur in the audience. "Was that 3.1 million, madam? No? Oh… 3 million and 50,000 pounds. Thank you madam. So the bid now stands at 3 million and 50,000 pounds. Do I hear 3 million, 100,000 pounds?"

People in the audience were now looking around trying to spot the next bidder. Ian's palms were as wet as his forehead. He could only see the back of Emma's head, but guessed she might just have her eyes tightly closed.

"Thank you, sir. On the telephone, I now have a bid of £3.2 million! Do I hear 3.3 million?"

The audience now gasped out loud! People began talking about the bids to their neighbour.

"Do I hear £3.3 million?" The auctioneer now had to raise his voice to be heard.

Previous bidders were now declining and shaking their heads.

The auctioneer glanced around the seated audience and then to the bank of telephones. Finally, he said, "I'm selling, then… at 3 million, 200,000 pounds… Once… Twice… Sir? Was that a bid? …No? …So for the third… and final time…" Bang! The auctioneer hit his gavel onto its matching hardwood block! He then announced, "Lot 15. '*Meeting on the way to market*' by Thomas Gainsborough, sold for £3 million, 200,000. Board number 254." However, only the people in the first two rows could hear his announcement over the loud chatter of the audience!

At the end of the auction Ian tried to catch up with Emma. She was slowly being carried along in the throng of people as they were all trying to leave the room.

Emma was a little concerned with the pushing crowd, but then spotted Ian waving and trying to ease his way towards her. She stopped, stepped aside and waited for him. When they finally got together they embraced tightly. After they released each other, Ian looked at Emma. She was crying!

"Why are you crying?" asked Ian, not really surprised.

"That was fantastic, Ian!" replied Emma, wiping her eyes. "So nerve racking, but also so exhilarating… and exciting! Oh wow, and £3 million!"

"I don't think I've sweated so much since my last summer in Hong Kong!" replied Ian. "Just look at my shirt, it's wet through!"

They both laughed out loud.

Chapter 48

After Emma left Sotheby's auction rooms, she made her way to the nearby underground station. There she caught a tube train to London Waterloo station, and then a South Western train back to Esher station, where she'd parked her car in the station car park. During the train journey she could think of nothing except the Thomas Gainsborough painting and the excitement of the auction. She loved having such a quality picture on the wall in their dining room and although she had persuaded Ian to arrange for a similar copy to be painted, she knew it would never be quite the same. Nevertheless an extra £3 million, she decided, would definitely come in very useful!

After she arrived back at Esher railway station she collected her car and drove off in the direction of Robert's school. Yesterday afternoon, when Emma had collected Robert, he had run over to her with a note clasped in his hand. It was from Mrs Barnsdale, Robert's teacher. The note asked Emma if she could arrive at the school 10 minutes earlier the next day as she had some good news to tell her about Robert.

During the 30 minute journey to the school, Emma wondered what the teacher's note meant. She pondered on all sorts of possibilities, but as she approached the school gates, she decided to just wait and hear what Mrs Barnsdale had to say.

Emma drove through the main gates and along the familiar long gravel driveway until the large red brick Georgian building came into view. The large schoolhouse and its grounds were once owned, just over a hundred years ago, by a famous Lord. It was used as his private residence. However, when the Lord died, and in order to pay the government's death duties, the inheriting family decided that the property needed to be sold off.

The estate was subsequently auctioned and eventually purchased by the very rich, Sir Edgar Brookfield. It was his ambition to save the building and grounds, and to convert it into a private boys school. Sir Edgar had acquired his wealth in South Africa after successfully investing in both gold and diamond mines. 'Brookfield School' became his legacy to boys' education. It was not until 2003, however, that the school also started to accept girls as pupils as well.

Emma parked her car in the large visitors car park at the rear of the school building. Arriving early she noticed that there were only three other cars already parked. At the time when Emma usually arrived to collect Robert there could already be upwards of 30 vehicles parked, waiting to collect children.

She closed and locked the car door and then walked around the side of the building towards the front entrance. It was a warm, sunny day and Emma spotted Mrs Barnsdale when she appeared from the main doorway. She walked over to join Emma.

"Hello, Mrs Caxton. I thought we would take the opportunity of this lovely sunshine and walk for a few minutes." They both turned around and walked towards the tennis courts. The large area of playing fields were just beyond.

"Your note was a little puzzling," said Emma, removing her sunglasses from her handbag.

"Yes, I wanted to explain, 'face to face' as it were, rather than try to put it all in a letter."

"Okay," said Emma, none the wiser.

"You will recall that we had a small problem with Robert's behaviour and then found out that it was due to the subjects he'd been asked to paint." Emma nodded. "Well I'm pleased to report that having moved Robert to another group for his art lessons he's had a transformation. Whereas he always complained and became disruptive, well, now art is one of his favourite subjects."

"I've noticed he's spending a lot more time now at home drawing different animals. I'd assumed things had finally settled down," said Emma, pleased to hear what the teacher was saying.

"More than that, his enthusiasm generally has improved as well. Quite a little star with his reading and writing. He is by far the best reader and speller in his class."

"Well that's super news," said Emma, beaming at the thought of her little hero.

As they reached the entrance to the tennis courts, they both stopped walking and turned around, continuing the walk and their discussion. As they approached the main school building again, the bell rang for the end of the day's lessons. Within seconds, children started to exit from the main doorway and run towards the main car park to be collected by parents.

"No running!" shouted Mrs Barnsdale. Some children listened and started walking, others carried on running once they were out of sight.

"Well, thank you, for that information," said Emma. "Robert's father will be pleased as well when I tell him."

"Goodbye, Mrs Caxton and thank you for arriving a little earlier today. Ah... here comes Robert now."

On the car journey home Emma was asking Robert about

his day at school. She could tell from his positive reaction and the enthusiasm in his voice, that he was now enjoying all of his subjects.

"Are you enjoying your art classes now?"

"Oh, yes. It's great fun. Mr Collins is excellent at drawing dinosaurs and animals and it all starts from drawing circles. It's so easy to follow."

Robert had not mentioned maths at all so Emma asked him, "What about maths, do you like that subject?"

"Mmm, it's okay. A lot of it's quite easy though, lots of numbers and things. I prefer reading and writing."

Interesting, thought Emma. A lot to discuss with Ian tonight.

Later that evening after Robert had gone to bed, Emma joined Ian sitting on the sofa in the lounge.

"I had another chat with Robert's form teacher this afternoon. She is now saying that Robert is excelling at school."

"Hey, that's great news," said Ian, sitting up to take better notice. "I've seen him drawing some dinosaurs, they are very good for a four year old. Better than I could do. Things must have changed at school."

"He's got a new art teacher. Mr Collins. He likes him."

"There we are. I bet he's not bored now!"

"No, just the opposite. Mrs Barnsdale says she's seen a transformation. He's the best reader and speller in his class."

"That's good isn't it? I know it's very early days, but I think we need to arrange some sort of treat for him."

"What a good idea. I'll ask him what he would like." Emma already had a couple of possible ideas.

"Talking of treats," said Ian. "After this morning's auction result, I think we need to treat ourselves as well. Any ideas?"

"Mmm. I've been thinking about that. You know, Ian, these last few weeks, especially with the role I had with the

Thomas Gainsborough painting… well, I found it all really exciting. Maybe we ought to consider reinvesting some of the money on more paintings."

Is this really Emma talking!? thought Ian. He then answered, "Well, yes, but it takes some time to find really good quality paintings that are either undiscovered or underpriced."

"Mmm. I've been thinking about that too."

My, you have been thinking a lot lately, thought Ian,

Emma continued. "Maybe it's time for us both to work at it full time!"

"You're serious, aren't you?" queried Ian. He was certainly seeing Emma in a new light.

"Of course, I'm serious!" said Emma, with a slightly raised tone in her voice.

Chapter 49

Viktor was finally paying his debt to Penny. He had to accept that she had got Ian's reserve price for the Gainsborough painting, spot on. However, he did wonder if she had benefited from some 'insider information'! After all, Ian was her boss and she'd put the auction catalogue together!

They were enjoying a lovely meal at their favourite restaurant in Covent Garden. Viktor had taken Penny's email to heart and insisted on the expensive menu. This evening, he did not mind the expense – he had an ulterior motive – a plan for the end of the evening!

"Seeing as I'm paying for this lovely meal that we've just eaten," said Viktor, after they had finished their dessert course. He picked up his glass of wine. "I think we ought to have a toast… a toast to, Ian."

Penny stared at Viktor with a surprised look on her face. Why, she wondered, did he specifically want to make a toast to Ian… and also why at this particular moment? "Okay. You've lost me. Why Ian?"

"Well, my dear, it is very simple."

Oh it is, is it, thought Penny. You've had too much to drink!

"Of course," continued Viktor. "Without Ian, where would we be?"

Penny was still none the wiser and just shrugged her shoulders.

"Penny, we are talking about your boss here! Ian Caxton!"

"Viktor, you have had too much to drink!"

"Penny, I promise you I've not!"

"Well it sounds like it to me."

"Penny, you are spoiling my big build up!"

"To what!?"

"Okay. What I was trying to say is… Ian has been a massive factor in my life… in yours too… but to a lesser extent. He pushed me. He challenged me. He believed in me. He saw in me that there was more to my career than just a safe role at Sotheby's. He was the one who persuaded Bob Taylor to take me on! He is the one person in my life that thought I could really achieve something. My parents wanted me to have a solid, boring and safe career. I am their 'only child' and they want to protect me from what… adventure, ambition, challenges, the bogey man?"

"Vic, you're rambling."

"No, I'm not, Penny. Just wait and listen, please. Ian drew the two of us together. We worked well together and he helped us build up a super working relationship and, more importantly, a great friendship. And now? Our relationship… well to me, anyway, it's the best thing that has ever happened to me!"

Penny just looked at Viktor with wide eyes and wondered what he was going to say next! His voice was obviously being heard by the people on the neighbouring tables.

Viktor put his hand in his jacket pocket. "Penny, I love you so much. Would you do me the most wonderful honour of becoming my wife?" Viktor pulled out of his pocket a small blue box.

From the small group of people sitting at the next table there was a lovely cheer.

Penny was totally embarrassed, but she gently took the small box from Viktor's hand and slowly opened the lid. Inside was a lovely diamond cluster and emerald engagement ring.

Her eyes moved from the ring and looked up and into her favourite person's face and looked deep into his green eyes. She smiled and then looked back at the ring. She lifted the ring out of the box and inserted it onto the third finger of her left hand. She then held her hand up to inspect the ring much better. Still the big smile, but a tear appeared in her left eye. "Vic, you are the best thing that has happened to me, too. I love you with all my heart. Yes, I would love to become your wife!"

More loud cheers came from the people sitting at the neighbouring tables. Both Viktor and Penny were both embarrassed now! However, this did not stop them both from standing up, leaning across the table and giving each other a deep and heartfelt kiss. More cheers and applause from the fellow diners! Even two of the waitresses had stopped their work and applauded.

Next morning, Penny was in the office about two minutes before Ian arrived. When her boss entered Penny's office area, she was sitting at her desk.

"Good morning," said Ian, as he approached the side of Penny's desk.

Penny did not respond but just held her left hand high in the air and wiggled her fingers. She had a large smile on her face.

What's all this? thought Ian, but when he saw Penny wiggling her fingers, he also spotted the extra piece of jewellery.

"Hey! So, Vic's finally popped the question. Let me see."

Penny stood up and pushed her left hand towards him.

Ian gently took hold of Penny's hand to inspect the ring.

"Wow. The boy's got good taste. Congratulations." Ian kissed his PA on both cheeks. That was a first, he thought! "Tell Vic from me that he is a very lucky man. A very lucky man indeed!"

"It's all thanks to you, Ian."

"Me!? What have I done?"

"Well that's what Vic said last night," said Penny, by way of her explanation. "We even toasted our drinks to you!"

"I've done nothing. Just brought two very special people together, that's all."

"So do I call you Cupid from now on?"

"Miss Harmer, soon to be Mrs Kuznetsov," Ian said sternly. "We have work to do!"

Ian marched towards his office and Penny just laughed out loud.

When Ian arrived at his desk he whispered under his breath, "Well done, Vic… and about time too!"

Chapter 50

When Ian arrived home that evening he told Emma about Viktor's and Penny's engagement.

"Well that's nice," she replied. "They looked very fond of each other when they came here for dinner a few weeks ago."

"Mmm, I'm pleased for both of them."

"Have you thought any more about what I was talking about last evening?"

"You mean going into business together?"

"Yes."

"I thought about it last night and again this morning whilst I was travelling into the office. I think it has a lot of merit…"

"But!"

"No, no buts. It's all a matter of timing. I want to leave Sotheby's at the right time. They do not deserve to be dropped in it. I'm also training Penny up to replace me as head of the department. She will not get my directorship, but she is quite capable of running the department. Also I think that you need to gain more experience, especially understanding what constitutes a 'good deal', when we buy paintings. I think we ought to go forward on a part-time basis… just for the time being."

"A few weeks ago you were seriously fed up at Sotheby's."

"I know. It was a bad day. But nothing has changed. I still want to try something more testing, more adventurous. But the timing has to be right. I owe it to Sotheby's so I want to leave when it is best for both parties."

"I see," said Emma. She was a little disappointed, but not dismayed. At least Ian still sounded positive and, of course, it didn't stop her from exploring the art world more on her own. Mmm, she thought, it would also be extra special if I could surprise Ian with a bargain, or two, achieved solely by my own efforts.

"Have a look at the paintings that are traded by the partnership. They will give you some ideas on valuations and also what artists and pictures are popular at the moment." Ian decided now would be the ideal time for Emma to be more directly involved in the partnership.

"Do you want me to be more involved with the partnership business?"

"Yes, of course. Everything is now working really well. I'll show you how the system works at the weekend."

Oscar was making his usual short walk back to his villa. He'd just finished his regular early morning swim in the Caribbean Sea. It was just after 7.15am. He enjoyed getting up early in Antigua. It was always warm and it rarely rained at this time of day. He was less keen on the middle of the day, because the direct sunshine was much stronger and often the humidity was much higher. He also thought his brain worked better after his early morning swim. Problems from the previous day seemed much easier to sort out over breakfast. Now he was pondering on a particular painting that Gladstone had suggested might be ideal for the partnership. Gladstone had told him that the asking price was far too high for his own means. However, the artist in question was a new one to Oscar, so he hoped it was not going to be another Whistler situation! More research was needed, a new job for this morning.

"Hi, Oscar, man." It was Garfield, his next door neighbour calling him from over their joint boundary fence.

The voice immediately interrupted Oscar's thinking. He looked up and spotted where the voice was coming from. "Hi, Garfield, are you off to work?" Oscar knew Garfield was a partner with a small legal firm based in the financial area of St. John's. He mainly dealt with commercial contracts and related issues.

"In a few minutes," replied Garfield. "Fancy popping round for a drink tonight? Some of the guys are coming over. Ella's visiting her mother's. I'll be doing a barbeque."

Ella seems to be at her mother's quite often, thought Oscar. "That would be great. Yes, thanks. What time?"

"About 7.30. Is that okay?"

"Yes, that's great, Garfield. I'll be there. I'll bring some beers."

"See you later, man," said Garfield and disappeared.

Oscar walked across the patio towards his villa. Might be a good evening, he thought. He went into his home, showered and changed into dry shorts and a clean tee-shirt. He made himself a bowl of cereal to which he added milk and some chopped fruit. He carried his breakfast outside and onto the patio area. The sun had just risen above the horizon. Mmm, he thought, sitting down on his lounger with his food, it's going to be another warm day. Lovely!

Just after 7.20 that evening, Oscar could hear some chattering and laughing coming from Garfield's side of the fence. Time to join the party, he decided.

He collected the two six packs of lager from his fridge and walked the short distance to Garfield's property. He made his way straight round to the back of the villa, where he immediately met Frank Hall. Frank was the man he had sold some Boscoe Holder paintings to several months ago.

"Hi, Oscar, how's things, man?" Frank held out his hand and they both shook hands.

"Yes, good thanks, Frank. You busy at the hospital?" Oscar remembered Frank was a consultant surgeon at the main hospital in St John's.

"Yep. People still getting themselves ill!" replied Frank and both men laughed.

"Hey, Oscar, come on in." It was Garfield who had joined them. "Let me take those tins before you drop them!" Another sound of laughter erupted from a group standing near the barbeque. "Your buddy Gladstone, he's over there."

Oscar looked across to where Garfield had pointed. He guessed there were about 10 men standing around, chatting in two groups.

Oscar and Frank walked across to join one of the groups. This group consisted of four men, each of them slightly hunched over and with their backs to Oscar and Frank. A committee, it seemed to Oscar, who were trying to get the barbeque started!

Frank raised his voice deliberately. "Hey, Oscar, how many men does it take to get a barbeque going?"

"More than four, by the look of this lot!" replied Oscar.

Another blast of laughter.

"Do you know any of these guys, Oscar?"

"I know Gladstone, and of course Roy, from the cricket match day," replied Oscar, nodding to them. He was pleased with himself that he had been able to remember Roy's name from just that one meeting. Oscar was then introduced to the two new faces.

Later that evening the barbeque food had been eaten and nearly all the cans of beer had been consumed. It was still a warm and balmy evening, but a refreshing breeze was beginning to blow. Gladstone and Oscar had not really had an opportunity to chat earlier in the evening, but they now stood together on the patio. Oscar with his fourth, or was it his fifth, lager, but Gladstone was holding a glass of tonic water.

"I didn't know you knew this group," said Oscar.

"I don't really. Last minute thing. Charlie, who you met earlier, is my neighbour and I owe him a few favours. He asked me if I would take him to this party. So here I am."

"I was wondering why you were not drinking. You could have stayed at my place this evening."

"Another time, Oscar, but thanks. I've still got to get Charlie home."

"Must go to the boys room, Gladstone, be back in a few minutes." Gladstone nodded and Oscar went in the direction of the villa's downstairs toilet.

Gladstone watched the party and listened to the loud discussions and laughter. One of the group decided to walk over to join Gladstone.

"So, Gladstone, man, what do you do for a living?" asked the man. Gladstone remembered he was one of the men in his group when they'd earlier been trying to start the barbeque. He also remembered that the man had introduced himself as Sheldon Murray.

"I'm in the art world, Sheldon. Buying and selling paintings mainly. What do you do?"

"Nothing as interesting as you. I work with Garfield, I'm one of his legal partners."

"Okay, so what area do you specialise in?"

"I mainly deal with personal issues, divorces mainly. Our partnership is based in St John's, but I work all over Antigua and occasionally in Barbuda," said Sheldon. "Tell me, do you specialise with any particular artists?"

"No, not specific artists, but the main period I get

involved in is with paintings from about the last 200–250 years. Occasionally older, but not very often."

"Do you do valuations as well?"

"Yes, why? Have you got some pictures you want to be valued?"

"Not me personally." Sheldon had now reduced the volume of his voice to a whisper. "But I have a client, he's currently going through a messy divorce and is looking for someone to give him some low valuations. Is that something you could do, Gladstone?"

Chapter 51

Bob and Zoe had adapted well to the new system of sharing their time during the gallery's opening hours. Zoe mainly picked up the middle period of the day, between school runs. Bob covered the other periods. The exception was when one of Zoe's clients either wanted an early morning or a late afternoon appointment. Then it would be Bob's turn to drop off, or collect, the children from school. He didn't mind, because he could often link this in with a delivery, or a visit to one of his customers. Today was one of those days. Zoe was finalising the sale of an up and coming French artist's painting to Mr Willoughby, a rich British expat, who, now close to retirement, was spending more of his year in his villa, situated on the French coast, just south of the Monaco border.

"Are you happy with this painting, Mr Willoughby?" asked Zoe, eager to complete the deal.

Mr Willoughby still looked at the picture and rubbed his chin with his right hand. "I'm a bit worried if it's, err… a bit too blue."

"No, I don't think so. It's a beautiful Mediterranean sea blue. Refreshing and cool for our type of climate. It's also typical of this up and coming artist's unique style. I'm very positive it will be a good investment."

"As you know, my wife, she really does like it. It's a bit modern for me though." Mr Willoughby still pondered on his final decision.

"Was your wife expecting you to be taking this picture home with you?" Zoe was now trying to sow a possible problem in Mr Willoughby's mind if he decided to go home empty handed.

Mr Willoughby considered this complication and the possible repercussions. He rubbed his chin again. "Mmm, okay. Yes, I'll take it." He was still not convinced but, heck, better to keep the little wife happy.

"Good decision. Now do you want to take the painting with you or would you prefer it to be delivered?"

Another decision! "Better deliver it, I think. Yes, delivery, please. I've got a few other things to do before I go home. When can it be delivered?"

"Well let's go over to the desk and we can sort out payment and I can then look at my diary." said Zoe. She started to walk back towards the desk with a satisfied grin on her face.

It was ten days after Sheldon's proposal to Gladstone, at the barbeque evening, that Sheldon was now driving Gladstone in his sports car along the sweeping driveway on one of the largest properties on the island. Sheldon had earlier spoken to Gladstone about his client in general terms. He'd given him a brief outline of the client's current marital position and had also mentioned that the client also enjoyed a celebrity status. However, it was not until they were only a few minutes away from the property that Sheldon revealed to Gladstone the client's name. Gladstone was suddenly shocked and very nervous about the forthcoming meeting. The client was, after all, one of Gladstone's all time heroes!

Gladstone leaned forward and peered through the car's

windscreen. Gradually the large whitewashed mansion came into view. Wow, he thought, there is a lot of money here!

Sheldon parked his car at the end of the driveway, about ten metres from the front door. Both men got out of the car and Gladstone shielded his eyes from the sun. He looked straight across to the manicured garden, noticing the large lawn slowly dropping away creating an infinity view with the Caribbean Sea. Gladstone just stood and stared. He thought the view was seriously amazing!

"Pretty special, isn't it?" said Sheldon, reading Gladstone's mind.

"Magnificent. Fabulous property and location," replied Gladstone. He was trying to think if he had ever seen a better view.

"Good afternoon, gentlemen," said a male voice from behind them.

Both men immediately turned and Gladstone instantly recognised the famous Jamaican reggae singer, Clancy Hobbie. Retired for about 15 years, Clancy's peak performing period was in the late 1970s and early 1980s. He was often compared with the likes of Bob Marley and other similar performers of his day. Now in his early 70s, Gladstone thought he was still looking pretty fit for his age. The long black dreadlocks had now gone and what was left of his hair had been clipped quite short. It also had a few grey streaks. Gladstone was still impressed though. He saw that Clancy had still largely kept his body shape and certainly looked at least 10 years younger.

"Hello, Clancy, man," said Sheldon. Clancy joined the two men and shook hands with Sheldon. "I would like to introduce you to Gladstone Clive," continued Sheldon. "He's the specialist art dealer, I told you about. He's going to value your collection."

Clancy released Sheldon's hand and held out his large hand towards Gladstone. "Pleased to meet you, Gladstone. Know your art do you, man?" The two men shook hands and Clancy gave him one of his big smiles, showing he still had a fine set of original teeth.

"Pleased to meet you, Mr Hobbie. I've still got some of your records," blurted Gladstone, part embarrassed and part star struck.

"That's nice, man. A person with good taste. Rare nowadays!" Clancy laughed. "Come on in, I've got some cold drinks. No alcohol, I'm 'fraid. Gave that up… must be what… twenty years ago? Time flies when you're sober!" Clancy laughed again and Gladstone just grinned in awe.

The three men walked into the house. Gladstone was immediately struck by the number of gold and platinum framed discs hanging on the hallway wall. He slowed down to read the titles of each record. When he'd finally stopped reading his two colleagues had disappeared, but he eventually caught up with them when he heard their chatter from the kitchen. As Gladstone walked into the room he was amazed by its size. He thought it was probably bigger than all of his own downstairs property! He walked across to join the other two men standing next to the large kitchen island.

Clancy asked, "I've got some fresh orange juice, lemonade or pineapple. What does everyone want?"

Gladstone could not believe his ears. This was a guy that once prided himself that he could perform before tens of thousands of adoring fans having just consumed a bottle of rum! "Er, orange juice would be fine. Thanks."

As Clancy poured three drinks and topped them up with ice, he started to speak. "Millie's not here, not been here for 'bout a month now, so we can chat freely. Gladstone, I need your help, man. This gold digger wants to take me for every penny she can. We've been married for only five years and she's found a younger stud, some 'toy boy' in St John's. Well, good luck to him, but she's not taking all my money. I worked damn hard for many years before I even knew that bitch. I bought most of my paintings back in the 1980s and 90s... long time before she came along. I don't want to lose them, man. We gotta sort her!"

Gladstone looked at Sheldon and waited for him to speak first.

"Okay, Clancy, we've talked about all this and, as I've said before, she won't get everything, but you need to accept she will get quite a bit. Now, Gladstone here, he is going to value your collection and we'll then see where we are. Okay?"

"Okay. Sorry, Gladstone, man, but she's a right sh…"

"Come on, man, calm down," interrupted Sheldon. "Time to show Gladstone your painting collection. Some respect for our guest!" Sheldon was deliberately trying to calm Clancy down. Not an easy task at the best of times!

Over the next 90 minutes, Gladstone was shown a collection of 22 paintings spread around the villa. He took numerous photographs and made copious amounts of notes. In his mind he estimated that just the lowest value picture was probably worth at least US$1 million!

After the tour the three men returned to the kitchen and to the remains of their drinks on the island. Clancy offered top ups and they both said yes.

"Right then, Gladstone," said Clancy, once all the drinks had been refreshed. "What's the score, man?" Clancy was eager to get an understanding of the situation.

"Well, I need to do some investigations, but…" Gladstone looked at his notes and did a quick mental calculation. "Your collection is probably worth at least US$70 million, maybe more!"

Clancy shook his head, looked at Gladstone and then to

Sheldon. "Man, that's about three, maybe four times, more than what I paid for them."

"As I say, I would need to do some investigations first. It could be less… but I very much doubt it."

"Could you do a valuation for about 40 million?" asked Clancy, who was looking at Sheldon as he asked the question. Sheldon remained still and quiet.

"As I say, I still need to do some more investigations," replied Gladstone. He could now feel his forehead beginning to perspire. He drank the last drops of his orange juice.

"Okay, Gladstone, you do your investigations, but don't be too long eh, man?"

The three men walked across the kitchen and into the hallway. Sheldon was in the lead and opened the front door. Both he and Gladstone stepped out and into the hot sunshine. Clancy stood in the shade inside the doorway. The two visitors shook his hand.

"We'll be in touch, soon, Clancy," said Sheldon, as he and Gladstone stopped on the middle step.

"Okay. Thanks, guys. Sorry, Gladstone if I was a bit rough. Not personal, man. You know, thinking about it, it would be much cheaper just to have that bitch rubbed out!"

"I'll pretend I never heard that, Clancy," said Sheldon. He looked at Gladstone. "He's always saying things like that, some day he'll say it in front of the wrong person."

Gladstone stared at Clancy… and just wondered!

Chapter 52

Emma was spending more and more of her time looking on the internet and reading Ian's books about artists and the art world. The more she delved into the history of paintings, artist biographies and the buying and selling of pictures, the more she began to understand the interrelationship between all these three main factors. The art market, she decided, was definitely similar to share dealing, stamp collecting or whatever. There was still the personal judgement, a gamble and hopefully a good long term investment! There were lots of people trading paintings, but it was usually only the final link in the chain, the wealthy customer, who was often the only person who had a serious passion for the quality of art. The rest were in it for the money!

Gradually, Emma also realised that as well as being an exciting financial challenge, the art market was also notoriously full of crooks, fraudsters and con artists! A world where 'caveat emptor', 'let the buyer beware', was a major factor and a big consideration, when looking at any possible art purchase. The importance of 'real' and traceable provenance was now more crucial than ever. Nevertheless, and despite knowing more than ever that experience was so important, she still intended to demonstrate to Ian that she was fully committed and was learning fast. Her aim was to unearth her first small 'find'… and to accomplish it as soon as possible!

Over the next few weeks Emma visited small antique shops in the hope of discovering a forgotten Constable or a hidden Monet. However, she soon realised that these rarely, if ever, really existed. So instead, on the bi-weekly Sunday morning, she got up very early and was out of the house before Ian and Robert had stirred. She had heard that, sometimes, a surprise could be found at the local Sunday morning car boot sales.

This particular Sunday, Emma drove her car into a large green field about 20 miles away from her home. She was so early that a number of stallholders were still unpacking their vehicles. Sunrise was still probably 30 minutes away.

She wandered between the stalls, trying to disguise her main aim, by picking up odd objects that caught her eye. At the same time she kept a keen lookout for any watercolour or oil painting that was not either a print or a reproduction.

When the car park began to fill up with other hopeful bargain hunters, that was usually her cue to leave and return back home. Sometimes she would arrive back home even before Robert was up and asking for his breakfast.

Today, however, was different, she had spotted a small watercolour painting which really interested her. The painting had very strong colours showing a sunset in the background and a rough, scrub-like, arid country scene in the foreground. It reminded Emma of Turner's type of work, especially the vibrant colours in the moody sky. When she saw the stallholder talking to a lady about a small brass statue of a horse, she picked up the painting and took a much closer look. She didn't recognise the signature, but on the back a small, old note said '*Sunset nearby the Grand Canyon*' and on a separate more modern sticker was written the price of £30. Emma looked again at the painting. She liked it a lot and for £30, well the frame was probably worth about that amount on its own!

The stallholder had now sold the brass horse and walked across to speak to Emma. "Nice picture isn't it?" he said, without adding any further detail.

"Is this your best price?" asked Emma. She had learnt that everyone negotiated on the advertised price at car boot sales.

The stallholder looked at the price on the back. "For you, lady, £25, but I can't go any lower than that."

Emma looked at the picture again. "Okay, I'll take it," she said. The stallholder wrapped the painting in two sheets of old newspaper. Emma had removed a white plastic bag from her handbag and the £25 from her purse. She handed over the money and slipped her parcel into the plastic bag.

"Thank you," said Emma. She then walked away and back to her car. She was back home just as Ian was making a cup of tea. There was no sign of Robert.

In Antigua, Gladstone had completed his investigations into the Clancy Hobbie art collection. He had also asked Oscar for his opinion. They were now sitting at their regular evening bar and were sipping their lagers and discussing the Hobbie painting collection.

"So, Oscar, what do you think, man?" asked Gladstone. He was seriously worried that maybe this challenge was a step too far.

"Mighty good collection. The guy is obviously pretty wealthy and has good taste," replied Oscar.

Gladstone had already explained the background to Clancy's musical career. Oscar had to admit he had never heard of Clancy. He also told Gladstone that reggae had never been the hot music in Hong Kong!

"Tricky this one," said Oscar, shaking his head.

"Valuations and divorces are always bad bedfellows! Difficult. One thing's certain, you are never going to please both parties."

"Well, I don't know Clancy's missus. She's certainly not my concern. If I value the collection at US$40 million, as Clancy wants me to do, then I'm putting my reputation at risk. His wife is bound to appoint other valuers and they would just shoot me down in flames! I reckon the collection has got to be nearer US$75 million. Probably more at a New York, or London auction."

"So have you told these figures to his legal rep? What's his name, Sheldon?"

"Sheldon Murray," interrupted Gladstone. "No, not yet. Wanted to get your thoughts first."

"Me!? Well to be honest, I don't think I would have wanted to be involved from the beginning! Why did you say you would value the collection at well below market price?"

"I didn't. Sheldon just asked me if I would consider it. Events then dragged me along. Clancy was a hero of mine in my teens and early twenties. Once Sheldon mentioned his name, I just wanted to meet the guy and try to help, if I could. I didn't make any promises."

"Okay, then, so why not just tell them the truth? The guy is so rich anyway. A few million here or there is not going to make him destitute."

"There's also another angle to this one that I've not told you about, so far. Not really sure if I should do so now."

"Hey, come on, Gladstone. You can't say that now and then keep quiet. Let me get us some more drinks and you can think about it."

Oscar rose to his feet, picked up the two empty glasses and headed towards the bar. A few minutes later he returned to their table, but Gladstone wasn't there.

Oscar sat down and wondered where his colleague had

gone. Had he decided not to face Oscar with this extra information after all? He sipped his own drink and looked around the bar area. A minute later Gladstone re-appeared and sat down.

"Thought you had run out on me," said Oscar, pushing the second glass of lager across to his colleague.

"Needed a pee, man! Thanks for the drink." Gladstone picked up his glass and took a large draught of his lager. He then put the glass back on the table and looked at Oscar.

"Well? Are you going to tell me?" said Oscar, now becoming annoyed.

"It's difficult, once you know… well you'll know!"

"What's that supposed to mean?"

"Alright, I'll tell you, but you must keep it to yourself. Promise?"

"I can't promise something I don't know anything about!"

"It's about Clancy. When Sheldon and I were leaving Clancy's house, the last thing he said was that it would be much cheaper to 'have the bitch just rubbed out'! He was talking about his wife."

"Men in his situation can often say things like that. Divorce is, well, messy. People's thinking gets mixed up. Things are said in the heat of the moment… get distorted."

"Mmm, I know. But I could see it in his eyes, Oscar, this man really meant it."

"Okay, so what's that got to do with you?"

Gladstone looked all around him. Satisfied nobody else was within hearing distance he leaned forward towards Oscar and whispered, "It would get me out of a tricky situation with him if she was 'rubbed out'… plus." Gladstone looked around him again. Oscar leaned closer now to listen. "I know someone who would do it for only US$2 million!!

Chapter 53

The partnership had now been established for just over a year and Ian was in his home office calculating the income, outgoings and the resulting profit for the year. As he'd kept a close eye on all the ongoing activity, his current task was made a lot easier and it was all quickly finalised. He leaned back in his chair and a small smile appeared on his face. Yes, he was very happy with the figures and now hoped the partners would be similarly pleased with the results.

Ian attached his spreadsheet to a short report and sent them by email to each of the partners. He hoped none of them would have any grumbles about going forward together for at least another 12 months and suggested a further video conference in two weeks time.

"Ian?" It was Emma calling him. "Have you got a minute?"

"Yes," replied Ian. "I've nearly finished here. Where are you?" He pressed the 'send' button on his email and switched off the computer.

"In the guest bedroom," replied Emma, from upstairs.

Ian left the home office and walked upstairs. Robert had now appeared from his bedroom to see what was going on. Both Ian and Robert walked into the guest bedroom together.

"Well, what do you think?" asked Emma.

Ian immediately spotted the new addition to the pictures on the far wall. He walked over to have a closer look. Robert decided there was nothing of interest for him, so he departed back to his bedroom.

"It could do with a good clean," said Ian, rubbing his finger gently on the glass. "But it looks like a watercolour painting by Thomas Moran. I've not seen one of his pictures for ages. Where did you get it?"

"Last Sunday, at the car boot sale!"

"You're kidding!" Ian looked closer. "It's probably an original... but it could be a good copy though. How much did you pay?"

"£25."

"What? Wow. If it is a real Moran, it's going to be worth maybe tens of thousands of pounds! Well done. What made you decide to buy it?"

"I thought it looked like an original painting and... well, I just liked it!"

"Well done you. What are you going to do with it now?"

"I was hoping you would suggest something."

Ian laughed. "Okay. As I say, it needs a good clean and needs to be checked out properly for authenticity... and re-framed."

"I like the frame, I thought it goes well with the painting."

"No, no. I wasn't suggesting we change the actual frame, we'll keep the frame. The picture has slipped on the right hand side, so it needs to be adjusted and presented properly. There might also be some additional information hidden inside. Leave it for now, I'll have a good look at the weekend. Anyway, well done you."

Emma smiled back at Ian. That's what she wanted to hear, 'well done you'! Now she just hoped it would turn out to be an original Moran. "So who is, or was, Thomas Moran?" asked Emma.

"Have a look on the internet for his full details, but from what I can remember, he was born in England but his parents took him and his brother to America when he was quite young. As an adult he moved to New York and became part of an art movement, 'Hudson river' or some such name. Can't remember exactly. However, as you can see here, many of his paintings featured western American country scenes, particularly around the Grand Canyon and the Rocky Mountains. I think two of his Yellowstone paintings were bought by the US government and were part instrumental in Yellowstone becoming a National Park. If this picture is a real Moran, then it would have been painted at about the end of the 19th century, or maybe, the beginning of the 20th."

"Thank you," said Emma. She had a big smile on her face. "I'll look him up and do some more investigations."

One week later Ian had received replies from all of the partners. With the exception of Sergei, they all agreed to continue for at least another twelve months. Sergei said he wanted to take all his allocation of profits, but would be passing his investment share of the partnership onto Viktor. Ian was pleased that Sergei was now stepping aside. Whilst he hadn't played any part in the art trading activity, Ian was still suspicious of Sergei's motives. Indeed he even wondered about any potential threat from any of Sergei's Russian connections.

All the remaining partners duly linked into the video conference call. Ian summarised the number of trades the group had been involved in and reiterated the return on each partner's investment. In total the Swiss account now held the equivalent of £84 million, a little less than Ian's plans to 'double your investment in the first year', but this did not take account of two paintings recently purchased for a total of £17 million. Predictions from Yuki and May Ling were that they were likely to achieve sales totalling £22 million. If these prices were achieved, then the overall profit would increase by another £5 million and the bank balance, when the £22 million was added, would show £106 million. Just above Ian's target!

After much healthy discussion it was finally agreed that each partner would take 15% of their profit as cash and the balance would go forward and be re-invested to boost the fund for the new business year. A couple of suggestions were also made, discussed and eventually agreed. One was to improve the communication channels more directly between the partners, but otherwise everybody seemed happy and enthusiastic about the future of the partnership.

When the meeting finally ended, Ian switched off his computer and looked at Emma. She'd been sitting at his side, but out of view of the other partners.

"So, what did you think?" asked Ian.

"It looks as though you've established an excellent business. Very profitable and all the partners seem to be very happy. The only thing I am questioning is why didn't you tell me about the partnership when it was first set up?"

Although Ian had explained, some months ago, the workings of the partnership, he was, in Emma's mind, still reticent to explain fully why he had not told her about the establishment of the partnership from the beginning.

"It was a big risk, Emma. The biggest investment that I've made in my life," explained Ian. "I thought the idea would work, but I wanted to make sure it was doing so before involving you. I thought you might worry and maybe have reservations. I wanted to concentrate on making it all work out successfully first."

"You didn't trust me!"

"I never said that! Of course I trust you. It's, well… it's what I just said."

"Mmm. Well next time I would like to be involved, or at least be aware, when you're investing our millions of pounds."

"Okay, point taken, but I hope you can see my dilemma? Anyway, most of the investment was from my Swiss bank account and the money I'd made from the Tobar collection."

"No, I don't really see your dilemma, but it's done now. Let's move on. I've found out some more information about this mysterious Thomas Moran painting."

"Oh great. Tell me more." Ian took a deep sigh of relief and tried to focus on what Emma was about to say.

Emma picked up her notebook and flicked through the pages until she came to the page she was looking for. "I've tried to find out more information about the history of this painting. There was a painting produced by Thomas Moran in 1898 which was entitled '*Sunset nearby the Grand Canyon*'. But during that period he also painted a number of watercolour and oil paintings around the Grand Canyon area, lots of which had similar titles. Many of these paintings subsequently changed hands over the years. The oil paintings have achieved prices between two to seventeen million dollars, whilst the watercolours have achieved much less." She flicked over a page and continued. "The provenance of our picture is a bit blurred. It looks as though it was originally sold privately early in the 20th century, but then it disappeared. Most of Moran's paintings have exchanged hands in America. I've checked both Christie's and Sotheby's American auction records of sale in New York, but our picture does not appear in either of them."

"Presumably you did not get the man's name at the car boot sale? Or, how he managed to be in possession of the picture in the first place?"

"No. At that moment I didn't think it would be such a valuable painting."

"No, of course. Anything else?"

"I would recognise the man again. Maybe I'll go to next week's car boot sale and see if I can spot him and get any extra information I can."

"Good idea. In the meantime, I'll try and find out if your picture really is an original painting by Mr Moran."

Chapter 54

Oscar was in Antigua's capital, St Johns, walking towards Redcliffe Quay, close to the waterfront promenade. He knew the area dated back over a hundred years and it contained many preserved buildings of a bygone age. It was an interesting part of the capital and when he had the opportunity he enjoyed wandering along the alleys and passageways. As he did so this morning he glanced into a number of the shop windows. When he was passing a television shop he noticed that the three televisions on display were all switched on and transmitting the same local news channel. He half gazed at one of the screens but then suddenly stopped dead and looked at the news item being shown. Whilst he couldn't hear the commentary, he was sure the typed sub-title had highlighted the name of Millie Hobbie! The television picture was now showing a photograph of a middle aged black woman. Quite attractive with long black curly hair. He briefly turned away and wondered why that name rang a bell. When he looked back at the television screen, unfortunately the programme had moved on to show the highlights of yesterday's cricket action from the Sir Vivian Richards Stadium.

Now why do I know that name? Oscar said to himself. I'm sure I've come across it before!

Oscar left the front of the television shop and continued his walk along the pavement. However, he couldn't get the woman's name out of his head. He was certain he hadn't recognised the woman's face, but the name? Why do I know that name, he wondered.

After a short distance Oscar stopped to cross the road at the junction with Market Street. Whilst he waited for the traffic lights to change he looked around him. Directly behind him, he noticed a newsagent shop. He wondered if any of the newspapers for sale would give him more information about the name Millie Hobbie. He stepped back and entered the shop where he picked up a copy of *The Daily Observer*. There on the front page headlines was the announcement, **'Millie Hobbie killed!'** He quickly paid the shopkeeper for the paper and walked out of the shop. Back in the sunshine he immediately started to read the article's details.

Millie Hobbie, the 47 year old wife of former reggae icon, Clancy Hobbie, was found dead this morning in her parked car. She had been shot three times in the head. Police suspect theft was the motive as her handbag had been discarded at the scene. However, her purse and all credit and debit cards were missing. Police are asking the public for...

Oscar stopped reading. The penny had dropped. Oh my God, he thought. Clancy Hobbie! That's the guy Gladstone went to see! What did Gladstone say? 'Clancy would like his wife rubbed out'! Wow! And what else did Gladstone say? Something about knowing someone who would do the job for US$2 million! My God, Gladstone, what the hell have you got yourself into... this time!?

On the following Saturday morning Ian was in his home office. He had removed the painting '*Sunset nearby the*

Grand Canyon' from the wall in the guest bedroom and was in the process of removing the picture from its frame. The thin wooden backing had been sealed to the frame by old tape so he was being extra careful whilst removing it. For added protection he'd already covered most of his desk with a large, thick cloth. He certainly didn't want to damage the frame, glass or, more importantly, the painting. Slowly the old tape was eased off. Sometimes a small strip came away easily, other times it refused to budge until he'd scratched the difficult pieces off with his fingernail. When all the tape was finally removed, he picked up a small pair of pliers to gently pull out the holding pins. Laying the painting face down on the cloth, he then slowly lifted off the wooden backing and placed it down on his right hand side. This activity immediately revealed many years of accumulated dust and general debris. However, it was a small piece of torn paper, stuck in one of the corners, that caught his eye. With a pair of small tweezers he gently eased the piece of paper out and laid it on the cloth next to the wooden backing. A further faded white sheet covering the rear of the picture was next to be removed. Then finally the actual picture was gently lifted clear of the frame. He turned the painting over and laid it on the cloth, face upwards. Carefully, he looked at the general landscape scene and blew a few specks of debris away using a can of compressed air.

With the use of his magnifying glass he closely inspected all the picture's details. The picture certainly looked old, he said to himself. Almost every brushstroke was then examined and the signature – *T Moran, 1898.* The distinctive capital M with a capital T inserted on top, was typical of the man's signature. Not, on its own, conclusive, but a good start, he thought. He put the magnifying glass back on the table and pondered on what he had found. Mmm, he thought, the picture is still in very good condition, for its age, so if it is a copy, then it is an excellent one!

Ian's next job was to ease the glass out from the frame. As well as being dirty, he could see it was quite thin and very delicate. He gently sprayed a small amount of liquid from a different can onto both sides of the pane and rubbed gently with a soft paper tissue. The glass was quickly cleaned of the decades of grime. The frame was then similarly cleaned.

After putting the frame back on the cloth he decided to look much closer at the torn piece of paper. With the use of his tweezers he then inspected the small fragment. It had obviously been torn from a larger sheet of paper as its edges were ripped. However, all it revealed was the handwritten words, *'dham. 1898.'*

After taking two photographs of the scrap of paper, he then pondered on what the rest of the word could be that ended in *'dham'*. Was it the end of someone's name? A place name? Part of a receipt?

Gently, he rebuilt the picture as it once was, including the scrap of old paper. He decided to only secure the backing with the original pins as he wanted a better expert to have a proper look first. Finally he cleared his desk and put the picture aside for Emma to see when she returned with Robert from her parents later that day.

When Emma arrived home, Ian explained what he'd been doing and also told her what he'd discovered. Emma was impressed. With the glass now clean it was much easier to see the details of the painting and, importantly, the 'possible' signature of Thomas Moran.

"So, what happens now?" she asked.

"I've made an appointment for Bill Milburn to see the painting on Monday. He's a very good judge on American artists' work. Are you going to see if you can spot the seller at the car boot sale tomorrow?"

"That was the plan. Why? Do you want to come with me?"

"No, I don't need to. I know you'll do just fine. I'll take Robert out somewhere."

The next morning Emma didn't get up at the crack of dawn. She assumed that if the man was going to be at the car boot sale again, he would still be there until at least lunchtime. She therefore arrived and parked her car at just after 11 o'clock. She wandered amongst the stalls looking for his friendly face. Unfortunately, he wasn't on the pitch he'd occupied two weeks ago. She carried on looking along the stalls, but already some of the stallholders were re-packing unsold stock and putting them back into their vehicles. She was just about to give up when she suddenly spotted him standing at the coffee trailer. He was chatting to the lady who was selling the coffee. Emma wandered over to speak to him.

"Hello, love, can I help you?" he said, using his cup of hot coffee as a hand warmer.

"I hope so," said Emma. "Two Sundays ago I bought a watercolour painting from you and I wondered if you remembered where you got it from?"

"Not from the police are you?" said the man, followed by a laugh.

"No, nothing like that. I bought the picture as a present for my husband and he asked me, something to do with provi... provenance, I think he said."

"Okay. Which picture are we talking about here? I've sold a few lately."

"It was the one showing a colourful sunset, possibly in America. You wanted £30 but we agreed to 25."

The man scratched his chin and thought. "Obviously I sold it too cheaply. Mmm, yes, now I remember. You were very early. I'd only just finished setting out my stall when another lady wanted a brass horse and then you bought the picture. It started a good day for me."

"And the picture?" asked Emma, hopefully.

"Oh, yes. Well that's easy. I bought a box full of odd paintings at our local market, about two months ago. I think there were about 18 or 20 pictures in total in the box. A man was just trying to get rid of his surplus stock. Not seen him at the market before. Hope that helps."

"Okay, thank you," said Emma. She tried to hide the disappointment in her voice.

"Must be worth more than £25 if you've come all the way back here again to ask me questions. Don't forget my 10% finders fee when you sell it!" said the man, laughing again.

Emma smiled and then waved as she walked away.

"What's that all about then, Tony?" asked the lady, leaning out of the serving hatch of the coffee trailer.

Tony turned back to face her. "Looks like I might have missed out on a valuable picture. Ah well, some you win, some you lose."

When Emma arrived back home, Ian was upstairs supervising Robert's change of clothes.

"What's going on?" said Emma, as she arrived at the doorway to Robert's bedroom.

"We went to the park and Robert decided he could jump a narrow section of the stream. Unfortunately, he just fell short and finished in the water... up to his knees! His wet clothes are laying in the bath at the moment. Anyway, I hope you had better luck than this rascal did?" asked Ian.

"No, not really." Emma then explained the conversation she'd had with the stallholder.

"Oh well, good try. It's not the end of the world. Hopefully I'll have a better result with Bill Milburn tomorrow at lunchtime."

Chapter 55

Bill Milburn was a partner in an art gallery located in the West End area of London. Although he sold all sorts of paintings, his personal specialisation was in the American art market and American artists. He had slowly built up a good name and reputation for this unique area of the market and Sotheby's had often used his talents and experience on a number of occasions.

Ian had telephoned him the previous week and Bill had told him that he was happy to look at Ian's painting. He suggested Ian brought it into the gallery at lunchtime, on Monday, as that was usually his quietest day.

Ian duly arrived at the gallery at 1.15pm and, after briefly chatting about the art market, Ian was now removing the framed painting from his bag. He then handed it over to Bill to examine it. Bill was in his early sixties and even he would admit, somewhat overweight! He was perspiring and it was not even a warm day!

"Okay," he said. "Let the dog see the rabbit." Bill placed the painting on the counter and pulled out of his coat top pocket a small eye loupe magnifying glass. He leaned closer to the picture and put the magnifying glass up close to his right eye. "Mmm, you've given the glass and frame a bit of a clean. Looks like Moran's style. Signature looks authentic.

Not sure about the dark foreground, though. Moran likes his colours, but… well, it's not a deal breaker. The title is a little odd, but so were the names of some of his other paintings. I guess you run out of ideas when you're painting a lot of similar places and scenes."

Ian stood quietly and let Bill ramble on.

"Can I take it out of the frame?"

"Of course," replied Ian. "It did have some old tape on the back but I decided not to replace it until you'd inspected it."

Bill nodded and pulled out a pair of pliers from his right hand pocket. He gently eased the pins away from the frame and lifted off the wooden backing. He then removed the slip of paper, the faded white sheet of paper and finally the painting itself. He put the painting face up on the counter and peared at it much closer. "You say there's no provenance."

"None that we have identified… yet. We think it was sold privately early in the 20th century, but it disappeared until Emma purchased it last week."

Bill continued to examine the painting closely. "I see." He continued to examine the painting with the magnifying glass and then the picture's reverse side.

"Tell you what, Ian, I'll give you £75,000 for it. I'll probably get a hundred, maybe a hundred and twenty grand with one of my clients. Could be more at auction."

Bill's offer caught Ian by surprise. He'd only popped in for Bill's opinion of the painting's authenticity.

"Even without the full provenance you are prepared to pay me £75,000?"

"Yes, that's right. You might get £100,000, or more, selling it yourself, but maybe not," said Bill, putting his magnifying glass back into his pocket. " Will you accept my cheque?"

Ian smiled. That would have been his strategy. "Okay, Bill, you have a deal."

As Ian exited the gallery he left Bill putting the picture back together. He had a cheque for £75,000 in his pocket and a big smile on his face.

When Ian returned home that evening, Emma was eager to know how the meeting with Bill Milburn had gone.

Ian looked at Emma and smiled as he reached inside his jacket pocket and pulled out the cheque. He held it out in front of Emma.

"What's this?" she said, before reading what was written on the cheque. Once she had noticed the name of the payee and registered the amount, her eyes and mouth suddenly became wide open. She was elated and threw her arms around Ian and gave him a big kiss.

Ian explained the details of the conversation he'd had with Bill at their meeting.

"Wow," said Emma, still elated.

"We might have got £100,000, based on Bill's estimation, but that's if we could find a buyer... and we would still incur other costs. Bill knows his market and my guess is he's already got a buyer lined up. Sometimes you take the easy option and avoid being greedy. In this instance we have a win-win situation and Bill remains a very useful colleague for the future."

"You know, Ian, I think we work pretty well together!"

In Antigua, Oscar had been trying desperately to make contact with Gladstone. However, Gladstone's mobile was not switched on and he was not replying to Oscar's emails. Oscar was afraid for his friend. He'd even visited Gladstone's small villa on the other side of St John's, but nobody answered the front door and the property looked deserted and had probably not been occupied for a few days.

The local reports, both in the newspapers and on television, were still giving daily updates on any developments in Millie Hobbie's death. The police were now aware that Clancy and Millie were in the process of divorcing and they had interviewed Clancy on three separate occasions. Clancy proved that he'd been staying in Jamaica for five days with some friends when the death occurred. It was the anniversary of his group's first number one hit record and he and the remaining members of the group had celebrated this achievement every year since 1978.

One news report stated that an inside source had suggested the police had come to the conclusion that the death was a deliberate act of murder and the theft of the purse, credit and debit cards, were just an elaborate cover to hide the real motivation.

Oscar followed the progress of the case closely and noted all the names of people the police had interviewed. However, no mention was made of them interviewing Gladstone Clive. Oscar was worried and wondered where Gladstone was and why he'd disappeared. He still continued to try to contact him on his mobile phone, but concluded the device was either still switched off or the battery must be completely dead.

It was two days later when Oscar received a brief text message. At the moment he heard his mobile phone ping, Oscar was sitting in Wesley's office, in the 'Shell gallery.' They were discussing a new local artist and Wesley was wondering if Oscar might know of any potential buyers in the UK or South East Asia. Oscar said he would make some enquiries.

After they had finished discussing this new artist, Oscar asked Wesley if he had seen Gladstone recently?

Wesley said he hadn't, but he'd heard that Gladstone was in Jamaica, something to do with visiting his son.

"His son!" exclaimed Oscar. "I didn't know he had a son?"

"Yeah. He must be about 30 now, I reckon. Gladstone's wife died, cancer I think it was, about 10 years ago. Roy, that's his son's name, well, he married a Jamaican girl and they settled near her parents' house. Somewhere near Montego Bay, I think. Why? Are you looking for him?"

"No, just curious. I haven't seen him for a while. Anyway, I must go. As I say, I will make some enquiries about this new artist for you."

As soon as Oscar had left the 'Shell gallery', he opened up his mobile phone and checked for incoming messages. To his surprise the earlier text message was from Gladstone.

Hi Oscar,
Am in Jamaica. Just become a grandfather!
See you soon.
Gladstone.

Well, well well, thought Oscar. A minute ago I was informed he was a father, now he's a grandfather! Doesn't sound like he's on the run! Maybe I'm worrying over nothing. Just a coincidence, probably. Hopefully!

Despite the innocent text from Gladstone, Oscar did think there were still a few questions he wanted answered!

Chapter 56

It was four days later when Gladstone arrived back in Antigua and the first person he telephoned from his home was Oscar. Oscar was pleased and relieved to finally hear from his colleague and they agreed to meet later that evening at their usual bar. Gladstone said he would then explain everything... and show him a photograph of his new grandchild.

Oscar arrived early for their meeting and bought the usual two pints of lager. The table where they normally sat was also conveniently free.

Gladstone arrived about five minutes later. The two men greeted each other as though they had not seen each other for many months, not just a few days. Oscar was anxious to know what Gladstone had been up to, but decided to ask about his family first.

"Well, Gladstone, I found out the other day that not only are you a father, but now a grandfather, too! You are a dark horse!"

"Being a black man I guess that comment is quite apt," said Gladstone, laughing.

Oscar smiled at Gladstone's joke.

Gladstone continued once he'd stopped laughing, "I guess we've never really talked much about the past, or families, have we? I don't know if you're married, or have any children, either."

"Okay, point taken. Anyway, congratulations." Gladstone smiled and nodded. "So is the baby a boy or a girl?" asked Oscar.

"Sophia is my granddaughter. She is my first grandchild and she is beautiful, man. Look, this is a photo of her with her mum and dad," said Gladstone, handing over a printed colour photograph to Oscar.

Oscar held the photograph and looked at it, "Yes, she is beautiful. You are a lucky man."

"I'm really pleased for Roy and Ellie. Ellie has had two miscarriages in the past, so this is a bit extra special."

"Well that's great, Gladstone." said Oscar, handing back the photograph. "Now then why didn't you answer my emails and texts?"

"I didn't know you were trying to contact me. I lost my phone somewhere on the way to the airport. My son, Roy, he telephoned me the previous day at home to say the baby was on the way and would I like to stay for a few days? I immediately agreed and rushed around getting a few things together, to put in a case. I was then able to get a flight to Montego Bay early the next morning. In all the rush I seemed to have lost my phone somewhere. It was definitely in my pocket when I left the house and when I climbed into the taxi, but when I arrived at the departure desk to collect my boarding pass and check in my case, it was missing. Could have dropped it in the taxi or whilst I was getting out. Either way it went missing. I decided I'd replace it once I got back to Antigua, or buy a new one in Jamaica. Too late to do anything about it at the airport"

"Have you heard about Millie Hobbie, Clancy's wife, being murdered?"

"Yeah. Spooky that, isn't it? Especially after what Clancy

said to me and Sheldon. It was on the TV news in Jamaica. Clancy is still a very big name in Jamaica. Apparently he's been in Jamaica for the last week or so."

Probably there to set up his alibi, thought Oscar. "You told me you knew someone who might kill her for two million dollars!"

"I know, but honestly, it had nothing to do with me. As you know, I was in Jamaica."

Oscar was not totally convinced with Gladstone's answer but decided not to challenge him any further. After all, it was none of his business. "The police have been interviewing Clancy and others. Have they contacted you?"

"No, man," replied Gladstone, in a raised voice. "Why would they do that!? I don't know anything. I only met Clancy the once, and I didn't shoot her. I'd never even met her!"

"I think the police are now sure that she was murdered to prevent her from benefiting from the impending divorce from Clancy. I'm sure they think Clancy paid someone to have her killed."

"Well, as I said, it's nothing to do with me. I just valued his paintings."

Oscar sipped his beer. Gladstone's story was plausible, but at the back of his mind, he just wondered if Gladstone was really telling him the whole truth. What was the full story about the US$2 million mercenary? Why did everybody seem to have, or need to have, an alibi in Jamaica? Maybe he would never get to find out the answer... the whole truth!

The next morning, Gladstone finally completed his valuations of all of Clancy Hobbie's 22 paintings. He had been delayed from finishing his work by the surprise telephone call from his son and the subsequent trip to Jamaica. Now his typed report was placed in an envelope and addressed to Clancy's home. A further copy and his invoice, he put in a separate envelope and addressed it to Sheldon Murray, at his office in St Johns. He then left his villa and walked the 200 metres to the main road, where his nearest postbox was located. He dropped both envelopes into the box... and took a deep breath. Gradually a small smile appeared on his face!

Walking back towards his home, Gladstone thought about Clancy and the valuations. No worries now, he thought, about needing to produce an undervalued report totalling $40 million. Hopefully anyone wanting to challenge my proper estimates, now totalling $82 million, will have a tougher job and my reputation will still be fully intact. Better keep well away from Clancy now though, at least until all this blows over. Never meet your heroes, someone once said... and they were right!

Over the following days less and less importance was being attached to Millie Hobbie's murder. Articles published in newspapers, or reports on the television news channel, were reduced and then they eventually disappeared altogether. There was just no new news now to report. The police appeared not to be interested in interviewing Gladstone, and Clancy was still a free man. However, Clancy was not yet fully exonerated of any involvement in the crime and still remained officially under suspicion. But, in reality, there was just no new evidence, or proof, to be found, and also there were no additional people coming forward with any extra information. One television programme in Jamaica even went as far as to present a defensive case for Clancy. They'd discovered old black and white footage of Clancy performing in his prime and also highlighted the huge amount of charitable work he'd been involved in since his retirement. Little was mentioned of Millie, and when it was, it was not very flattering and even inferred that Clancy was much better off without her!

Needless to say, this television programme sparked protests by some of the more radical women's groups. They shouted that Millie hadn't done anything wrong and her treatment was a typical example of how the authorities behaved, so biased and unfairly, towards their gender. Unfortunately for them, their actions only encouraged newspapers to divert their reporting from Millie, to highlighting stories of the protesting women's loud and disorderly behaviour!

Oscar watched some of the demonstrations on the television news channel. He really didn't understand why these women were making such an issue, after all, Millie was dead and all the shouting in the world wouldn't bring her back. Besides, wouldn't their efforts and wasted energy be better channelled into helping the police to bring the murderer to justice? Instead they were perversely tying up valuable police time with their protests!

Gladstone, meanwhile, largely ignored all the commotion. His mind was elsewhere. He had decided that he would spend some of his recently acquired extra income on some new baby clothes and bedroom furniture for his new granddaughter. He had discussed these details on the telephone with his daughter-in-law at length. Ella was pleased with Gladstone's gesture and suggested some items for him to buy. For the baby clothes she suggested that she would obtain them locally and Gladstone could pay the bill. Gladstone told her that he was very happy with this arrangement. He also decided that he would open a special savings account for Sophia. This money would be available for her to use when she attained the age of 21. He got out his cheque book and wrote out a cheque for US$200,000. He picked up the cheque, examined the written details and smiled. He would set up a new account tomorrow.

Chapter 57

Ian was travelling home on his regular commuter train. As he sat and stared out of the window he pondered on his future. He had become more and more certain that the time was now right to be handing in his letter of resignation. His annual performance review meeting with Michael Hopkins, was due in two days' time and he was weighing up all the pros and cons of waiting until that meeting. After all, he was aware that there were some internal changes currently being considered at Sotheby's and he wanted to be in control of any impact and any changes they would have on him and his department. He was certainly convinced that Penny was now ready to take over his role as head of the department. For the last nine months he had pushed her and she had responded positively to the extra responsibility and the added pressure and exposure of handling a number of issues and tasks directly for Michael Hopkins. He was also a lot happier now in his own mind that his resignation would not be the major issue for Sotheby's that it might have been just six months ago. Although he was now ready to leave Sotheby's, he still felt he owed them and they would not now be left in the lurch.

When the train slowly pulled into Esher station, Ian picked up his briefcase and headed towards the exit. The train finally stopped and very quickly the quiet platform was swarming with commuters heading home to their families and their usual evening routines. Tomorrow, Ian thought, it will all be the same again. As he walked along the platform he glanced at his fellow commuters. He recognised a few faces, but knew nothing about their lives, or even their names. This is a sad existence, he thought. Life has to be a lot better and more exciting than this. I wonder what most of these people would do if they had been given the same opportunity that I have? Jump for joy no doubt and grab it with both hands? Almost certainly. So why am I still messing about!?

Later that evening, Ian and Emma were sitting in the lounge drinking their mugs of coffee.

"I have a meeting with Michael in two days' time," announced Ian, placing his mug on the coffee table directly in front of him. Relaxing back on the sofa, he continued. "I think it's now time to hand in my notice."

Emma immediately placed her own mug down and looked straight at Ian. Somewhat surprised at his sudden outburst, she asked, "Are you sure? The timing is now right?"

"I don't think there will be a better time, Emma. A lot of things are coming together, and yes, the time is now right."

"Well, Ian, I'm with you," she said, excitedly. "You know I'll support whatever you decide."

"Thanks Emma. I really need your support. We've got a great future together... and lots of good things ahead of us."

Two days later at two minutes before 3 o'clock, Ian walked into his boss's outer office. He had his letter of resignation in the inside pocket of his jacket. Michael's PA smiled and said, "Good morning, Ian. Go straight in, Mr Hopkins is expecting you."

Ian smiled back, took a deep breath and walked towards Michael's door. He knocked and walked in, closing the door behind him. Michael stood up, walked around his desk and over to shake Ian's hand. He suggested they sit on the two easy chairs in the bay window, which had a view looking down onto Bond Street. Ian briefly glanced through the window. This was the view the Managing Director of Sotheby's had. He'd seen it many times before. More buildings and traffic on the road! Still not that impressive, he thought to himself.

The two men sat down. "Well, Ian," began Michael. "How's Emma and young Robert? I gather he's started school. Time flies, even more so, when you get to my age."

Ian smiled. "Emma's fine. Thanks for asking, Michael, and yes, Robert is in his introductory year, but he starts primary school next term."

"That's a nice age, an exciting time for you both. Take my word, it doesn't get any easier as they grow up!"

Again Ian smiled.

"Now, Ian. You know we have been looking at the possibility of some internal changes." Ian nodded. Here we go, he thought. "Well one of them includes me! At the end of this financial year I will be stepping down and taking early retirement. It's not official, just yet, so keep it to yourself. The chairman is the only other person who knows. It will be officially announced next Friday."

"Well that is a big surprise, Michael. I had no idea you wanted to retire."

"Business is becoming ever more demanding. It's a young man's game now, Ian. Besides, Jean keeps asking when I'm going to retire, 'before we are all too old to enjoy the benefits', she keeps saying. She's right though. Our children and grandchildren are spread out all around the world and we haven't really had the time to see them properly. So, anyway, I've chatted with the chairman and he's accepted my decision."

Ian nodded and wondered why he was being party to all this privileged information!

"The other point the chairman and I discussed was my successor. We've both come to the same conclusion, Ian. It should be you!"

This time Ian was seriously shocked. This is not how he envisaged this meeting would go at all! He'd still got his letter of resignation in his inside jacket pocket! What the hell was he going to do now!?

"Michael, are you sure?"

"You are the best and most suitable candidate, Ian. Yes, we are both sure. I don't expect your answer this minute. Speak to Emma. This is a big opportunity, Ian, but I make no bones about it, it is also very demanding on all of your talents… and especially your time… and on your family's life too. It's not for everyone, so you really need to get Emma's full support and commitment too. Without that, everything, and I do mean everything, could easily fail. Jean has had to put up with quite a lot over the last 12 years, but she has supported me all the way. I couldn't have done it without that level of support."

Ian just stared at Michael, he didn't know what to say. Had this offer put a whole new perspective on his and Emma's plans and lives going forward, he wondered?

"Look, Ian, I know this has all come as a surprise. Chat it over with Emma this evening and over the weekend. If you have any queries or questions, then both the chairman and I will be available to answer them. However, I do need your answer on Monday morning at 9 o'clock. The new MD should ideally be announced at the same time as my retirement announcement. As I said earlier, that's planned for next Friday. We can talk separately about the terms of your appointment if you decide you want to go ahead."

Michael rose to his feet. As far as he was concerned the meeting was now over. He held out his hand. Ian stood up and, by instinct, shook Michael's hand. However, his mind was wondering what's going on!? What do I now say to Emma!?

"Remember, Ian, except for Emma, this conversation is for your ears only."

Ian nodded. "Thank you, Michael. I've got a lot to think about." Ian immediately thought about the letter in his pocket again, but this development had suddenly put a whole new twist on his plans. Lots, yes LOTS, to think about… and to discuss with Emma!

When Ian arrived home Emma was preparing dinner. She heard him come in through the front door, so she turned down the dials on the hob and met him in the hallway.

"So how did Michael take your resignation?"

Ian put his briefcase down next to the home office door and walked over to where Emma was standing. He smiled and then kissed her gently on the lips. He put his hand into his inside jacket pocket and pulled out the still sealed envelope that contained his letter of resignation.

Emma looked from Ian's face to the letter and then back to Ian's face again. She was confused. "So you've not resigned!?"

"Emma, you are just not going to believe what happened today!"

Ian and Emma went into the kitchen and Ian started to explain the surprise conversation he'd had with his boss that afternoon. At the same time he poured two glasses of white wine.

When he'd finished Emma asked, "So does this now change your thinking about resigning… and our future plans?" There was definitely a disappointment in the tone of her voice.

Ian sipped his wine. He genuinely didn't know. Five years ago, both he and Emma would have been 'over the moon' with his promotion, but now... well, life had moved on. Emma had changed. He had changed, but he still wanted more freedom.

"We need to discuss it, Emma. I don't think I've changed my mind, but we need to spend some time this weekend and analyse all the pros and cons. This promotion was not part of our original discussions when we made our decision. Does it change our thinking now? Also, Michael wants my answer on Monday morning," replied Ian. He could not have sounded more unsure of himself if he tried!

Chapter 58

It was late Sunday afternoon and both Ian and Emma were still discussing the two options for their future. They had analysed all the pros and cons but were still not 100% certain of the correct choice to make. It really was a tough decision. They'd been able to spend all of the weekend concentrating solely on their discussions because Emma's parents had offered to take Robert to a special science exhibition in Oxford and he was staying at their house overnight. Ian and Emma were now waiting for them to bring Robert back home.

How things could seriously change in just a few days, Emma thought. She'd assumed that everything had been sorted and agreed about Ian's job at Sotheby's. Ian was going to resign and they would both concentrate on building up the art business and would also be able to spend more time using the apartment in Monaco. Now with the offer of the Managing Director's job at Sotheby's, all this now appeared to be in jeopardy.

Ian had explained to Emma the benefits of taking the Managing Director's role. A much improved and secure salary, larger eventual pension, more benefits and considerably improved personal status and prestige. Yet, despite all these attractions, Ian could not convince himself, never mind Emma, that this new option was the right decision. Indeed the serious warning words of Michael Hopkins continued to bounce around in his head. He could almost remember Michael's words exactly:

'This is a big opportunity, Ian, but I make no bones about it, it is also very demanding on all of your talents… and especially your time… and on your family's life too. It's not for everyone, so you really need to get Emma's full support and commitment too. Without that, everything, and I do mean everything, could easily fail.'

There it was again thought Ian, 'A Big Opportunity'! The very same words that Andrei had quoted all those years back. <u>Two</u> big opportunities now! People keep quoting it to him, telling him, advising him, giving him the big opportunity! It was all beginning to drive him mad with frustration! But of course, when he'd finally calmed down, he knew that without his involvement with Andrei, he would not now have the extra money in the Swiss bank account, the apartment in Monaco and the 10 years guaranteed annuity income that Andrei had provided. This, he also knew, was a very generous gesture by Andrei. It would easily cover, and more, the costs of owning and running the apartment. Then there was the extra money from his private art sales and the success of the partnership. Was he now prepared to throw all this hard work away? Hadn't he put in all this time and effort in order to set both himself and his family 'free'? To finally grab the future he'd planned and wanted for such a long time!

Emma could feel Ian's frustrations and anxiety. They had both experienced broken and sleepless nights since Ian's meeting with his boss. It was a big decision, a huge decision! Even she was beginning to have second thoughts. After all, there were no guarantees when you stepped away from a secure employed role and into the world of self employment! No more regular income that they'd been used to… and, to some extent, had taken for granted! Robert's school fees and a large mortgage would still have to be paid. Usual domestic bills, food, two cars, holidays, entertainment, the list went on and on! They would have to be very, very successful in the art world to get even close to the income and benefits the Managing Director role at Sotheby's currently enjoys. Maybe, they were being too adventurous. Were they really cut out for this uncertain existence? Yes, they were reasonably financially secure – at the moment, but what about illness, another world financial crisis, that could well see the bottom fall out of the art market once again. Where would they both be then!?

Ian knew he had about 16 hours to make his final decision. The biggest decision of his life! The decision that he might eventually live to regret! His excitement and enthusiasm, just a few days ago, had now changed to anguish and apprehension. How was he going to finally decide?

The tension in the house relaxed a little when Robert, and Emma's parents, arrived from their trip to Oxford. Robert was excited and eager to tell his parents about all the scientific exhibits he'd seen. However, neither Ian nor Emma, could really join in with his excitement. Their minds were still very much focused elsewhere.

When Ian and Emma finally fell asleep, just after midnight, it was due to exhaustion, not a gentle drifting off to sleep. They had gone to bed at 10.45pm with the decision still in the balance. Emma suggested they try to summarise their many discussions by listing all the benefits and downsides they'd decided came with each of the two career options. Just before midnight they had finally, yes finally, jointly agreed and had come to 'the decision'. They both then kissed and snuggled down under the duvet.

At 6.45am the following morning, the bedside alarm clock rang. Ian switched it off but Emma had not been disturbed. He got out of bed, showered and shaved. He then put on his best suit and his lucky blue tie. A quick bowl of cereal and he was then on his way, walking towards Esher railway station. Again, he recognised a number of the 'regulars' standing on the platform waiting for the same commuter train to London as him. He still didn't know any names, no occupations, nothing about their individual lives. He only recognised their faces.

The announcement over the tannoy system saying his train would be 'approximately 10 minutes late' was no surprise. He smiled when he heard people around him give their familiar sighs and groans. The train was never on time, Ian knew that. There were always various excuses for the delays, but it still meant the train was usually anything between five to 30 minutes late in arriving. He then wondered if the same people would cheer if the train did actually arrive at the correct time? Probably not.

Eight minutes after the announcement of the delay the train slowly pulled into his platform. Unfortunately, instead of the usual 12 carriages, today there were only eight! When the train finally stopped there was a rush to the entrance doors. Fortunately for Ian, he found a seat but some people were already standing and this was certainly not the last station before London! Ian pushed back into his seat and closed his eyes. He hated commuting – with a passion!

It was 8.35am when Ian walked into his outer office. Everything was very quiet. Penny was usually the first to arrive, but then he remembered, she'd told him on Friday, that she would not be in the office until about 10 o'clock, as she had a dental check up.

Ian walked into his own office, stopped just before his desk and then looked all around the room. This was not going to be his office in the future, he thought. He placed his briefcase on his desk, walked back to the far wall and hung up his overcoat. On the wall immediately next to him, was the large colour photograph he had taken some years ago. It was the view across Victoria Harbour from Kowloon to Hong Kong Island. Such a lot had changed in his life since the time he'd been working there. Great times, so many happy memories, he thought.

He checked his watch, 8.40am. He took a deep breath and wished this was all over and done with. But of course it wasn't, not just yet. Suddenly he smiled and remembered the old black and white cowboy movie, *High Noon*. Yes, his meeting with his boss in a few minutes' time, was going to be his own *High Noon*. He could now feel 'butterflies' fluttering in his stomach.

He walked over to his window and looked out. The street was still busy with commuters hurrying to their offices, shops and elsewhere. Like ants going about their daily business, he thought. He checked his watch once more, 8.44am. He decided not to waste any more time and strode out of his office and walked along the familiar corridors. His mind was trying to focus on the right words he was about to deliver to his boss. His stomach was still churning, the palms of his hands felt unusually damp. He hoped that the tension he was feeling in his body would not develop into a horrible headache. As he passed the mens lavatory he quickly popped in and washed his sweaty hands. He dried them and re-checked his watch, 8.52am. Two minutes later he walked into his boss's outer office where he found Michael Hopkins standing near his office door, talking to his PA.

"Ah, Ian," said Michael, looking across and a little surprised. "A little early, but come on... into my office."

Ian smiled and nodded at Michael's PA. He then followed his boss into his office, gently closing the door behind him.

"Sit down, Ian. Did you have a good weekend?"

Ian smiled. If only he knew!! He sat down opposite his boss and said, "I've had a lot to think about, Michael, and of course, I've also had numerous discussions with Emma! We really didn't have much time to do anything else."

"Yes, of course," said Michael, more seriously. "A big decision. So then, what have you both decided?"

This was it! thought Ian. He shuffled a little in his seat and nervously rubbed his hands together. Finally, he looked across to his boss and started to speak, "Michael, your offer of the Managing Director's position, last week, came as a total surprise. I had no idea that you planned to retire so soon or that I was being considered by you and the chairman to be your preferred successor. Your wise words advising me to discuss all the implications with Emma before I made my final decision were very astute. A strong warning that the role was not for everybody, whatever their qualities and skills. As I mentioned earlier, Emma and I have discussed nothing else all weekend. Emma did, however, confirm that she would support me in whatever decision I finally made." Ian took another deep breath before he continued.

"However, I have to tell you, Michael, that it has never been my ambition to become Sotheby's Managing Director. Over the last few days I've found it very difficult to change that view. I accept that careerwise, it is a massive opportunity and you're also paying me an enormous compliment, but... I'm sorry to say, Michael, I'm refusing your offer."

"I see," said his boss, a little shocked, but not totally surprised. "And that is your final decision?"

The story continues in

'The Gamble'

Volume 4 in the Ian Caxton Thriller series

DISCOVER THE FIRST TWO VOLUMES OF THE IAN CAXTON THRILLER SERIES

'THE OPPORTUNITY'

Ian Caxton is a senior manager at Sotheby's. After successful career moves to Sotheby's branches in New York and Hong Kong, Ian is now based in London and earmarked for the top position. However, following a chance meeting with Andrei, a very rich Russian art dealer based in Monaco, Ian suddenly reassesses all his plans and ambitions. Even his marriage is under threat. The Opportunity charts the tumultuous life and career of Ian Caxton as he navigates the underbelly of the art world, one of serious wealth, heart-stopping adventure and a dark side. The big question is, will Ian take The Opportunity? And if he does, what will the consequences be, not only for him, but also for his wife and colleagues?

'THE CHALLENGE'

The art world is full of pitfalls, mysteries and risk. It is a place where paintings can be bought and sold for millions of pounds. Fortunes can be made... and lost! For those whose ambition is to accumulate wealth beyond their wildest dreams, expert knowledge, confidence, bravery and deep pockets are certainly needed! Ian Caxton is being tested by fake paintings, a financial gamble on the artwork of a black slave, his wife's life-changing news and a series of mysterious emails that suggest he's being watched. More dramatic events, mental conflicts and soul searching decisions. How will Ian cope with all these extra demands?

This is the big question, that is The Challenge.

Printed in the USA
CPSIA information can be obtained
at www.ICGtesting.com
LVHW101557190823
755704LV00006B/413